Double Life

A Ghost Story set in Derbyshire

by

Narvel Annable

British Library Cataloguing in Publication Data
A catalogue record for this book is available
from the British Library

ISBN: 978-0-9530419-7-8
E-book: 978-09530419-8-5

Published by
Narvel Annable
44 Dovedale Crescent
Belper
Derbyshire
DE56 1HJ

http://tinyurl.com/narvelannable
www.twitter.com/NarvelAnnable
narvel@narvelannable.co.uk
www.narvelannable.co.uk
narvel@btinternet.com

Tel: 01773 824483

Cover Design

Interior Formatting

Terry Durand

This novel is dedicated to all LGBT teachers who have been isolated and harmed by institutionalised homophobic attitudes still prevalent in 21st century classrooms

Another intriguing, compelling and informative novel from Narvel Annable

He reflects across the decades of his double life: the joys and sorrows of an isolated and sometimes painful teaching career.

We empathise with the LGBTs he now helps at the Belper Golden Rainbows support group which grows from strength to strength.

Narvel constantly campaigns. Over the years, letters to the press and radio interviews have inspired the lives of gay people in deepest darkest coal encrusted Derbyshire.

Narvel now gives talks to audiences in the Derbyshire Police Force as a part of their in-service training days on Hate Crime - and does not shy from including a harrowing account of his arrest and imprisonment by plainclothes police in the war-torn 1960s Detroit riots.

Blending fact and fiction with gay history, this is a ghost story set in the harshness of the Thatcher era and the moral panic about AIDS in the 1980s. All set against a blighted colliery landscape after the fall of once mighty King Coal.

Peter Tatchell, human rights campaigner

www.PeterTatchellFoundation.org

CONTENTS

Introduction to *Double Life*

This novel will receive inspiration from the period 1978 to 1995. This is when I was a history master at the Valley Comprehensive School in Worksop, north Nottinghamshire. I taught as I was taught in the 1950s. I was too strict, too formal, too unwilling to modernise and reluctant to embrace progressive trends in state education which arrived in the 1980s. This 'Mr Chips' mindset was a cloak to conceal the continuing anxiety of leading a double life. Inside, I was a frightened homosexual trying to look like a confident heterosexual on the outside. It had to look like a teacher easily fitting in with pupils and staff.

For about 16 years, for the most part, Mr Annable succeeded in dodging disapproval and maintained a mask of po-faced respectability hiding inside a house in the ultraconservative colliery village of Clowne in north-east Derbyshire. Like most isolated, closeted gay men, I spoke little of myself and was constantly on guard. It became a way of life.

From time to time there were alarming incidents at school. Our staffroom, predominately macho male, was a hotbed of football fanaticism, strong language and laddish crude humour.

One afternoon, a colleague lazily leaned back in his seat and insouciantly yawned out –

'Nothing much to do. I suppose we could go out and beat up a queer.'

Probably disappointed at a lack of response, he repeated the bait several times over the following weeks. Others took notice. One of them gave advice -

'You know, Narvel. You really should make more effort to socialise. Try to fit in. Come to the pub with us after school once in a while.' He lowered his voice in earnest. 'Get yourself a girlfriend: talk about her. Better still, get yourself married. If the boss [headmaster] thought you were queer, he'd have you out of here so fast your feet wouldn't touch the ground!'

The final two years saw gay hate terminating a teaching career. Although my private life continued to remain very private, some pupils began to speculate on Mr Annable's sexuality. They turned him into an object of fun inflicting humiliating hurtful episodes. I might have survived a few, but, at the end, there were too many. A steady torturous drip destroyed my credibility and confidence. At the edge of a breakdown, a shell of my former self, there came a point when my position was untenable.

I was unable to discharge professional duties. These appalling disrespectful attacks were never taken seriously by senior management. One culprit was told –

'That was a silly thing to say.'

On Thursday, April 6th 1995, a colleague commented on my continuing melancholy, my appearance and exhaustion. She earnestly advised 'a few days off'. I walked out of that classroom and never returned.

So much for reality. The fiction for Simeon Hogg detailed in *Double Life* will be a *return* to work after a period of recuperation and counselling. In a halfway house between several months of lesson preparations and actual teaching, he is installed in a small classroom adjacent to his old classroom where the daily life of a busy school down a long corridor can be observed. This is the vehicle for a novel which explores all the above issues. Mr Hogg will be reflecting back on his years at the Valley Comprehensive School. His story, in part a ghost story, will be told in flashbacks as he tries to make sense of a repressed and difficult career.

Much of the text will be told by Simeon himself but also in the 'third person' sometimes described as the authorial voice. This voice will have the viewpoint of 2019 when words like homophobia are commonplace. I first saw 'homophobia' (meaning homosexual hate or fear of homosexuals) in *The Times* in 1981. It was first coined by a psychologist, George Weinberg, in the 1960s.

As with previous titles, nearly all names in *Double Life* (even nick-names) have been changed. Like previous titles, it is autobiographic, a blend of fact and fiction – essentially telling a true story. The following events took place in real places peopled by a fictitious cast. The following caricatured composites were inspired by a selection of the characters I met many years ago. However real flesh and blood the original model, who ends up on these pages (after being processed through my brain) is far from being a real person – alive or dead.

In an attempt to maintain the flavour and accuracy of the 1960s, occasionally I refer to African-Americans as Negroes.

Chapter 1

Invisibility

The lesson plans were making poor progress. Sadly, Simeon looked down at a few untidy handwritten notes together with a scattering of textbooks and judged that he should have made more headway in the time available. But how much time had that been? Was it weeks, or months, since his nervous breakdown? His counsellor euphemistically referred to this life changing event as a 'break-*through*' rather than a break-*down*. In order to answer his own question, he perused assorted typewritten sheets with little success and, to tell the truth, little interest.

The problem was memory. Everything was in a haze. When did he last see his counsellor? He tried to remember his face. It was a blur. Fragments of their conversation floated in and out of his consciousness. He'd been warned the therapy might often feel this way. Did he admit to that counsellor that he was homosexual? He couldn't remember. Sometimes he doubted there ever *was* a counsellor: so confusing, like living a dream, swimming in treacle.

Where was it all going anyway? All this nonsense; wouldn't it put him right back in the classroom, *again* to endure all the familiar misery? At least in his present situation, Simeon appeared to be protected by a shield of invisibility.

He was still Mr Hogg. But this was a pathetic Hogg who had lost his power. The nasty elements had lost interest and simply ignored him as they might ignore a caretaker or a cleaner. There was no fun in attacking ancillary staff. Simeon had become invisible – and was that such a bad thing? He was located next to his old classroom. He was established in a small room all to himself with a view down a corridor the full length of the block shared by Humanities and the Sixth Form. Nearly two thousand pupils filled the Valley Comprehensive School staffed by nearly a hundred teachers. Here he could observe school life passing by.

There was the problem of his pension. Simeon would have pressed for a clean break with teaching altogether. He wanted out. However small, he needed an income to survive and was forced into the option of therapy and counselling for six months on half pay. And then what? The mounting uncertainties exacerbated his mounting anxieties. But at least, regarding his erstwhile tormentors, Simeon was at peace. Simeon was invisible.

For most of the late 1970s, 1980s and early 1990s, like most secretive gay men, Simeon had always sought invisibility. He spoke little of himself and avoided social contact in and out of school. In a staff of a hundred, there was a probability of at least four other gay teachers. He easily identified one in the Art Department, one in the English Department but other masculine men could hide and blend in with the generality. They might be bisexual and appear to he happily married. They could stay hidden forever, except, of course, when Simeon came face to face with a butch colleague from the Technical Department at a Manchester gay sauna. After fleeting eye contact, both were in denial at that venue. Back at school, they conscientiously avoided each other.

Simeon might have met other members of staff (including lesbians) had he been a frequenter of queer pubs - or, if he had been a 'scene bunny', at a gay disco. His revulsion of late nights, alcohol and loud thumping music had limited his activities to public toilets, certain notorious woodland walks and Turkish baths. As his 30s blended into 40s, the dangers of toilets and woods became more and more unacceptable making the Turkish bath a favourite comfort zone.

The Harrogate Royal Baths, a safe distance from Worksop, were like an eastern temple dedicated to the god of pleasure and sensuality. There was the richly tiled Plunge Pool, together with Hot Room Chambers - Tepidarium, Calidarium and Laconium. The bather entered the dry area, padded over soft, thick pile carpets and progressed through exotic, tranquil halls. These areas of rest beds were resplendent with crafted wooden partitions sporting occasional Arabian motifs to complete the fantasy for recumbent fat bathers – most of them retired with all the time in the world.

These were the guilty ones, the soft, flabby, shapeless, old men who furtively observed any firm body in that plush silence, that serene restfulness which could have been a gentleman's club in London. Much was hanging in that humid air, but little was said.

Simeon knew the rules. Like the Derby Turkish Bath, the Harrogate Baths were open to the general public - caution and discretion were the watchwords. According to Kinsey's figures, 5% of the population were exclusively homosexual, but the reverse was almost always true inside any British Turkish Bath where perhaps one in 20 male bathers attended exclusively for the pleasures of hot steam, relaxation and therapeutic benefits. For many decades before the advent of 'the gay bath house', poorly paid bath attendants gladly accepted big tips to look the other way should they stumble upon any illegal activity.

Most baths had a café area where tea, coffee and tasty main meals could be enjoyed in the comfort of hushed peace and quiet. Here, polite conversations were whispered between gentlemen who might have recently been carnally acquainted.

In and around elaborate oaken cubicles with luxurious maroon curtains, Simeon soon encountered Mr Bill Bulman who was a regular fixture and gentleman of character with a rough manner, but very popular with the staff. Underneath a hard shell, he was courteous and always generous.

Pushing on a heavy door, a bather was hit by an angry, gurgling hissing which seemed to emanate from the subterranean depths of Harrogate. Gingerly, he moved into an opaque blinding fog of hot steam with visibility further limited by inadequate, low powered, amber bulbs. Carefully, slowly, step by step, his eyes gradually became accustomed to the nebulous atmosphere. A cavern was discerned, longer than it was wide, occupied by occasional lumps of flesh, Lords of Lard who silently lurked on stone benches, in dark Turkish recesses on either side.

Simeon selected a vacant seat and sat down. The heat felt good. The shower was great, but after hours cycling in cold rain, these lovely minutes of hot haze penetrated deep into his cold bones. Warmth and relaxation brought him to a point where he closed his eyes, drifted into a lethargic reverie and, for a few minutes, came very close to sleep.

Suddenly the touch of flesh! He looked up to see a fat face smiling encouragement to engage in … well, Simeon was no innocent. It reminded him to progress further. He was expected in deeper, denser steam and had yet to reach his objective. He advanced into an even darker section of the long, dimly lit chamber of erotically charged vapours. The first indication of an oversized bather was the faint glint of something shiny and metallic leaning next to the mosaic wall. On closer inspection, it resolved into the top of an expensive, stout, walking stick – silver, in the image of a bull's head.

Peering into the vapours, he could hazily discern the vague outline of what appeared to be two figures. The first was no fat man and [unusually in that establishment] he was anything but soft. It was the rear view of what Simeon usually described as 'a real, solid bloke'. A well tanned hairy torso was well supported above perfectly formed muscular buttocks. Strong tattooed arms suggested a rough working man, the sort often referred to as 'hairy arsed miners' by coarse, drunken slags who staggered over Heanor Market Place in Simeon's early teenage days. He never thought he would see such a macho bloke, standing to attention, mouth wide open, intoxicated with carnal delight.

The voyeur drew closer and was excited hearing a deep purring of mounting rapture. At the same time, this real rugged bloke started to arch his back, surrendering his manhood for the delectation of another macho man, a big man, who was seated. Two hands, big hands with pleasure-giving digits, were busy, wantonly stroking those firm beautiful buttocks. They wandered further, around dangling genitalia and sought out secret places out of sight. Also out of sight, hidden deep inside a fat throat, was a stiff cock. It was begging for release inside a salivating grotto, complete with an experienced muscular tongue, greedily extracting drops of dribble before the final bliss – that final, creamy jet of completion.

None of these extracurricular activities could ever be discussed with colleagues at the Valley School. When the public corporation baths in various provincial towns and cities began to clampdown on their homosexual bathers, the exclusive gay sauna emerged and grew in popularity.

Chapter 2

Ronnie, Bobbie and Freddie

Simeon taught as he was taught in the 1950s. He was too strict, too formal, too unwilling to modernise and reluctant to embrace progressive, child-centred trends in state education which arrived in the 1980s. This 'Mr Chips' mindset was a cloak to conceal the continuing anxiety of leading a double life. Inside, he was a frightened homosexual trying to look like a confident heterosexual on the outside. It had to look like a teacher easily fitting in with pupils and staff but more often than not, the stern schoolmaster was sabotaging his efforts to look human and come across as an effective educator.

In two decades, only once did he achieve a breakthrough and enjoy a friendly, meaningful relationship with a group of pupils. They were a boisterous bunch of ruffians with an appalling reputation throughout the school. Progressive staff referred to the Ronnie, Bobbie and Freddie mob as 'challenging behaviour'. Hard-nosed traditionalists abused them with loutish language and occasional violence to keep order and impose discipline. Mr Hogg identified himself with this 'old guard' but never condoned corporal punishment.

This gang of three, by popularity and sheer force of personality, imposed on the rest of the class an influence which could make life very difficult for a teacher who took his work seriously. On one occasion, after an onerous hour, Mr Hogg dismissed the class but detained the terrible trio. Unwisely perhaps, they were ordered to remain behind, explain their disruptive attitude and suffer a reprimand. Simeon had little confidence in his strategy - but it was worth a try.

Many years on, without success, he tried to recall and reconstruct this extraordinary conference of four and locate the exact point when everything changed between the teacher and his charges. The sea change happened during a moment when a criticism of Ronnie was interrupted by an effective heartfelt defence from his number two – Bobbie. In plain language normally considered disrespectful to a member of staff, despite limited articulation, Bobbie managed to paint a picture of his best friend who was experiencing all the stresses and chaotic adolescent miseries which could have been a 14-year-old Simeon.

Effectively, the atmosphere of this detention, this coerced punishment suddenly transformed into a voluntary and valuable meeting between four equals. It was a magical moment, a sudden switch from monochrome into glorious Technicolor where three boys wanted to stay and further explain their lives to an adult who was now more counsellor than schoolmaster.

It was a dodgy situation for Mr Hogg! He was hearing confidential information about his colleagues which was verging on 'unprofessional conduct'. He was hearing distressing details of their home life. His sympathetic ear encouraged further trust to the point that his teacher status had morphed into the confidentiality of the confessional. Now treated like a newly acquired friend, Simeon was begged to guard the secrets which had been entrusted to him for safe keeping.

Were these revelations true? Were these boys telling lies? In the weeks which followed, cautiously and casually, Simeon cross-referenced the accounts with a few friendly colleagues and one trusted deputy head who had access to private files. Although the boys hid behind a veneer of defiant swagger, their new confidant concluded that there was indeed a case to answer. They were victims of an insensitive system all too willing to exploit youths from a deprived background and give three dogs a bad name. Bobbie said,

'I can't help the way I speak, sir. It's me voice, it irritates folk. It's not my fault, sir. Honest.'

Simeon had always been annoyed by a certain element of insolence in the utterances delivered by Bobbie. There was a sardonic tone which, at a low level, challenged authority and continued to chafe. Notwithstanding, he accepted that the pupil's lilt of speech was natural, a part of Bobbie's personality. It was *not* intentionally disrespectful.

The new friendship was affirmed, enjoyed by all four, but did not really solve any problems. It reduced the stress of teaching in that particular class and, by osmosis; improved Mr Hogg's standing in the whole of that 4th Year.

So now, somewhere into the start of a new academic year, Ronnie, Bobbie and Freddie will now be 5th years. He had not seen them. And that was a pity. They were worth looking at, especially Freddie, the cute one. Of the three, he was the least assertive, not to mention his perfect bottom well displayed in close fitting trousers.

Simeon mentioned Freddie's tempting anatomy to a repressed married friend who, like himself, was carefully navigating around a secretive double life.

'I'm a bit concerned about your lust!' said the friend.

'What do you mean?' responded Simeon.

'Well ... As teachers, aren't we in a position of trust? It's not on is it - leering at boy's bums.'

'I was *not* leering. A lifetime of caution has taught me the art of the crafty shufti. *You* are a teacher. Are you telling me that a desirable teenage arse has never titillated?'

'I suppose it depends on thoughts *remaining* thoughts and never being put into action,' said the friend backing off. 'Anyway, what would you do with Freddie? You don't do back passage. You've been americanised. How did those butch numbers in Detroit put it - *hitting the dirt road*?'

'True enough. Penetration is not on my menu. What *really* irritates me is the inequality, the injustice, the double standards of our double lives.'

'What's that supposed to mean!' countered the gay colleague.

'It means *you*, a gay man, as randy as me coming over all moral, tut-tutting because I fancy Freddie's nice bum when *you* never said a dicky-bird after that odious performance we all witnessed in the staffroom last week!'

Simeon was referring to a few minutes of light hearted banter between a few macho, ribald, coarse colleagues. One, a senior staff member, had allowed his office to deteriorate into an unworkable state of chaos. He asked a much lusted after nubile 6th form girl to rescue him from his self-inflicted shambles. In a naughty narrative of soft porn proportions, he aroused his heterosexual all male audience into a raucous mob of salivating sinfulness.

Simeon was particularly revolted by repeated references to the girl being told to pay special attention to the lower shelves - making it necessary for her to bend down and bend over. The senior member of staff delighted in a graphic description of the way her knickers revealed her 'sexy bum'. Hoots, cheers and loud guffaws encouraged further indecent comment.

Simeon condemned and berated his hypocritical homosexual colleague for laughing along during this prurient performance.

'Well! Didn't you join in with them?

'I'll be damned if I did! *My* head was deeply buried in *The Guardian.* I'll admit to cowardice, but not to any complicity. I'll also confess to envy in that people like us could never enter into such banter... '

'*Which,*' interrupted the other, 'could not be condoned in a situation where a professional is employed in a *position of trust*?'

'Touché,' parried Simeon, concluding a rather fractious exchange between two repressed gay men.

During this time of the late 1970s in the Valley Comprehensive School, discipline and respect for masters was rapidly deteriorating. Corporal punishment was still available to the Head and his Deputies but, to the relief of Simeon, forbidden to other teachers. A minority of macho 'old guard' staff regularly applied a violent fist to quickly correct any irritation such as casual insolence. This type of transgression having reached the ears of senior management usually resulted in a gentle reprimand and advice along the lines of - 'Don't get me wrong, I know Bobbie and his scumbags can infuriate, but just go easy. Stand back. It's not worth it.'

Detention after school was used with increasing frequency. But it was a *formal* detention of one hour from 4 to 5pm. To punish a pupil required the completion of a detailed Incident Report in triplicate to the Head of House who would send a letter to the parents. Overwhelmed with work and stress, most staff already bogged down by red tape simply could not find the energy and time to cope with ever mounting bureaucracy. Some hard cases (like Bobbie) would make sure the letter never reached his parents anyway; or he might simply refuse to attend the detention. In the mid 1980s in Mrs Thatcher's Britain, to Simeon and many of his beleaguered colleagues, it just felt like the world was falling apart.

Some months after that extraordinary impromptu detention, which magically morphed into a constructive conference of equals, a history master was whispering with the terrible trio in the library. Seated in front of written notes and open books, it was intended to look like a teacher helping his pupils. Actually, it was Simeon enjoying a casual chat with Ronnie, Bobbie and Freddie when the subject of school punishments came up.

'Do you remember that time, big bust up, when I ordered you lot to stay behind in class?' asked Simeon.

'We'll never forget it!' responded chief spokesman Ronnie, slightly abashed. The others displayed a degree of embarrassment and a short silence forced Freddie into respectful speech.

'We're sorry we upset you, sir. Honest.'

'Yeah,' mumbled Bobbie.

'It's just that ... well ... I wondered ... well, you, all three of you, could have just refused to stay behind. You're known for refusing detention. Not to mention disrupting other detentions. You could have simply walked out of the room. Why *didn't* you walk out?'

They looked at each other for a lead.

'I expect ...' started Ronnie.

'I think it's because we liked you, sir,' said Bobbie.

'Liked me! After I'd pitched into you all!'

'Well, we knew you'd got a temper ... I mean ...' stumbled Freddie.

'Tantrums don't amount to good discipline or good teaching, lads. I wish I *was* a good teacher. Afraid I'm not.'

'I'll tell you what, sir,' said Ronnie, 'We were sorry to have upset you so much. We felt bad about it. That's what it was.'

This thoughtful exchange with boys from a rough, chaotic, dysfunctional troubled background was very affecting to Simeon. He thought on it deeply. So, all along, could it have been that the trio unconsciously engineered this extraordinary reconciliation? For this stern master, it was a sort of Damascene moment, one shining flash, the most significant instant in his whole teaching career. The mask of Mr Chips had slipped and revealed a useless stressed-out Mr Hogg who had suddenly stepped back and was staggered by the futility of his position.

Fast forward ten years and see an older broken Hogg in a small classroom, half-heartedly presiding over untidy notes spread out on a table before him pondering that special conversation with Freddie, Bobbie and Ronnie. By coincidence, suddenly, *there was Ronnie!* It *was* Ronnie, large as life, mischievously grinning at Mr Hogg through the glass door. Immediately Simeon summed up the situation. The disrupter had been ejected from his classroom. He was bored, wandering around the block heading for even more self-inflicted aggravation, not only on himself, but staff who already suffered enough from that terrible trio.

'Get in here, Ronnie!' barked Simeon. 'Kicked out of class again?'

'Well … not really, sir …' ventured the boy eternally in denial attempting to justify his conduct. Recalling good relations and the need to build on past success, he smiled and put the lad at ease.

'Never mind. I'll take responsibility if questions are asked. Sit yourself down. I could use a bit of company. Nobody seems to notice me these days. How are you?'

'Not too bad, sir,' beamed Ronnie, settling into his chair, clearly delighted to be back with his former teacher. 'Not teaching this period, sir?'

'I've been poorly, Ronnie. Took bad, as we say in Derbyshire. Not physically, it's ... well ... a mental breakdown. You lot have finally driven me crackers,' smiled Simeon enjoying his own joke. 'Seriously, I've been in this room for months scribbling away at this stuff. The idea is to get me back into the classroom eventually, get me better - something like that.'

'I'm sorry ...' said Ronnie, concerned, sincere, inadequately trying to express himself. Writing stories?' asked the visitor after noticing an untidy spread of papers.

'Supposed to be lesson plans, but I'm thinking it's all a waste of time. Perhaps I should be writing my life story.'

'*That* would be interesting! When you come back you could read it to us. We'd enjoy that, sir.'

Simeon smiled a sad smile.

'I don't think I'll be back here teaching you, Ronnie.' Briefly, in simple terms, he explained his breakdown and problems of memory. 'But enough about me. Tell me *your* news.'

'Got meself stabbed, sir!'

'Stabbed! You mean …'

At this, the victim jumped to his feet, lowered his trousers and jerked up his shirt proudly revealing his milky midriff and several inches of ugly scar just above an adolescent waist. This was serious violence, and recent violence at that.

'My God! Cover yourself, lad, *quickly*. Anybody walking by will wonder what's going on in here. How did that happen?

'Knife fight.'

'Oh Ronnie! Will you ever learn? It must have been a hospital job.' Recalling the brutal reality of this boy's chaotic life, Simeon was alarmed. 'Were your mates involved? Did they get hurt?'

The reference to Bobbie and Freddie seemed to discomfort Ronnie who slumped back down in his seat.

'I can't remember.'

'You can't remember! But you *must* remember!'

'I was in hospital a long time. Do you still live in Clowne?'

Now it was Simeon's turn to be discomforted. The abrupt change of subject turned his mind to recurring anxiety. Had he locked the door when he left his house that morning? Why was he plagued with visions of piles of unopened letters and a neglected overgrown garden?

Another unwelcome thought intruded: the cycling club which was strangled at birth by a deputy head. He was alarmed on hearing about an impromptu visit to Mr Hogg from three enthusiastic cyclists. Ronnie, Bobbie and Freddie turned up at his door urging the formation of a school cycling club run by their favourite teacher. Affording them hospitality demanded by basic courtesy, Simeon, serving up three mugs of tea in his living room, knew he was on dodgy ground – and told them so. But exuberant innocent youth could see no such subtle obstacles. The boys wanted to experience the mysterious nooks and crannies of the High Peak Simeon often mentioned when describing his weekend excursions. Bobbie and his cheerful claque often greeted Simeon with friendly banter regarding his sexy McEnroe shorts when cycling into school.

'Ope ya didn't mind that bit o' cheek this morning, sir? It's just us being a bit daft.'

'Don't worry, Bobbie. I know the difference between genuine disrespectful abuse and a compliment - albeit inappropriate. Anyway, a bloke my age should be grateful his legs get noticed. Don't wolf-whistle; that's all I ask. It might catch on and be embarrassing.'

Did Simeon cycle to school this morning? If so, did he still park his bike in the history book cupboard, the usual place? He had no memory of how he had arrived at school, no memory of parking his car.

Thoughts went back to the deputy head incident.

'Try to see it from my point of view, Simeon. You, a single man living alone, were entertaining male pupils in your home. Of course, *I've* full confidence in your professional conduct. That goes without saying. Fortunately the three lads concerned, carefully questioned, spoken to separately, breathed nothing of any impropriety. It's not me; you have to see how *others* might interpret this visit to your home.

'You must also consider the reputation of these rogues. They *begged* me to permit this cycling club. Of course, it's out of the question. They were dismayed when I pointed out the need for an extra member of staff - even if I were to tolerate such a club. It's nice to be popular but, believe me, Simeon, unless this business is squashed at the outset, you are on the road to disaster! I've made it clear that no further visits will be sanctioned and expect to hear no more on the subject.'

Simeon was annoyed. He had no intention of agreeing to such a venture and hoped the surprise visit would have passed without comment. Senior management had seized an opportunity to indulge in unacceptable, unchallenged homophobia. Walking down the corridor, minutes after the reprimand, too late, he rehearsed a defence of several sound bites. Simeon's weekends were precious. His time was valuable. Solitary cycling in the Derbyshire hills was restorative, his way of recharging the batteries, combating stress and building up fresh reserves for Monday morning. The boys might have been congenial company, but the main purpose was fresh air and exercise *away* from school and responsibility. Cycling in a group also constituted an unacceptable risk of collision with possible grievous results. All these points Simeon should have made in his defence. Under the threat of bigotry, prejudice and ignorance, he was paralysed into an abject silence.

During these lengthy cogitations, Simeon realised he had not answered Ronnie's question.

'Yes, I still live in Clowne.'

'Good! I'll bike over and see you like last time.'

'I'd enjoy that but … your last visit gave me a bit of bother with the bosses.'

'It'll not matter now, sir. Who'll see us?'

Before he could respond, Simeon, with a sudden rush of realisation, was overwhelmed by the profound truth of that statement. Who indeed would know? He had been reduced to a nonperson, a former teacher who simply did not matter anymore. Then he noted the singular 'I'll bike over'. The other boys were not mentioned. Ronnie responded,

'I don't see much of them these days.'

'That's a shame. Friends are important. You, of all people, need as much social support as possible.'

'Yes. I get lonely since the hospital stuff.'

'They came to visit you – I hope!'

'I saw Bobbie and Freddie there once, just once, but they couldn't find me. I was too weak to call out. *You* were there, sir! That meant a lot. You were the only teacher who cared enough to bother. But it was the same thing; you looked straight at me, but didn't recognise me. I must have been a bit of a mess with tubes and stuff in me.'

Simeon had no memory of such a visit. In truth, he was experiencing his own difficulties at about the same time, but did not have the heart to disillusion Ronnie. Possibly he was reliant on that mistaken belief.

'Anyway,' thought Simeon, 'for all I know, I might well have shot off to that hospital on hearing such dreadful news. If only my memory were not so bad. I'm sick of this perpetual fog.'

Ronnie came back to the subject of his teacher's lesson plans which inspired such little enthusiasm.

'Forget this stuff, sir. If nobody's checking up on you, what the hell! Write about something we'd all like to know about. Best part of your lessons was when it became personal, when you spoke about yourself. That's when it was real! Sometimes you used examples, your mates, that American bloke Walter who was brainwashed by the Jehovah's Witnesses.'

Too true! That was *real* all right! It triggered another painful memory. A girl in the class, who was a Jehovah's Witness, complained with the result that Simeon suffered another reprimand from the Deputy Head.

But there was something odd about this teenager. Teacher studied pupil. Something was wrong. After a few seconds, he realised it was his speech. It was a touch too sophisticated for Ronnie? He was never so articulate. Yet it *was* Ronnie. As he stared, momentarily Ronnie aged – and then returned to normal. Was Simeon going mad!

'Something wrong, sir?'

'Nothing really. It's just that … look … my memory's horribly vague. It *is* correct, isn't it; I was teaching you, Bobbie and Freddie last summer? Or was it the year before? I can't seem to reconcile the good times with you chaps and those appalling incidents with the sixth formers which, well let's face it, drove me out of teaching.'

'Driven out!' Ronnie was genuinely horrified. 'It's news to me, and I'm sorry to hear it.'

Simeon took a deep breath. He made a decision. It was motivated by increasing loneliness to the point of desperation. Emboldened by the boy's maturity, his compassion and heartfelt empathy – for the first time ever, Mr Hogg would admit his homosexuality to a pupil.

'We all knew that, sir,' said Ronnie in some sadness and a wan smile. 'But it made no difference,' he added cheerily. 'You've always been well respected and well liked.' In a sudden change, he spoke softly in low menacing tones, more to his hand as it became a fist. 'Course, we 'ad ta give a bit of strong advice to one or two youths, just now and again, you know, when they forgot their manners. Those sorts, well, they learn quick – never said it again.'

Simeon looked at his bodyguard with mixed feelings and chose his words carefully.

'Yes. I'm fully aware of your considerable influence in the school,' he said sardonically. 'Much better to have you, Bobbie and Freddie with me rather than against me. It made life easier. It was a brief golden age in my career.'

'You should have told us about them yobs. Why didn't you? We could have sorted it in seconds.'

Simeon explained. He detailed gay hate at the Valley Comprehensive School in Worksop which, effectively, terminated a 17 year teaching career.

'You see, Ronnie, my private life had to remain very private. I was leading a double life, but some pupils began to speculate on my sexuality. They turned me into an object of fun. In the last months there were humiliating hurtful episodes. I might have survived a few, but there were too many. A steady torturous drip destroyed my credibility and confidence. At the edge of a breakdown, a shell of my former self, there came a point when my position was impossible. I couldn't do my job properly. These appalling attacks were never taken seriously by senior management. One culprit was told – "That was a silly thing to say." A colleague commented on continuing misery, my appearance and exhaustion. She advised a few days off. At the end of that day, I walked out of that classroom determined never to come back.

'All those years, I did my job quietly. I kept my head down, kept my private life very private and did nothing for the gay cause.' Ronnie looked a question.

'Gay cause?' Simeon tried to explain.

'Some brave folks in far off cities were sticking up for me and others like me. Homosexual teachers are isolated, terrified of being exposed as queer, frightened of being humiliated by ignorant pupils and colleagues especially in Worksop, a deeply conservative colliery community.'

'I don't remember anything like that,' said Ronnie in puzzlement.

'No,' replied Simeon slowly. 'Look here, Ronnie, we have both endured trauma and both have memory problems. Let me ask you a simple question: can you remember who the Prime Minister was when I taught you and your mates?'

'Mrs Thatcher.'

'Mrs Thatcher indeed! She was the PM in the 1980s. What year are we in now?'

'I'm not sure,' said Ronnie - after a troubled pause.

'I'd say 1995 - sometime in October - but I'm not sure.'

During a difficult silence, they looked at each other for some moments. Simeon broke the silence.

'I might be having difficulties, but I've not lost my critical faculties. You see what it means? If I'm right about the current year, I'm in conversation with a man in his early twenties! I thought you'd been kicked out of a class? Is that right? Or have you just walked along Valley Road and into the building?'

Ronnie, mystified, was stunned into silence. In that silence, Simeon cast his mind over the Thatcher years. He grieved for people who suffered under her appalling 1988 law, Section 28. It was the first anti-gay legislation passed in a 100 years! Like living in a police state; it prevented any positive mention of homosexuality in schools, banned Local Authorities from publishing material expressing the acceptability of homosexuality as a 'pretended family relationship'. In other words, it told gay children, lesbian and gay parents – 'you are not a real family, you are unacceptable, you are inferior.'

At the 1987 Conservative party conference, she mocked people who defended the right to be gay in her keynote speech, insinuating there was no such right. During her rule, there was an explosion of queer bashing and murder, whilst gay men were demonised for the AIDS pandemic. In that year, after a bout of flu, Simeon returned to his classroom and was greeted by a scrawl on the board – 'Hogg's got AIDS.' Simeon felt under siege. It was a dreadful time. The Conservative government's 'family values' and 'Victorian values' campaigns whipped up hysterical levels of homophobia aided by the moral panic over AIDS which was dubbed the 'gay plague'.

Ronnie attempted to answer Simeon's question.

'*You* thought I'd been kicked out of class, so that's what *I* thought. I'm not sure which class it was … I *might* have walked in from the street?'

'Aren't we a pair of crocks?' replied Simeon with a wry smile.

The bell sounded for the lunch hour. Immediately corridors filled up with youthful humanity pressing and crushing to exit the building. Ronnie turned round to see if he recognised anybody. Columns crowded towards the main exit on the left colliding with pupils emerging from classrooms down the corridors on the right. At times the jam came to a halt. Nobody took notice of the two men observing from that small classroom.

And it **was** two men. Ronnie was no longer a boy. As if by mutual consent, both were reluctant to pursue further the taboo subject of mental problems. They had pushed the analysis as far as they dared. In silence, teacher and pupil assessed areas of agreement and gave voice to a safe way forward. Simeon, the more articulate, spoke first.

'I'm delighted to have been reunited with you today, Ronnie. We've agreed I'm wasting my time with lesson plans and should write an autobiography. It'll be a lot easier to do that if I can tell it to somebody. Will you come again and discuss it with me?'

'Of course! I like your company and, let's face it; I've nothing else to do.'

'If you can ask the occasional question, make the odd comment from time to time, it'll be really helpful. Don't be reluctant to criticise. I'm on my own in this eternal fog and need feedback. Steer me in the right direction if you feel the need.'

It seemed like the present spate of conversation had been exhausted. Warm goodbyes were exchanged in the comfortable knowledge that a framework for future meetings had been established. Ronnie was excited by new responsibility which gave his life new meaning. With youthful enthusiasm, he declared his intention to return the following morning. Even so, he was reluctant to leave the room. Slowly, very slowly, he walked to the top of the stairs and descended at a snail's pace.

Simeon became painfully conscious of their shared loneliness as an excessive melancholy descended on him. Had he dismissed Ronnie too soon? Where would he go? Would he know *where* to go? Would he remember the arrangement? Would he remember anything? Yet again a great emptiness intruded together with a fear of that taboo subject – don't question, don't try to analyse, don't dig too deep. The truth might be too dreadful.

Chapter 3

Winter of Discontent

The following morning, sunny and bright, was a complete contrast. At the first sight of Ronnie, Simeon jumped out of his seat and very nearly hugged him. A firm hand shake was probably the first time he had ever touched any pupil. As a gay man, he had to be especially careful with boys. Ronnie's face, wreathed in smiles, displayed equal enthusiasm.

'I must warn you that these meetings will uncover personal details which might embarrass you. Hope you can cope with that?'

'No problem,' replied Ronnie, 'I've knocked about a bit meself. I've had *my* bit of fun.'

'I wasn't particularly thinking of sex, although, I expect that will come into any homosexual biography. No, I was thinking of the sensitive issue of our shared memory problem. For example, I can tell you that I'm haunted by a horror of my pigeon hole.'

'What?'

Simeon explained the communication system of pigeon holes, more than one hundred small mail boxes located on the wall in the main office block next to the headmaster's office. Staff were expected to check them every morning. Vaguely, he recollected going there a few times on his return after the long absence. Was it embarrassment? Or his increasing tendency to reclusiveness which accounted for a fear of going near the main office? Mr Hogg's pigeon hole might well be overflowing with dozens of uncollected notes and general staff instructions. Somewhat hesitantly, Ronnie offered to walk down there and pick up his mail.

'No! Thank you, it's ... err ... a kind thought, but I don't want to know what's in that bloody box. Anyway, if seen, you'd likely get into trouble. And another thing, what do I want? I want out. I should have got the hell out when I was *really* bad, when they bullied me into those counselling sessions. Do you know, Ronnie: as time goes by, I remember less and less about those meetings.'

'Fine,' said the other, eager to diffuse increasing anxiety. 'They've probably forgotten you anyway.'

A short exchange of ideas established Ronnie's preference to keep the biographical focus on Simeon's teaching career.

'When did you start?'

'I'd lived in America for 13 years, qualified out there and just wanted to settle in England teaching English history in a cosy school,' concluded the master with a grim cynical snigger. 'I was looking for a quiet, comfortable life - some hope!'

'Why didn't that happen?'

'Several reasons. Firstly, Worksop is a provincial colliery town where every 'proper' bloke is expected to fit in. You had to be keen on football, swill beer with the lads in the pub and, most important of all, be able to fancy a lass. I always thought I'd be safe in a community of educated schoolmasters who'd respect a gentleman's privacy. The British have a reputation for accepting the status of a bachelor. Intrusive questions are considered bad form; not so at *this* school. It simply wasn't possible to keep up a double life. I was in for a rude awakening!

'Double life! It's a joke. When you think about it, I had all on to lead a *single* life.'

Simeon never invented girlfriends to satisfy his curious colleagues. As far as possible, he was honest about his personal life, waxing eloquent about his love of cycling and walking in the Derbyshire hills and dales. Tea shops were sought out and, where possible, public houses avoided. Occasionally he stayed at youth hostels, more often at a Bed and Breakfast. It was in his nature to retire early and rise early - after being assured his accommodation would be quiet.

Homosexuality had turned him into a recluse. Indeed, Simeon's austere lifestyle of healthy abstinence hindered his efforts in meeting other homosexuals. The Turkish bath was the best way. Other venues such as notorious lascivious lavatories or certain infamous woodland walks were, to his cost, found to be much too dangerous.

Ronnie was intrigued about how a gay made contact with another gay.

'Catching a kindred eye,' said Simeon, philosophically recalling a line from a half forgotten poem. 'I've spent my whole life doing just that. Pretty boys in the street or even here at this school. Briefly you snatch a quick look at a handsome face and instantly look away - for safety. I ask myself, is it lust? Will I be satisfied with a simple kiss, a fumble up an alley or a minute in the steam room? Or do I want something more, something more edifying - a relationship?'

'I expect most men like you would want that, to actually get to know and love another man,' said Ronnie.

'Yes,' sighed Simeon, in a faraway voice.

His mind went back to 1966 in a gay sauna. A slight turn to the right revealed the profile of a light skinned young Negro who, after a few seconds, turned a beautiful full face. It was an appraisal, a close-up to confirm his selection for the evening. Here was a boy of stunning good looks fixing Simeon with his considerable power. Here was a chicken-hawk who was accustomed to hunting the chickens of Detroit City. Here was a boy who was accustomed to getting exactly what he wanted - and he wanted Simeon. In those few magical moments, Derbyshire eyes scrutinised Detroit eyes. Both pairs were full of wonder, full of desire. Under pressure of enchantment, each countenance melted, slightly, very slightly into a half smile. Simeon was drawn into an alluring face. He supposed that this strapping lad with an Adonis body was about his own age. It was a face of softened Negroid features: not a wide nose: lips not thick, yet temptingly full: coal-black hair, not exactly frizzy, yet with short tight curls, suggesting African ancestry. And big round eyes - yes - beautiful brown eyes, firm of purpose, holding, bayoneting their prey.

Later that evening they were walking the streets of Detroit when a turn took them into a narrow street. He stopped. Simeon stopped. They looked at each other - enjoyed the look when, suddenly, roughly, the Adonis pushed him into a recess, up against a dilapidated doorway and, with arms outstretched leaning on the door, he created a small area of confinement. Simeon was in a trap. It might have been a mugging. They looked at each other. Easy, sweet and slow, the hard strong youth breathed out a few words.

'You think ... I'll lock you in a cage like a little bird, all for myself?' He smiled, leaned closer and kissed his captive, oh - so - very - gently. 'And, if I opened the cage door ... would you fly away? Would you?'

Simeon was frozen mute by the greatest sexual power he had ever encountered. It was a thrilling combination of menace and magic. He could not run, had no desire to run. Seizing the initiative, with supreme poise and self-assurance, the ruffian continued to weave his enchantment.

'I don't think so. Know why? Because I can get *inside* you. I can eat you up. I can drain you ... and, yes, boy, you'll beg me for it; you'll love me for it. Does my boy love me? Does he?'

As if with a broken spirit, Simeon heard himself whisper an affirmative as the lover dropped his arms, descended to a squat, fumbled and concluded his magic spell with physical expression and physical expertise, ending in a long, slow, paroxysm of acute pleasure which the English prisoner would remember all his life.

'Hello!' said Ronnie, trying to be cheerful but noticing the abstraction and sudden moist eyes. 'You're miles away! Come back. Hope I didn't upset you?'

Quickly Simeon rallied and returned to the task at hand. He was pleased the biography was disciplined and focused on the period of 1978 to the present day. He took a breath and lunged into a start. More correctly, *they* made a start. Simeon knew he had suffered a catastrophic collapse of confidence. Ronnie's encouragement was essential. It would be a conversation. One would occasionally chip in whilst the other made rough notes to write up later. The reality was two people, isolated by recent trauma, needing the warmth and comfort of companionship.

Simeon couldn't recall much about his first months of the 1978 autumn term, but had vivid unpleasant memories of the dreadful 'winter of discontent' in early 1979.

'Is it *all* going to be misery, sir?' complained Ronnie.

'Absolutely not! Despite many difficulties in a life dodging daily assault, the slings and arrows of constant bigotry, prejudice and ignorance, there's a lot of fun and laughter in the gay world. The very nature of hardship compensates with comedy acted out by some bizarre people. As we go along, you'll meet my circus of curious characters. It was the same in Detroit. Black people could be most amusing. By the way, do you know my first name?'

'Simeon,' said Ronnie, slightly embarrassed as if he had uttered a taboo word.

'It's just that it's beginning to feel a touch silly, a bit pretentious being addressed as a master. Those days are long gone. We're now equal. We're friends.'

'Okay, Simeon,' replied the former pupil with a cheeky grin. They both grinned like two naughty boys.

Ronnie remembered with some pleasure the chaos and disruption caused by the period coined 'winter of discontent'. It was so cold the school occasionally closed due to a shortage of fuel. There were paralysing strikes causing Worksop's dustbins to overflow, its streets piled up with rubbish. Cemetery workers refused to bury the dead. Food and petrol supplies were disrupted.

Worst of all, Simeon recalled the stress and danger driving out of the pit village of Clowne, a scruffy coal blackened community exposed to the elements perched up high on a Derbyshire ridge. His fragile little Mini car precariously descended down an icy main road towards Worksop several hundred feet lower in Nottinghamshire. Surfaces needed grit but militant road workers were on strike and his tyres, fully locked, simply skated down and rubbed across the kerbstones. He hated being late, but often was during that dreadful winter.

Fear of a sharp tongued unsympathetic dictatorial headmaster locked into a 1950s mindset caused intolerable anxiety.

School closures, of which there were several, were a godsend. Some of this precious stolen time was due to lack of fuel. Striking ancillary staff gifted a few extra days for this beleaguered teacher to catch his breath. It was possible to manage without cleaners and dinner ladies, but caretakers, with boiler house expertise and multiple keys to navigate the buildings ... Well, they were essential.

There was mounting discontent with a dying Labour Government. An insensitive comment from Prime Minister James Callaghan infuriated a freezing strike-bound Britain shuddering to a halt. Returning happy and tanned from a tropical Caribbean summit, he exclaimed, 'Crisis! What crisis?' Little did Simeon know these blunders would pave the way for 13 years of a right-wing homophobic Thatcher Government taking gay people back to an age of prejudice and bigotry, even worse than their current malaise.

During Margaret Thatcher's time, the few enlightened teachers were afraid to challenge homophobic bullying. Indeed, the word homophobia had yet to be coined. From that time, up to and into the 21st century, 41 % of gay pupils were beaten up and were six times more likely to commit suicide. From 1978 to 1995, at the Valley Comprehensive School in Worksop, fearing exposure and humiliation, Simeon Hogg kept his head down, said nothing about his private life and tried to be invisible. It didn't work. A series of painful incidents, homophobic abuse from some pupils together with the indifference of senior management effectively terminated a teaching career. The repeal of Section 28 in 2003 came too late for 20th century teachers who shared same-sex attraction. Such was the Thatcher legacy. Her eventual passing in 2013 provoked an outpouring of adulation from some and scenes of ecstatic dancing in the street from others. *Ding Dong! The Witch is Dead* from the *Wizard of Oz* shot to the top of the pop charts in the days prior to her funeral.

But Britain was not the only country to inflict retrospective punishment on its gay population. Simeon's gloom increased when the Shah of Iran was deposed by violent gangs of religious fanatics followed by the dread arrival of Ayatollah Khomeini who plunged that nation back to a medieval darkness. This evil, grim-faced pitiless old man precipitated a gay hating witch-hunt of executions devouring untold numbers of hapless homosexuals.

Simeon was horrified by distressing reports of Iranian gay men who suffered their anuses being medically sewn up closed by doctors. The inevitable result was a slow agonising death. When it came to light that a compassionate surgeon cut through the stitches to help some of these victims of rabid homophobia, that brave doctor was promptly arrested by the (extra judicial) Religious Police and thrown into jail.

A combination of Thatcher, Khomeini and the forthcoming AIDS epidemic released an unprecedented wave of terror driving the gay community back to an abyss of bible blackness.

In spite of this decade of stygian gloom, gay men like Simeon were getting on with their lives. Religious fanatics need to recruit new members whereas those who share same-sex attraction are born at a rate of one in ten if bisexuals are included. Most of them are able to hide within the heterosexual majority by marrying and / or repressing their natural urges. Many years later, a sympathetic policeman said -

'Let's face it, Simeon. You were *born* illegal.'

A shining light in such bleak times was the entertaining Mr Toad, an old friend from the 1960s. One weekend in early 1979, Simeon was invited to meet Toad's notorious mother, known in gay circles as Mother Ghoul, nicknamed after her home town, the busy Humberside port of Goole, 50 miles inland from the North Sea.

'Good!' said Ronnie, 'This is getting interesting.'

'Not so good for me. It was a big mistake. I'd been warned she was a harridan of the first order. A monster of a woman!'

She was a hideous version of her ugly son. The first sight of Toad some 14 years before was a never-to-be-forgotten experience. Yes, certainly a toad. His pupils had christened him well. He looked like a toad. His exuberant bulging eyes, full of ardour, were set wide over a tight mouth which seemed more like a long crack. 'Crack in a pie' was a regular comment. He inspired something of the repulsion felt at the nearness of a reptile. Like Kenneth Graham's Mr Toad, he was comical, eager, impatient and entirely puffed up with his own importance. Catching sight of a teenage chicken, the little creature ran, actually ran up to Simeon who, trying to look innocent, sauntering around a certain public park, was forced to retreat several steps.

After a few minutes conversation, Toad registered a childlike delight when the newcomer found this funny little man interesting. Years later, Simeon had grown fond of his toad who was utterly repulsive and, at the same time, utterly compelling.

Toad loved to laugh. He was a funny man and could show surprising erudition in quoting the classics with a homoerotic subtext. Boasts about his sexual conquests included '*Where the bee sucks, there suck I*' and *'There's corn in Egypt'*.

Mischievously, Simeon amused Ronnie with an account of an outrageous episode in a gay bathhouse one busy afternoon. Toad was crowing about his tremendous success in the orgy room. Having completely drained himself dry after servicing so many willing bottoms, oral activity was the only possible option left. Keen customers were queuing up for quick relief from his talented muscular tongue of exquisite skill and the thousand thrills delivered by dexterous digits delighting dozens of onlookers anxiously awaiting their turn.

'I sucked, slurped and slobbered,' bragged the reptile, 'completely satiated with a tummy filling with spunk. How does that song go? *Yummy, yummy, yummy I've got love in my tummy ...*'

The audience loved it as much as the participants, but repetition was getting a little tedious when, not wishing to disappoint his adoring voyeurs, he was inspired by a scene from a comedy film seen a few years before in 1960 - *Bottoms Up* staring Jimmy Edwards as the corrupt incompetent Headmaster of a failing school with abysmal standards.

Entirely consistent with the standards of the day, harsh discipline was brutally imposed by thrashing a boy's bottom with a bamboo cane. Toad was titillated seeing Edwards (a gay man himself) wantonly striking the buttocks of five boys selected for a public punishment in front of the whole school. Just before the beating, sadistically, Edwards carefully aligned each backside to make a neat row to improve the presentation.

With this arousing memory in mind, Toad carefully picked out five alluring bums to be presented to his crude crowd in the orgy room. With instructions, he arranged them into a neat, straight line.

'Number two in a bit. Number four out a tad ... Yes that is perfect! Ready gentlemen? I'll now begin.'

Unlike the Headmaster, Toad was inflicting exquisite pleasure by rimming each anus in turn with his powerful prurient tongue. After a few minutes, his face buried in buttocks, all, moaning in ecstasy, were brought to a delicious milky conclusion assisted by clever toadal fondling fingers.

'That is vile!' complained Ronnie who had never before heard of this particular sexual activity.

'Agreed. I was shocked when it was first done to me by Ahmed my first love in Detroit. I could hardly believe it was happening at all. It is extreme and can be dangerous with a risk of contracting hepatitis. Come to think of it, Toad was put out of action for several months in the 1970s with that disease. But, Ronnie - aren't we missing the point?'

'What do you mean?'

'Toad boasted his sexual prowess to me in 1965. It was not until sometime in the 1980s that I actually saw *Bottoms Up* on TV and realised that his bragging was inspired by that 1960 film.'

'So he was lying!'

'Possibly, the bit about neatly lining them up. I would use a different word. I would call it fantasising. Don't get me wrong. I've seen Toad rimming in the Brighton bushes in front of an audience. It does happen. You, Ronnie, are horrified by your perception of a disgusting performance. I can understand that.

'I too am sickened and nauseated - but not from an act which gives pleasure - from an act which inflicts pain with impunity. In this very school, the Valley Comprehensive, it was normal practise to punish boys by beating them on their bottom or hand with a stick. *You* should know!'

'Too right!'

'My point is this - it was considered OK, quite legal, to impose discipline by inflicting physical suffering on little children and even teenagers. On the other hand, if those teenagers or grown men expressed affection by fondling, fucking, sucking or rimming - *they* were breaking the law! If caught, they would be thrown into prison. Once in that confinement, it was considered quite reasonable to stand back and let other 'disgusted' inmates beat the shit out of them. Reduced to emotional wrecks, many self harmed. Some committed suicide and some were murdered.'

Ronnie was staggered by his former teacher's descent into the use of foul language. His countenance clearly showed sufficient disapproval to elicit an apology - which was given fulsomely.

'Sorry, Ronnie. You are quite right to expect better of me, but I feel very strongly about this issue,'

After a slightly tense interval, the conversation returned to Mr Toad, a deeply damaged man after a lifetime hiding his true nature from the heterosexual majority. Tragically he was also reviled by many of his own kind. Trendy young men, familiar with the gay scene, viewed him as a piece of slime creeping around the dance floor - but to Simeon, oh no, his funny little friend was more than that - much more.

In the years of their friendship, Toad became quintessentially the very essence of old-fashioned Englishness in its purest form. He was as salty and as vulgar as a seaside postcard. The best times in Simeon's life would not be in the company of intolerant chickens. No. The best times would be spent with his old friend being tossed and blown about on the North Sea on board the Yorkshire Belle. Toad was quaint. Toad was funny. Toad was a bundle of fun, a barrel of laughs. He represented an amusing character in caricature - perhaps one of the last of the type. He did not know it at the time, but for Simeon, these precious hilarious moments were the beginning of a lifelong friendship with Mr Toad, nay, a love affair; a love affair which would last for decades.

Toad was one thing, Mother Ghoul was something else! Weekends away from the daily slog of teaching were precious, especially in the spring after the winter of discontent. One Friday after school, Simeon heard the approach of an ugly little 'toadmobile' announced by a constant and urgent - toot toot, toot toot. He liked his tooter, all part of an immature pushy personality pugnaciously huddled over the wheel. It was a hideous slug-shaped foreign contraption which suited the slug-shaped owner.

Eventually they reached the best part of an otherwise grimy town. Mother and son lived in a substantial Victorian town house overlooking the narrow town park bordered by the River Ouse. This pretty well-kept park dramatically terminated in a black confusion of cranes - massive long arms, beams, cables and cruel looking hooks blending into the darkness of a cold winter evening.

The invitation from the son was given gladly, but, unbeknown to the guest, had to be wrenched from mother who gave Simeon a reception as icy as the inky blackness from whence they came. When he complained, Toad said:

'Don't take it personally. Mother hates my gay friends.'

'But I *did* take it personally,' he told Ronnie. 'I'd heard of her reputation but at least expected a modicum of formal courtesy if not warmth. Scowling in tantrum, she plonked down my dinner in an ill lit ancient kitchen grunting a half audible - "Folks can't afford to entertain at these prices."'

'I'd have told her to stuff it,' said Ronnie. 'It'd choke me!'

'It nearly did. This was Friday evening. I was going to be in Goole all Saturday until Sunday evening when he would drive me back home. I was determined somehow to escape that obnoxious woman. If necessary, I'd get a bus or train back to Clowne that evening.'

'Did you manage it?'

'No I didn't. I was trapped and had to sleep in the maid's accommodation in the attic area.'

The one time maid had escaped her miserable servitude in the 1950s when Father Ghoul, a bank manager, suddenly died. Mother Ghoul decided she would pocket the miserly £4 per week and sacked her wretched little servant who had suffered abuse from mother and son for the previous two or three decades.

The next morning, brilliant sunshine illuminating a hard frost, was a welcome contrast to the lowering Dickensian atmosphere within that soot blackened edifice.

'Thank you for that nice breakfast, mother. I'll take Simeon on a Grand Tour of Goole starting with our park.' She received this cheery toodle-oo with a grimace and grudging grunt of disgust. In a vain attempt to sweeten the old battleaxe, Toad added - 'Don't trouble to make any lunch, we'll have a bite at the pub and Simeon will pay for himself.'

'Aye, see that he does,' she snapped.

Yes - he fully intended to pay for himself and, if possible, not to return to further insults with the help of his trusty rucksack. Toad was used to seeing his friend clad with that familiar accoutrement on his back and did not notice the complete removal of all personal items from the residence of Mother Ghoul. Effectively, Simeon had checked out.

A few steps from the front door, the neat park presented itself with a well preserved bandstand and several ornate comfortable benches thawing under the warming sun. The two friends progressed through the park until an ivy clad public lavatory came into view. In sudden excitement, Toad broke into a run. His little arms came up to shoulder level, podgy hands gesticulated with waggling fingers as he disappeared into his favourite and conveniently located 'cottage'.

He was so candid. It was this childlike honesty which always impressed Simeon down the years. A total contrast to the pretentious types he knew in Derby and Nottingham. It was too early. The cottage was empty but it afforded an opportunity to boast of wonderful days in which he sat next to that wonderful glory hole in that wonderful lavatory.

'I'm never refused! Lorry driver after lorry driver, van driver after van driver, I can get *real* men in this place. Quite adequate for my needs. I'm not ashamed to admit I'm often here with sandwiches and two flasks of tea. You've to be here early before an old queen gets in. They won't budge once they get established - so I beat them to it!' He giggled and gloated.

As they made further progress, the cranes loomed larger and the park deteriorated into a scrubby area of weeds and shrubs fighting against the pollution of a place which had worked for its living over the previous 200 years. It was protected from the treacherous tidal river by an embankment nearly twice human height. This levee, stretching many miles inland, supported a footpath giving views on swirling dark waters to the southeast and the town of Goole to the northwest. Toad mentioned several notable tragedies of victims swallowed up by merciless mud banks. Remorselessly, sluggishly, the central murky current flowed on. Suddenly, they were startled by screaming birds swooping overhead.

'They say seagulls are the tormented souls of sailors long dead. I'll introduce you to a regular fixture in the tavern. He can spin a few yarns about folklore and legends of bygone Goole.'

'An old seaman?' suggested Simeon.

'An educated chemist actually. Kenneth the Chemist, he's quite a colourful character. Knowing your inclination for ancient toothless types, you might find an opportunity for quick pleasure in the cellar.'

After negotiating a dreary muddle of cranes and untidy cables, they emerged into an intrigue of dismal warehouses and dwellings, derelict in appearance, linked by a tight knot of narrow cobbled lanes suggesting a culture of criminality. Simeon was seized with a curious mixture of fear and fascination. Isolated in a time warp, this bizarre little port appealed to his fondness of the weird and ugly. He had the same taste in men which is why he was with Toad rather than a beautiful young man. It was no mystery. As a 12-year-old, he had been sexually imprinted by a paedophile known in a Derbyshire pit town as Granddad to the boys at a Dickensian Church of England school. Several powerful pupils were regular visitors to his primitive terraced home almost completely smothered in ivy.

They walked past an inn which would not have been out of place in a horror film. A silent dark facade suggested closure for the last 100 years. Despite his aversion to alcohol, Simeon was pleased to learn they would be eating in that old ale house later. Equally as prominent as cranes on the Goole skyline was a tall slender spire, pointing to God, piercing a freezing heavenly vault of pure blue. In contrast to showing Ghouls (as toad dubbed the citizens of Goole) the way to a better world, the church itself had been blackened by decades of soot and smoke. Toad patiently followed his guest as he mooched around sombre grave stones perversely enjoying a sweet sadness in this strange haunting town. He perused names and epitaphs in a futile attempt to glean some meaningful understanding of the deceased. The monuments only confirmed ignorance and servile obedience to the bigotry and stranglehold of religion.

A short walk took them into the main high street where they enjoyed a pot of tea and a hot teacake in a plain but clean and popular cafe. It was so crowded, no tables were available. Toad and his chum stood uncertainly holding their trays, scanning empty tables where they might beg permission to share with others. One table with four chairs occupied by two men looked promising.

'Excuse me,' said Toad politely, 'do you mind if we sit here?'

'We certainly do!' came the alarming and unexpected response.

Toad's reaction was a surprise. He seemed not to notice this hurtful conduct and immediately asked at another table where two elderly women simply ignored the request. Silence was interpreted as consent and the little man plonked himself down, ordering his chum to do likewise. In a conversation later in that day, Simeon learned that Goole was a close knit community where almost everybody knew everybody else - and everybody knew the infamous Toad. The little man avoided pain by living in denial of nasty comments, pretending not to hear an insult. An empathetic instinct, common to most gay men, instructed Simeon not to interrogate or remark on this appallingly unkind incident. In this way the two homosexuals were protecting each other.

The two women speedily paid up and left the cafe, leaving the two good friends with their own table free to chat. Simeon asked about Kenneth the Chemist. A curious character in his late 70s made him about as old as the century. His well-known homosexuality had been cruelly established in the public mind by the tragic death of his 21-year-old lover decades earlier. An innocent friendship between two young men exploded into scandal when the boy's suicide note, intended for Kenneth's eyes only, was read by his outraged devout Pentecostal parents. So vehement were these flames of shock and disapproval that the secret of Kenneth's degeneracy leaked out of the family circle and became common knowledge in the town.

'With such a hostile population, how did your friend manage to become the respected chemist of Goole for over half a century?' queried Simeon.

Toad explained. Kenneth was the only son. There was no other option. From boyhood he had been trained to carry on in a trusted family business which had served the needs of the old port since the early 1800s.

'Pious heterosexuals are always prepared to hold their noses and accept services and skills from queers when needed. They tolerate me, don't they?'

Indeed they did. When Ghouls needed an organist for their weddings and funerals, they called on the talents of Mr Toad who was not only a music specialist in a good school, but also an acclaimed church organist whose fame had spread many miles beyond the small minded population of Goole.

Further perambulations took them into the afternoon through sombre deserted streets but for an occasional sad figure of bent back and uncertain foot. Vile alleys lurked behind high wharves. Simeon heard about slop shops and slut stops for quickies in this appalling place. Finally they trod across steps worn hollow by the ceaseless tread of drunken feet. Toad pushed aside a doddering loose-lipped senility who was blocking the tavern entrance.

It still looked forbiddingly derelict, but a creaky door which gave on to the hum of cheery companionship within. They were cold, so a large plate of hot food was welcome. A central table afforded views around assorted regulars, an equal mix of gender and types.

'Look at those rough looking women; they're known as Dock Fairies, prostitutes for the comfort of these gorgeous randy sailors. They also get comfort from *me* - for free!' added Toad salaciously licking his lips. 'It's true! Our crude cave is so black; they'll even accept pleasure from men they can't see at all! Such as that ancient pile of rags sat by the fire.'

Simeon noted a shabby old man deeply reposed in an arm chair carefully observing other patrons. Everything about him said - 'this is *my* chair next to *my* fire secure in *my* pub'. His was a face, worn with time and trouble, yet thoughtful and pleasant. Intelligent calm eyes studied Toad and chicken knowing full well that he was the subject of their discussion.

'You are looking at the famous Kenneth,' announced Toad.

'I don't understand!' Simeon was confused. 'Goole, as you've made clear, is populated by respectable small minded moral bigots, yet they tolerate prostitutes and homosexuals in an orgiastic room in a public house. How do they reconcile that situation?'

Toad talked his friend through that conundrum. In the Goole code of ethics, there was a distinction drawn between honest red-blooded sailors in need of quick heterosexual relief and filthy perverts who, unfortunately, might sneak in to assist in that process.

'It's grown up over the years,' explained Toad. 'The dark room at the back is for the girls where money is involved. Downstairs they get it for nothing in a cellar. Many seamen prefer a mouth and not too fussy who it belongs to. Sluts like me and Kenneth are highly skilled in the fine art of extracting semen from seamen. *They* know what a good time is! They come downstairs and often have to queue up - a line of tasty tars waiting their turn. Let me introduce you to Kenneth.'

They walked over to an old man who greeted with half smile and brief comment.

'Decided to slum it again, Toad?'

'This is my friend,' replied the complacent reptile. Leaning over, a lascivious whisper entered Kenneth's ear. 'Simeon likes your sort. You'll be able to have him.'

'What makes you think that I want him?' was the reply in a surprisingly cultured accent assisted by hands with an involuntary tremor.

'He'll want *you*. He's wanted to meet the talented toothless old chemist of Goole for several years.'

'Old chemist indeed! I shall have to see what Elizabeth Arden cosmetics can do for me. Would your friend care to ascend?'

At this point, Simeon understood that Kenneth's chemist days were long gone. In retirement, he occupied a small suite of rooms on the first floor making him the sole resident apart from the landlady who tended to his simple needs. Toad, *not* invited to ascend, informed his guest that he was honoured to be serviced above, alone, rather than in the cellar where others might be present. The honour was not appreciated. Simeon was more excited when hearing sounds of pleasure escaping the lips of fellow participants, not to mention anonymous touches in total darkness.

However, nobody was looking. Critical and disgusted eyes would never see Simeon sucked by this ancient Ghoul from Goole. They would never know. His reputation was safe. And, yes, it had to be acknowledged, there was, deep in his sexual psyche, a perverse desire to be touched by this vile, mouth-watering fossil reposed on his sucking stool, wanting and willing to work. And work he did. He worked well with tongue and clever, crafty hands. Naughty fingers sticky with drool searched and slid around the nooks and crannies of bliss, as the young man's half focused eyes idly explored the dark recesses of a dowdy, dreary room reverberating with crashing ecstasy. All these sensations were enjoyed, greatly enjoyed, safe in the knowledge that the worker would remain low, far away, far below navel level. After a few precious minutes of pleasure, Simeon finally succumbed. He succumbed to the succulent sounds of slurps and slobber. He succumbed to overwhelming touches, tickles, titillations and the distant sounds of a North Sea busy port. It all ended in that last familiar sound, that finality, the escaping sigh, the last, long, low murmur.

Back down in the tavern, Simeon was assaulted by quick fire questions.

'How did you get on upstairs? I had a marvellous time in the cellar without competition from Kenneth,' boasted Toad.

'He's a very interesting man, a survivor no less'

'Has he talked about that awful suicide, his boyfriend of many years back?'

'That and much more. I need extra time to hear that man's extraordinary philosophy on gay life. I don't want to offend you or your mother, but I've been invited to spend the rest of the weekend here. Now don't get upset! Face facts, your mother will be delighted to be rid of me and Kenneth wants you to be with us in whatever we do. I insisted on that - no exclusions. After all, first and foremost this is a weekend with my dear friend Mr Toad.'

On that Saturday afternoon they motored to a deserted and cold Bridlington where Toad spent an hour in a toilet leaving the others free to chat. Looking for a sympathetic ear, Simeon explored his suffering at school and mentioned Toad's behaviour earlier in the cafe which led to Kenneth making a comparison.

'You and Toad are like turtles. When bad things happen you both go into a shell. You go silent and stoic. It's the way you deal with hurt.'

'Is that bad?'

'No, it's natural to resent an unkind comment, but brooding on it should be avoided. That's the difference between you and Toad. I've only known you for a few hours, but you're inclined to mull over things. Toad just moves on. That's a good quality. He'll not fall out with anybody. I ignore people who offend me, Toad ignores nobody. In that way, never cutting anyone adrift, he receives more social support and makes better use of life. He can teach us both a lesson.'

Time spent with a new older, wiser friend was a valuable experience for Simeon. There were other weekends enjoyed at Goole, but always with Kenneth, never again with Mother Ghoul.

Chapter 4

Pupils in Distress

Simeon explained to Ronnie that teaching involves helping people at a social level. His older friends like Toad and Kenneth inspired him, where possible, to reach out and advise certain boys who were clearly troubled with personal problems. In a class of 30, on average there were likely to be three boys or girls who were either gay or bisexual. In a hostile homophobic atmosphere, most would keep their secret deeply buried. In 20 years of teaching, he was approached by only a few boys who, having heard rumours about Mr Hogg's private life, were desperate enough to reveal their sexuality and ask for some form of counselling. This was given, but always on the understanding that Mr Hogg never confirmed his own same-sex attraction. On the other hand, choosing his words carefully, he never denied his sexuality. To such pupils the schoolmaster presented himself as a man of the world who had met all kinds of people. He urged compassion, condemned prejudice and ignorance. These discussions always took place in his classroom during school hours or in the interlude following the last period when the campus was still buzzing with hundreds of dawdling, socialising and slowly dispersing pupils.

It was at just such a time when an adolescent with flame red hair, clutching his exercise book, nervously entered Room 76, the classroom of Mr Hogg.

'Can I have a word, sir?'

He was invited to take a seat directly in front of the teacher's desk. Fearing a request to re-explain the 1815 Corn Laws, Simeon was relieved when a completely different matter came up. The youth lowered his deep voice.

'In case anybody saw me, I wanted it to look like I'm asking about a history lesson.'

'You've every reason to ask, but I'm as much in the dark as you! Truth to tell, I've never really got my head around the economics and political chicanery of the Agrarian Revolution. It bores me to tears. It'll get better when we get on to canals and railways.'

Banter eased the tense atmosphere. Mark, with his healthy shock of shaggy hair, was a desirable butch working-class youth with heterosexuality written all over his lust inspiring bulges and curves. This beefy boy of mussed up red mop over freckled face had always intrigued, but sensitivity isolated him from other boys and nurtured a small measure of warmth between him and his teacher.

Simeon took pleasure from roundness of sparkling eyes and a child-like nose which had developed little from its original button-like charm. Suddenly, sunlight pierced the classroom spotlighting eyebrows and eyelashes rendered almost invisible on that troubled expression.

'What's up, Mark?'

The problem was preceded by begging. An earnest request for confidentiality was satisfied by cast-iron guarantees buttressed with references to the confessional of a priest. The schoolmaster made it clear: what is spoken in this room stays in this room. Mark was further assured that he safely belonged to a minority of boys whose internal difference would always be well concealed from others. Unfortunately this counselling took place in the 1980s, a time before the establishment of Lesbian, Gay, Bisexual and Transgender support centres such as the splendid Worksop Out on Wednesday at the Abbey Community Centre which started to help gay boys and girls in 2010. Simply being told that he could go through life as an invisible homosexual was small comfort to this youth unhappy with his new Saturday morning job.

'It's just to earn a bit of money, sir, get me out of the house and enjoy a bit of company. I've got no friends, no *real* friends I can talk to. I'm lonely - but I can't go back to that dirty workshop with its dirty talk.'

Feeling alienated, Mark described a greasy old shed at the rear of a cycle shop. It was decorated with pornographic female wall calendars and populated by rough uncouth youths spouting obscenities and boasting recent sexual conquests.

Simeon's advice was limited. Instead of a homophobic cycle shop, he suggested investing time with a writing group or amateur drama or both. In such an environment, Mark would mix with artistic people more sympathetic to his sensitivities and increase his chances of meeting that one significant person who could change his life for the better. A further visit to Room 76 to 'discuss the Corn Laws' was proposed in which the pupil could take possession of a newspaper which would certainly increase gay knowledge and enrich his life via the use of the Contact Supplement with a host of names and box numbers.

Mark's courage paid off. He didn't find a writing group but spent a few weeks with amateur drama which fizzled out. The big change came with making full use of *Gay News* which took him away from Worksop to rewarding years in London. After a series of encounters with different people, eventually Mark found the right man and settled into a loving relationship.

Not all unscheduled visitors to Room 76, given similar advice, were able to break out of the homophobic constraints of an old coal town - but Mark was the best successful example. During the oppressive Thatcher years, many Worksopians were less fortunate. Simeon was horrified to hear about two screaming queens who, in pursuit of sexual conquest involving a rough randy youth, chose to suppress their moral instincts. The threesome, all very chatty, were on their way to a derelict building where sex could be safely enjoyed. The rough youth was bragging about his new found scam of acquiring regular amounts of money.

'It's easy! I just keep an eye on a cash machine and follow a likely punter to a quiet place, show them a knife, and ask nicely for the dough. It works every time - piece o' cake.'

The effeminate youths were not evil. Indeed they expressed disapproval and remonstrated with the object of their lust. Notwithstanding, they still pressed on to the ruined house and indulged in a lewd act with this shameless rascal who justified his conduct on the grounds that he and his new friends were 'all queer anyway'. Simeon was particularly distressed with this example of self-hate which had embedded itself into the secretive gay community of his school.

Another pupil, lured to the canal side by an alluring ruffian, was knocked down unconscious.

'How long were you there?' asked the appalled schoolmaster.

'Don't know, sir.'

'You didn't report it to the police?'

'You're joking! Anyway, it could have been worse - much worse. At least he didn't roll me into the canal. I'd be dead!'

The inability to help these people was a cause of increasing anxiety. Beyond offering a sympathetic ear, giving out general commonsense suggestions and uttering platitudes, Simeon was incapable of making any real difference to a life racked by secrecy, pain, guilt and constant fear.

The stress of a double life was exacerbated during an epidemic which appeared in the early 1980s. Acquired Immune Deficiency Syndrome - (AIDS) - a new infection which destroyed the body's immune system - was common in homosexuals and increasingly infecting heterosexuals. The spreading 'gay plague' was an effective death sentence with no known cure. In 1985 it created a sense of moral panic in some parts of the general population. The government launched a £20m ad campaign to encourage safer sex with the slogan *'Don't die of ignorance'*.

The death of Rock Hudson in that year was followed by revelations of his homosexuality which shocked millions of his fans. AIDS eventually claimed the lives of Liberace, Freddie Mercury and Rudolf Nureyev. Health minister Edwina Currie tried to calm the growing hysteria uttering her infamous homophobic remark - *'Good Christians won't get AIDS.'*

Tension grew in the Valley Comprehensive School and was clearly etched on Simeon's ravaged face when he passed along a corridor near the main office, so much so that it alarmed and drew comment from the school nurse.

'Simeon! Good heavens, man. You look dreadful.'

She expressed alarm regarding his strained, pained expression and deep furrows of brow. This exchange took place following a full staff meeting about AIDS the previous evening which he had not attended as it was not compulsory. The passing of a film star, a glittering flamboyant pianist, a master showman of powerful voice from the world of pop and a star of ballet had concentrated ignorant minds of some Valley staff.

Before the word homophobia was in common use, with tact and sensitivity, Nurse told Simeon she was thankful that he had not been present to suffer such rank prejudice which would have been distressing, adding to this anxiety. It was a familiar scenario - the 'elephant in the room'. Nurse was tiptoeing around the issue; well-meaning comments were made, hatred condemned but the 'H word' never uttered.

Nevertheless, her acute perception was embarrassing, unnerving and paralysing. He stood mute, frozen, unable to respond to this act of kindness from a conscientious professional. He was typical. Many gay people lull themselves into a false sense of security, a comfort zone where they feel that *'nobody knows'* - where, in fact, almost everybody knows. Fearing exposure and humiliation, Simeon said nothing about his private life and tried to remain invisible. It didn't work.

Even his choice of house near Clowne was evidence of wishing to be invisible. Any visitor to Simeon's home near this remote pit village needed complicated directions if he was to have any hope of reaching his destination. Indeed, finding this secluded section of Derbyshire's extreme north east corner, in the 1970s, was a challenge for any explorer who was prepared to risk getting lost in a maze of narrow country lanes. It was a surprising achievement to see Ronnie, Bobbie and Freddie at his door on one occasion in the hope of starting a cycling club.

After years in ugly flat well scrubbed Michigan, in 1978 Simeon was a persistent cyclist in search of English ugliness in a craggy backwater of interbred crooked colliers.

In Clowne, he struck gold! Arriving at a lopsided, dirty bedraggled high street, littered with the slovenly and the dishevelled, he supposed this must be 'downtown' Clowne, a pit village of about 7,000 people situated in north-east Derbyshire close to the borders with Yorkshire and Nottinghamshire. Indeed, after he was established in his new home, the cycle ride from Clowne to Worksop (and back) took Simeon through three counties.

So now here he was in the middle of this craggy coal community. Flat caps and slatterns slowly shuffled around the scruffy shops uttering inanities in pit talk. This was a place of no consequence to those who did not live there. He was at the very centre of a primitive pit place evidenced by an ancient cross which had stood at this intersection of several roads for 800 years.

Abruptly, sudden silence descended as Simeon dismounted and looked around him. He was received as an alien from another planet. Small white close fitting shorts and a bright Palm Beach shirt provoked rude gawking from an assortment of fishwives, scarecrows, yokels, crones, hags, louts and simpletons, including the obese, the old and the misshapen.

A panic set in! In an effort to escape this uncomfortable ill-mannered scrutiny, he quickly mounted and furiously cycled out of the village for about half a mile until he had reached the edge of woodland. Catching his breath, he looked back over green fields at Clowne and noticed the spire of the rather charming old church surrounded by slowly rotting sunken graves.

It had been a dull day, but a break in the clouds enabled the rural idyll to be brilliantly spot lit. Yes - the people had irritated him. Yet he had been intrigued by this medieval scene and now wished he had enjoyed the tranquillity of that graveyard now beautifully illuminated in full sunshine. Perhaps another time.

His labours had taken him up an incline and the welcome sunshine born on a brisk westerly was racing towards him across the picturesque landscape. It was now warming his legs and also brought to life a haze of woodland bluebells. This pretty scene resolved into a rough bridleway winding into the wood. And then - something else - a faded For Sale sign about Magpie House.

How odd. A dwelling in the middle of nowhere! Beguiled by this inviting wooded bridle path decorated with bluebells, anemones and celandine; Simeon set out to inspect Magpie House. He was already in heaven! This ancient deciduous woodland of oak, sycamore, beech and birch was a riot of sweet scents and humming with spring birdsong. It was early enough to be well lit and nicely warmed by the April sun which, with increasing foliage, would be more heavily shaded from a July sun. Simeon had always dreamed of living in a fairytale forest where such magical contrasts could be observed and enjoyed on a daily basis.

As he cycled on, he came to appreciate the enchanting effects of human neglect which enhanced the natural allure of a mature wood. Areas of dark density and several trees which had fallen with a mighty violent crash were evidence of an unspoilt world where nature (and not the axe man) had laid low a great beech or ancient oak, which, with exposed torn roots thrust up! twice the height as himself, was now supporting mosses and fungi.

And there it was - the Victorian Gothic dwelling of Magpie House. And surely the possession of it must also be a dream? It looked totally out of his reach. But it was everything he desired. Strong and sturdy with stone mullioned windows which added character. Heavily covered with ivy and Virginia creeper, this house had all the camouflage needed by a damaged gay man in search of invisibility. Even before he set eyes on the house, the short ride through woodland put Simeon in mind of the Sleeping Beauty legend.

Every indication told him that this building was derelict and had been so for many years - totally devoid of human occupation. He knew there would be no sleeping beauty within. A good thing, since a sleeping prince (a handsome one) would be more to Simeon's taste. Anyway - it was the **house** sleeping and Simeon would, if he could afford it, kiss this house into a home.

He fully understood the psychology behind a multiplicity of emotions swirling around his head. In 1957 it was in such a home of dilapidation strangled by masses of foliage where Simeon found kindness and respite from the ongoing cruelty at Mundy Street Boys School.

Magpie House *must* be cheap! Rundown, certainly, nearly covered by a combination of ivy and Virginia creeper which nostalgically recalled Guzzly Granddad's house in Heanor together with happy erotic associations.

A large country house with land - impossible to afford! Yet, given current raging inflation at 20% +, his colleagues had advised him to go for something costing more than he could afford. Could it really *be* possible? Could he obtain a mortgage on such a crumbling old relic?

He walked around the house checking windows and tried to see if there was a sunken roof from the close encroaching trees. It appeared to be sound. The solid, sturdy front door proclaimed full security and was firmly locked - nothing wrong there.

A triple 'kaah' and shrill 'kyaw' forced his attention to the top canopies of nearby tall trees where a multitude of cawing jet black birds had built large untidy rough nests made up of twigs. Simeon had heard that some of these rookeries were centuries old as pairs of birds returned year after year to renovate the same nests. He looked hard but failed to see the distinctive black-and-white flash of the intelligent, cunning, thieving 18 inch magpie which had given the wood and his house its name. Further round the house, to his delight, the familiar magpie cackle announced, in full flash flight, the much welcomed sight - 'two for joy'.

He wondered about the previous occupants of Magpie House - distressed gentle folk who didn't have as much money as they once did? Two old spinsters and an elderly brother? Unearned incomes which had dwindled? Complaining bitterly about being reduced to one servant! Decayed ladies, nice ladies, well bred and gracious, who had *never* earned a living. Judging by the size of trees just yards from the front door, the old dears had departed many decades ago.

Woodland had encroached over a one-time garden right up to the house walls. A few daffodils and hyacinths had survived. There was an air of deep sorrow. This house was impregnated with melancholy. So sad - and yet, Simeon was excited! Why? Because Simeon might get exactly what he wanted - a tumbling down ancient dwelling, in an enchanted wood, with land at a cheap price.

'It's perfect!' he said out loud. 'I wonder if it's haunted. Ghosts can't hurt you. I think fairies can, if they put their mind to it. No matter, the ghosts and fairies around this place and wood are *friendly*,' he insisted. 'All the same, I'll be careful not to annoy them. Anyway, a house this old, so crooked, so decrepit ... well, it's bound to be a bit noisy. Especially in the dead of night when there's a profound silence. I think it's called *settling*.'

A few days later, Simeon had closed a deal with the estate agents who had welcomed him with open arms. A mortgage was quickly and eagerly arranged giving him ownership of land and the property. It was more a case that the agents were a go-between liaising with the buyer and the Church of England.

This property, quite sound according to the surveyor, had no discernible history of distressed gentle folk or decayed ladies. It was the old vicarage uninhabited since 1956 when a smaller more practical house for the incumbent was built in the village. Simeon was told that, from time to time over the years, the property became useful as a store house. Therefore it had to be properly maintained - in spite of appearances to the contrary. The Church of England even offered to finance the removal of numerous trees too close to the house. This offer was firmly declined by Simeon who said he wanted to preserve the Sleeping Beauty effect of neglect - and let it continue! Bring it on!

The affordability of the deal was sealed when Simeon uttered that every tree in Magpie Wood would die of old age and never by the violence of man. As custodian of these principles, his resolve to live in Magpie Wood for the remaining days of his life was also music to the ears of Church officials. A further generous reduction in price was agreed when Simeon willingly signed a covenant that the house and woodland would revert back to the ownership of the Church after his death.

Simeon's idyllic existence hidden in the tranquillity of beautiful Derbyshire woodland did not save him from the harsh reality of the Iron Lady of distant London.

In 1988, the Thatcher government passed the notoriously homophobic Section 28. Like living in a police state, it prevented any positive mention of homosexuality in schools and banned local authorities from publishing material expressing the acceptability of homosexuality as a 'pretended family relationship'. Teachers were afraid to challenge homophobic bullying. This was the Thatcher legacy for people of same-sex attraction. For decades a serious problem remained in our schools - 41% of gay pupils were beaten up and gay pupils were six times more likely to commit suicide.

At the 1987 Conservative party conference, the Prime Minister openly mocked people who defended the right to be gay. During her rule, there was an explosion of queer-bashing, whilst gay men were demonised for the AIDS pandemic.

'Mrs Thatcher again!' objected Ronnie. 'If I were a gay lad reading your life story, I'd want to hear less about a wicked witch and more about a handsome prince. What happened to the fun in your life? Being gay must have given you opportunities and a few adventures. Let's have some good stuff.'

'Point taken,' admitted Simeon. This comment from a young man plunged him into a morbid and unprofitable meditation. What was this schoolmaster after all? A dried up old man with neither child nor chick; no one to care whether he lived or died? Old? How old was Simeon? He had to work it out. If it was 1995, he was 50. Perhaps not so old. The previous day, Ronnie had estimated him to be a 30-something which might have been the case when he taught that class in the 1980s. Anyway, his life had been full of incident. Ronnie was interested and wanted 'the good stuff'. And there *was* good stuff. There was, for instance, the black youth in Detroit - Laurent - who we will meet later.

Chapter 5

Detroit Riots

From 1963 to 1976, Simeon lived in Detroit visiting the UK annually for as many weeks as funds would stretch. He had several jobs but was most content as a messenger at Detroit Bank located downtown. The pay was poor but duties undemanding and totally stress free. Most of the time he sat in the messenger room with other messengers waiting for instructions from Herb the head messenger. On an average day these sedentary intervals could extend from a few minutes up to half an hour, or more, depending on demand.

Other seated colleagues sat silent or might occasionally attempt trivial conversation. Simeon, much bored, soon found the quality of the job dramatically improved by the simple expedient of reading a book. Accordingly, in two years at that employment, he devoured dozens of improving titles which eventually led him to save for a university education.

Being a messenger in Downtown Detroit, around, up and down the skyscrapers, was educating in other ways. He was delighted when asked to take items to the Bhule Building, Hudson's Department Store or the Lafayette Building - *especially* the Lafayette Building. Each of these old towers housed an obscure, infrequently used public rest room which acquired a notorious reputation quietly disseminated amongst members of the gay community.

Simeon soon learned the rules of this secret society. Like other gay venues, it was a meeting place for homosexuals. Unlike other venues, these toilets were not for chatting, getting to know each other, sharing a drink or dancing together. Like 'cottaging' back in England, the Detroit skyscraper 'tea rooms' were used for quick silent sex. Simeon would simply come and go. It was very American, always oral: the fast convenient relief extending the errand just minutes. A delay so slight, Herb never noticed.

Cubicles were occupied by seated workers, patiently waiting for fresh young cream. They tended to be older African Americans eager to service standing visitors who were usually younger.

Doors and partitions had been removed from cubicles in the Lafayette Building, probably to deter 'inappropriate activities'. In fact, it had the *opposite* effect. Fat-faced cock-suckers were now in open view slurping on inflated weapons of impressive proportions. Simeon was greatly aroused at the sight of his fellow chickens wantonly sheathed in well practiced, well lubricated orifices affording supreme ecstasy. Fired by recalled pleasures of a toothless grotto from his schooldays, the 'orgy effect' was a powerful aphrodisiac. Like enjoying a good meal with friends, pleasure shared - was pleasure enhanced.

These public displays of obscenity were totally untroubled and uninterrupted thanks to a sign proclaiming 'Rest Room Out of Order'. Simeon suspected certain powerful men in authority probably had a carnal interest in keeping the Lafayette orgy going. And what an orgy! If not audible, concluding moments of high delight were indicated by evocative body language. An arching back, a bracing spasm of joy gripped the torso as an open mouth issued a silent scream of rapture from the very foundations of a stiff stake struggling to further impale a slobbering sitting slut. Deep guttural groans of gratitude signalled a milky gush, the reward for services rendered.

Simeon's chances of meeting other members of the gay community were restricted by his personal inclinations and life-style. Most gay men were city slickers sharing a different routine inhabiting late night bars, clubs and discos. With his aversion to alcohol and thumping loud music, he was early to bed, early to rise, ever dreaming of a return to the hills and beautiful Derbyshire Dales. The Detroit job had given him regular access to quick sexual gratification and would also open a door to the secretive world of gay culture.

Each morning at 8.30, Simeon stood on the sidewalk in front of the impressive Palladian frontage of the bank with its Greek columns and capitals asserting the confidence of American capitalism. It was his daily duty to meet the President of Detroit Bank who rejoiced in the splendid name - Oscar de Hammarskjold. As the massive Lincoln Continental gracefully glided to a halt before the mighty edifice of finance, a regular exchange was like a mantra -

'Good morning. Mr de Hammarskjold.'

'**Morning**,' came a grunt from the great man. It sounded more like a reprimand than a greeting. 'Tell 'em to wash it.'

It was the same every day. The six-foot-plus President eased himself out of the driving seat set for a tall man, quickly replaced by a humble five-foot-nine messenger who would not dare to adjust the power seating position. With difficulty, Simeon drove the stately beast. It was dangerous. He was deeply reclined with a restricted view together with inadequate control of the large vehicle. In these precarious circumstances, the Lincoln slowly moved to the corner, right and right again and first left into a narrow street dwarfed by two skyscrapers. A little way down on the right was the entrance to an expensive downtown multi-storey park used by executives. A young black guy was waiting to take the car to its usual reserved location.

'Mr de Hammarskjold would like his car washed,' said the driver.

This ungracious response to a polite request irked Simeon. The unwarranted attitude had been endured for several days when he finally decided to challenge the attendant. His rudeness was no mystery. An overnight sleep stealing low of unbearable humidity had not dipped under 70 degrees. Worse was to follow! Another miserable scorcher in the 90s was fast approaching this hazy polluted oven of concrete and cement. Even worst still, the atmosphere was thick with ethnic hatred. These were the 1960s when Detroit was gripped by racial turmoil eventually leading to an explosion of burning riots which left city blocks gutted resembling a war zone. Regardless, the humble messenger attempted a remonstration with the African American along the lines of their shared lowly circumstances.

'Look!' he implored, 'I'm no different to you! I'm not pretending that I'm better than you. We're about the same age and are probably paid the same. When I ask you to wash this car, I'm just following orders. There is no need to be so nasty to me!'

The black boy seemed to be startled by this outburst when the drama was interrupted by an older black man.

'Hey! Hold on there! What's this all about?'

The man turned out to be the boy's boss. Simeon reiterated his main points and tried to explain that he was not prejudiced against the attendant. In so doing, the two Americans were suddenly transfixed by an unfamiliar foreign accent known in England as broad Derbyshire.

'Where on God's earth is you from?' asked the boss man.

Simeon launched into another spiel describing a background and family of mine workers emerging from the bowels of the earth with faces encrusted with coal dust - so deeply ingrained - no amount of soap and scrubbing could ever remove the blackening which marked the lowly status of a common collier. He added his belief that at £8 per week, existing in a primitive terrace cottage, there was precious little difference between a coal miner and a cotton picking slave. For good measure, he threw in the fact that while Detroit Negroes drove around in huge beautiful automobiles, Simeon's kin folk got around on pushbikes.

This tetchy polemic was cut short by the boss striding forward with an air of menace. He was a big man, albeit with a benign expression signalling good humour, indulging a child throwing a tantrum.

'Well, Englishman, I guess that's better out than in,' he said, now in full smile. The smile faded addressing his subordinate, 'Laurent! It's your job to be nice to our customers. We don't sneer at them, we help them. You can start by explaining the pre-sets.'

The boss was referring to the complication of power seat controls. In past days he had noticed Simeon struggling to drive the Lincoln. Sullenly, with a touch of shame, Laurent slipped into the passenger seat and asked his customer to get back into the car. He was invited to push a button marked 'medium' which immediately raised and moved the driving seat forward to suit a man of average size. Both boys beamed at this sudden demonstration of electronic wizardry and made eye contact in that intimate space. For two youths looking at each other, the moment lasted longer than it should have done. Hostilities had magically evaporated and Simeon was now free to savour perfect proportions of quintessential African features. He scanned tempting thick lips, a wide nose and big, beautiful, wondrous round eyes. In return, the black boy was able to examine a Caucasian countenance so very enticingly close.

'Yeah! I guess we done some good here,' came a commanding deep voice from the big black boss's face which had abruptly jutted into the car. It shattered the tender moment of incipient mutual affection. 'You got time for a coffee?' Simeon declined. He had already exceeded the time quota for parking the President's car. 'Lunch?' Yes, he could return during his lunch hour. He shook hands with the boss (firm grip) and then accepted Laurent's gentler warm hand. Further embarrassing seconds passed before, reluctantly, it was relinquished; another exciting moment of extended duration.

At 12.30 the boys greeted each other with obvious enthusiasm after four hours apart.

'Boss man got us some goodies,' said the attendant through brilliant white teeth contrasted against smiling ebony. Simeon followed his former foe down a dark corridor noticing for the first time beautifully formed buttocks tempting with mesmerising motion.

'Do da wigger like dem sweet buns?' This surprise husky voice, in gentle whisper, intruded behind his ear. Boss, observing Simeon's lusting eye line, had stealthily joined the lads from an unnoticed junction on the right. The three turned left into a comfortable if drab staff kitchenette complete with small table, chairs and armchairs. Greasy walls, untidily adorned with a selection of scantily clad soft porn, announced to a heterosexual world the correct credentials of red blooded black Americans. But Simeon knew better. He had been admitted into the secret of a homosexual sect. All the clues had been given and understood.

In the circles of gay ghetto speak, a 'wigger' was a white kid with a taste for black meat and 'buns' described a tantalising black bottom in lascivious locomotion. At that moment, he realised why boss man was somewhat familiar. Of course! He was a regular worker in the Lafayette Building - and a good one too. Boss was one of several older overweight guys who always sat and serviced those who stood. Over the weeks and months, much of Simeon's seed had been pleasurably consumed by this noisy slobbering slurper whose spunk stained overalls testified to his erotic gluttony.

At the moment when Boss Man dropped into a dirty old armchair, those same familiar smears and discolorations daubed over his dark blue overalls sparked a strong invitation to both boys. In unison, they surged forward to that well practiced juicy grotto of ecstasy tantalisingly visible in an enormous wide-open mouth.

'Is it safe?' breathed Simeon, concerned that others might enter the kitchenette.

'Nobody come in this place,' said Laurent flashing a sexy smile. The executive car park was staffed with fewer employees than might be supposed. In fact, at that moment, there were only two more men in the whole building busy cleaning the Presidential Lincoln. Boss Man was *the* Boss, entrusted with daily management, hiring and firing. Consequently, staff were recruited from a social circle of young men who shared Simeon's secret sexual inclinations.

Current activities could continue because the big man was not just king of the car park, he was a power within the hidden homosexual underworld of downtown Detroit. In fact, there were two coexisting covert gay networks in the city. Simeon had stumbled into the Black Mafia and would eventually become acquainted with the Pink Mafia. Like all criminal gangs, as with the conventional Mafia, they protected themselves under a cloak of corruption and, when necessary, the infliction of violence.

Simeon took to Boss Man like a duck to water. His big glistening tongue fell out in lewd invitation triggering both boys to fumble for a quick trouser drop releasing two stiff stakes ready for action. In deference to his new friend, Simeon let the more impressive one go first. He took pleasure seeing the dark weapon wantonly sheathed up into that luscious cave of carnal delight, at the same time, up close, scrutinising Laurent's facial features contorted in ecstasy.

Nor was Simeon's hand idle. This was an opportunity to complement oral efforts by exploring that sweet black bare bottom (so much lusted after) with gentle finger-tip caresses in and around erogenous areas. From past experience, Simeon knew he would not have long to wait. Making a pig of himself, the glutton gorged on Laurent's black meat encouraged also by the aural effect of escaping sounds of bliss, quickly (too quickly) coming up to that joyful climax of several concealed spurts. Now drained and satiated, he withdrew his still rock hard slobber strewn manhood and triumphantly brandished it at the excited white boy. Somewhat aggressively, he panted out -

'Yeah, wigger! Don't keep Boss Man waitin'. Look!' He pointed to the yawning, glistening grotto now proudly brim full of semen eagerly awaiting a racial mix of second-helping. Lascivious past Lafayette images of that same electrifying scene flashed through a mental memory bank. On many a busy afternoon, Simeon had actually stood in a lewd line to get a piece of the action. This greedy gobbler, often dribbling love juice from preceding punters down the front of his overalls, revelled in his piggish practices. It was a big turn-on for him and patient customers (like Simeon) who had been imprinted by past experiences.

Boss was simply acting out his sexual fantasy. In other ways he was quite different. If not an educated man, he was intelligent and could articulate his thoughts and effectively communicate his extensive knowledge of a life blighted by institutional racism. In the weeks which followed, Simeon (the only white face in a small black harem) was invited to several social gatherings in which this dominant personality steered animated discussions around a labyrinth of what he termed 'double jeopardy' - the perils of being both black *and* queer. He encouraged thoughtful and tolerant debate - reminding his boys that Simeon was a guest, effectively a stranger in the US, and should always be treated with polite respect. Simeon emphasised this point to Ronnie, adding that Boss was as good as, if not better than, any professor at his university attended some years later.

On one occasion, this 'tutor group' was taken to see the 1958 musical *South Pacific*. Viewing was preceded by a short lecture on one important and controversial song - *You've got to be Carefully Taught* sung by sexy Lieutenant Cable.

'The lyrics say that racism is not born in you, it has to be taught,' explained Boss. 'This movie was badmouthed by Southern politicians. One redneck Georgian lawmaker said the song was inspired by Moscow!'

'How so?' asked Laurent.

'It justified interracial marriage. The bigots saw the lyrics as a threat to the American way of life.'

Simeon recalled his eight-year-old nephew enthusiastically up to the TV, goggling brutal white police officers inflicting unspeakable violence upon peaceful protesting African Americans as they huddled together in a vain attempt to avoid serious injury. The boy's words were painfully seared into his memory.

'Hey dad! Come and look at the niggers getting beaten up.'

The big man's philosophy was revealed in question and answer sessions.

'Have you noticed that we always have sex standing up? Why is that?'

'Don't know,' said one boy. 'I guess straight folks do it in bed.'

'Yes - but they don't face the dangers *we* do. Have you seen wild animals or dogs woofing down food? We do sex like that. Cops might come and lock us up, or hoods might put the boot in. We got to be quick, that's why I'm so good,' he smiled. 'Get ya jollies off before something bad happens.'

He justified group sex on the grounds that it was 'more fun' and in some ways safer than private activity.

'Let's face it; most stuff we do is done with strangers. You just don't know what kooks you're playing with. If everybody can see everybody else, you can jump in and help if somebody squeals or something don't look right.'

During these weeks of Boss gatherings, Laurent continued to look longingly at his new white friend and was ever at his side. But it never seemed to get better than that. In whispers, several times, Simeon asked if they could meet up away from the group in private. Each answer was much the same.

'It's like ... we stick together,' said Laurent. 'Boss keeps us on a short leash. We all do it together. Keep it simple. Boss calls it "schoolboy sex." We all get sucked together and we learn together. Boss don't go for secret romance. And he don't like the dirt road.'

This was a stark contrast to the gay scene back in Derbyshire where you were asked - 'Are you butch or are you bitch?' Butch giving it, bitch taking it. Most gay Americans were hostile to anal penetration which was more common in England. Simeon often heard offensive references to Europeans who 'hit the dirt road'. On the other hand, regarding the racial angle, he wondered if Laurent found Boss's rules a convenient safety net. Deep down, the boys knew that colour was an insurmountable obstacle to any realistic hope of a relationship. With that threatening cloud hanging over them, there was an ineffable sadness in the loving looks often exchanged.

They enjoyed the choreographed orgies sometimes put on to titillate Boss Man and his beefy bodyguards. Simeon found himself in the role of a white kid lost in the ghetto. Threatening black hoodlums descended on him grabbing, groping and extracting maximum humiliation. White kid resisted the lewd assault until he was overwhelmed by the strength of intrusive searching black hands removing his jeans. Many rude black fingers disappeared inside underpants (front and back) exploring private places, those hidden nooks and crannies of carnal delight. Here were buttons of bliss gently pressed and stroked by clever fingers winning the battle. The script called for the 'victim' to give up the struggle at a point when extreme pleasure defeated all useless efforts to resist. Boss insisted the moment was signalled by half closure of eyes, open mouth and, at the very end, protruding tongue. Simeon played it well, loved every second, and often obliged with a concluding orgasm.

It was fantasy, all too soon violated by the feared explosion of city violence. The long hot smouldering month of July 1967 burst into flames on Monday 24th. Like thousands of white workers from segregated suburbs carefully cleansed of Negroes, Simeon did not dare make the daily 20 mile commute from his home to downtown Detroit. There were fearful comparisons of the 1943 race riot in which 38 people were shot dead. Some commentators spoke of this current incendiary event as the first spark of a civil war. Since 1964, dozens of major American cities had already suffered riots and looting. After several city blocks had been gutted, beyond the control of regular riot police, Federal Paratroopers were sent in to restore order. A few nervous employees of the Detroit Bank started to trickle back on the following Monday and Simeon steeled himself for a return to work on the Tuesday.

His fragile link with Boss's black harem was entirely dependent on his daily duty to park the Presidential Limousine. From that morning routine, all invitations to other venues followed. He was never given a phone number or an address; indeed, he was warned against attempting any such contact. He would turn up each morning and receive instructions from the Big Man. On this first day after a week of racial turmoil, Boss and Laurent welcomed him with a heartfelt hug of affectionate relief and praise for doing 'the right thing'.

'Shit baby!' said Laurent, 'The Black Panthers had *road blocks* stopping and checking out everybody.'

'What then?' asked Simeon.

'Not much. No problem if you're black. They'd just let you go on your way.'

'What if you're white?' pressed Simeon. A few tense moments passed before Laurent, with sad eyes, sad voice and slow shaking head, responded.

'You in bad shape, baby.'

Those few grim words seemed to sum up Simeon's precarious position within the circles in which he moved. Boss Man was also thoughtful, sad and serious. He was fully aware that this new revolutionary, far left, Black Nationalist organization had no reputation for being gay friendly. It had not been put to the test. Few gay African Americans were brave enough to admit their sexuality to armed citizens' patrols who were giving out free breakfasts to poor children and other good works. Somehow, unbeknownst to Simeon, the riot and its aftermath had a catastrophic effect on Boss, his bodyguards and his harem - they disappeared! One morning in early August, he arrived at the park to be received by an indifferent stranger, who shrugged at the question -

'What happened to Laurent?'

Boss turned out to be a different boss with a personality so weak and gray he was almost invisible. Nobody was about to give a nosey white kid any information which was none of his business anyway. The shrug summed it up. Simeon was frozen out of any exchange with the black race. No small talk. After handing over the car, he walked back to the bank. Lafayette eroticism continued as before, but without Boss Man. There was the usual anonymous silence; the usual void of social exchange was unaffected. It was impossible to know if any of the nameless knew anything about the missing regular. Similar types were still there sitting and slurping on meaty manhoods offered to them.

Ronnie was appalled by this sad ending.

'You must have been gutted! After weeks of building up friendships with that black kid and the old man ... how could you not know anything, not be told at least something?'

'It was worse than that. I was in love with Laurent, and Boss, for all his dominance and bullying, was the centre of my sole social network - not to mention intellectual stimulation. That man was an education. I was back to square one. Lafayette and similar venues were good for sex, but I needed affection, emotional support and a degree of camaraderie. With no friends, estranged from my family, I needed to belong to something.'

'But folks just don't disappear! A workmate could have whispered something to you, or a sex mate, or a relative. Surely during all those weeks meeting all those people, *somebody* might have approached you with news?'

'You don't understand the reality of *my* world, Ronnie. You live in a heterosexual network where heterosexual friends get introduced to other heterosexual friends, heterosexual relatives and heterosexual colleagues. When something bad happens, people swap news, close ranks, offer help, support, advice, condolences - you get the lot. My family threw me to the wolves. I'm on my own.

'In 1960s Detroit we were the despised minority in hiding. We were known as fags, queers or degenerates. The race issue simply complicated an already difficult situation. Had the parking people been all white, I was still isolated from relatives and others who, in their view, knew there was something seriously wrong with me. Not a word was ever spoken, but the tension and shame was always hanging in the air. There's an expression, the *elephant in the room. I* was that invisible elephant, an embarrassment never to be acknowledged. *The love that dare not speak its name* was another reference to homosexuality. Humiliations were endured on a regular basis. At a funeral, a stranger asked me if I was a friend of the family.

'No,' I said. 'The man in the coffin there - that's my dad!'

Jack Hogg died in Detroit in 1972. After American custom, he was on view in open coffin for a few days prior to the funeral. Simeon wandered over to look at him. A stranger did the same and shook his head. They made eye contact.

'Sure makes you think, doesn't it?'

'Sure does.'

'Friend of the family?'

'He's my dad,' responded the son.

At this the stranger seemed shocked trying to make sense of baffling information. The questioner was aghast. During the uneasy moments which followed, much puzzled, he was struggling to find an appropriate response. He opened his mouth to speak - thought better of it - and then immediately closed his mouth. Clearly embarrassed, he tried to ease the tension.

'Your sister never told me she had a brother! I'm sorry ... it's just that, well, you see ... she never mentioned you.'

Having been the 'elephant in the room' for so many years, it might be assumed that Simeon had a strategy for dealing with this type of mortification. He had not. You never get used to pain. And, at 27, he was still young. He was painfully self-conscious, ill at ease, ashamed and humiliated. He did what he'd often done to preserve his dignity. He walked away from an impossible situation.

'Didn't you try to explain to that stranger that you'd been disowned by your sister?' asked Ronnie.

'No need,' responded Simeon. 'He just shuffled away in embarrassed confusion, no doubt drawing his own conclusions. I was a coward. I lacked the confidence to assert myself. The queerness of my miserable life had completely defeated me. It's made me bitter. I've wasted so many opportunities. It seems like this extended conversation with you, Ronnie, is about the best thing I've ever done. But I should do more like those gay campaigners. I should get involved.'

'Why don't you go to those meetings of homosexuals you mentioned the other day?'

'You mean the CHE - Campaign for Homosexual Equality. Yes, great idea. It's just this eternal, infernal mist. I'm lost in it, can't go anywhere, can't find anything, can't remember anything, can't think straight ... '

'I know what you mean,' breathed Ronnie in some discomfort.'

Man and boy thought about the ‘elephant in the room’ reference: something big and important which could not be acknowledged. But this something was not homosexuality. It was something common to them both, something deep dark and dangerous which frightened them both. At this stage, neither had the courage to confront that dreadful reality.

Chapter 6

Breakdown

'Why haven't you said anything about this counselling stuff they made you do? Can't you remember? Or - don't you *want* to remember?' asked Ronnie.

'Good question, Ronnie! I've bared my soul to you with, so far, good results - and I'll give this a go. Now then ... his name was Ian and, truth to tell, he was pretty good - make that 'very good'. To start with, I don't think it was *his* decision to force me back to school. He was part of a team and it was a team decision.

'Before you turned up, Ronnie, I had only a hazy memory of meetings with Ian. But, over the last few weeks, I've thought more about it and remembered more. Yes, Ian was a digger, and, during helpful conversations, he dug out some dramatic developments from my miserable childhood. Together we analysed the dark period which descended upon me in the last few months of teaching.

'Do you know what, Ronnie? He was very like you! Really! He encouraged a journal, very similar to your suggestion about the biography. You missed your calling. Become a counsellor. You'll be a good one.'

'Some hopes,' grinned Ronnie. 'How come Ian was so good?'

'He always referred to me as a "client" rather than a "patient" - thus removing the shame, the social unacceptability often associated with mental illness. Make no mistake; I *was* being treated for a mental disorder. He asked me about my thoughts - negative thoughts. I admitted to brooding hateful thoughts. They're no good. They drain energy and damage the psyche.

'Ian reminded me that hateful thoughts do no harm to those who hurt me years ago. Endlessly playing back mental tapes ... no good at all. It's a futile attempt to alter the outcome of what can't be altered. I was trying to change history. I'm not religious, but understand the psychological value of forgiveness

- letting go. I can't forgive or forget, but I will try to *avoid.* Ian said I should try to put back the lid - scab - on my historic horrors. But discussing these difficult matters with an understanding and caring professional was very helpful.

'Also to be praised was a nonjudgmental approach to all the embarrassing aspects when we explored the secret and dark corners of my memories. Ian had no problem with my homosexuality even when conversations explored erotic anonymity and orgiastic realities, common to many homosexual men.

'Repeated reassurances enhanced my confidence because I suffered a complete *collapse* of confidence in those terminal days of teaching. Trust is so important in professional counselling.

'Crucial to my recovery has been Ian's foresight and permission to keep a journal in which he's quoted. I still have it! Back at home ... I think? Anyway, it should help take the sting out of the stigma surrounding mental illness. This record of our conversations has evolved into a revealing family history.'

'Well? Are you better then? Are you cured now?'

'On the last session of therapy, we both concluded that there isn't much wrong with me, beyond gathering the strength of will to control anger. When I give pain permission to intrude into my conscious mind, I allow historic trauma to disturb my peace. I've always said my problem is not so much depression, it's more like fury. Accordingly, having thoroughly discussed these issues, we agreed to wind up the therapy.'

'What issues?'

'Ian has dug out childhood trauma. He's diagnosed Post Traumatic Stress Disorder - PTSD.'

'What?'

'Bad stuff. All the nasty things which happened when you were little. It screws you up.'

A silence descended. Ronnie became thoughtful. He was slightly embarrassed having noticed the near breaking voice and pain distorting the other's face.

It was a mutual brood, but brief. Simeon knew his former pupil was giving serious thought to the 'bad stuff' he himself had suffered during his rough, chaotic and dysfunctional childhood. The moment allowed for a discreet examination of small scars and various disfigurations on Ronnie's face and neck, evidence of early brutality.

'I wanted to *escape* from teaching,' continued Simeon, 'so I accepted this course of counselling sessions. It was okay, but it seemed to me that the solution was plain and simple - early retirement would soon restore me to full health.

'The decision went against me - and here I am back at school. Anyway, Ian and I got to chatting and the chat closely followed the sorrows of a life marred by ignorance. Such episodes included the exploration of many dark and dangerous recesses in my memory - but I coped.

'At Mundy Street Boys School in Heanor, a sadistic schoolmaster choreographed classroom situations in which I suffered excruciating humiliations. They wreaked emotional damage which will follow me to the grave. To this day, I endure vivid flashbacks, intrusive thoughts causing distress which still disturbs my sleep. If not branded into my flesh with a hot iron, the traumas inflicted by that ruthless Church of England regime are burnt into my psyche. Cruelty has a cost. I'm now paying the bill. Ian did his job. With my collaboration he picked at a hard scab which had afforded protection against the horrors of late 1957. Counselling sessions confirmed that, for safety, we repress agonising memories of childhood torture. I'm glad we did it. I wrote this harrowing account to put on public record what can happen to an abused boy who is seen as - *different*.

'So what happened to you?' asked Ronnie. 'Was it a mental breakdown? What exactly *is* a mental breakdown? Is it a *nervous* breakdown?

'Ian said I should see it as a break-through! The first hint of a problem came when a fellow teacher made a diplomatic and revealing comment.

"How can I put this, Simeon? You see ... this job we do, it can be tough at times, but for the most part it's fulfilling and quite often fun! You find no joy in this job at all, do you? It's destroying you, isn't it? Get real. Over the last few weeks we've seen you sink lower and lower. For God's sake, man, you've got to *do* something!"

'He had detected a haze of depression which was adversely affecting the quality of my work. I was falling down on the job. A number of unwelcome facts came into sharp focus. I'd stopped cycling at the weekends. I'd stopped going to the gay baths - full stop. Numerous personal correspondences ceased. Letters remained unanswered. I became reclusive, unwilling even to socialise with gay friends. In general, I'd lost my way - figuratively and literally. Car trips negotiating busy city areas became too much of a challenge.

'Counselling was helpful, but I resisted any suggestion of antidepressants. Hate drugs! I'd always stood firm against that stuff - recreational drug use, alcohol and tobacco.

'I was determined to emerge from this dark period by sticking to a healthy active lifestyle coupled with a wholesome diet. It's what I've always done. Anyway, after seven one-to-one sessions, a group course focusing on cognitive behavioural therapy was recommended. I wasn't keen. I'm not in the same league as potential self-harmers, you know, folks who might top themselves. But ... eventually, I was persuaded by the advantages of a group dynamic. They teach relaxation techniques. And that was useful.'

The therapist suggested to Simeon further counselling on completion of the group course. A new counsellor, Ian, interviewed him for an assessment. He proposed a fresh approach focusing on harrowing activity experienced at age 12. After several sessions, he diagnosed PTSD - post-traumatic stress disorder- equating Simeon with emotionally damaged soldiers who have endured excruciating experiences in the field of battle. He was surprised. Ian clarified.

'You shouldn't be. On a daily basis, in late 1957, you described physical attacks such as a blow to the abdomen (winding) rendering you temporally unable to breathe. You spoke of a sharp kick in the leg (dead legging) cutting you to the ground and ear screaming resulting in a life-long loss of hearing. All this in front of an audience, a mob of jeering bullies whipped up by a teacher who was supposed to protect you. You are a victim of torture, as terrible for a 12-year-old, as for a grown man in uniform. The agonising memories, vivid flashbacks and intrusive thoughts causing rage are symptoms of PTSD.'

Simeon feared Ian would attribute his current malaise to the sexual activity with the man known to Mundy Street boys as Granddad. Although adults having sex with children cannot be condoned, the therapist was prepared to acknowledge help and comfort received from the old coalminer who lived near Mundy Street Boys School. The problems had been clearly stated. Ian was fairly confident in having discovered the root of those problems. At this juncture, here was the question: will ongoing conversations with this professional therapist extinguish fires currently marring Simeon's life?

It occurred to Simeon that the 1957 trauma was an all male ordeal. If so, how could Ian explain a life-long tendency to misogyny, in that an acidic female comment could inflict a sting more excruciating and longer lasting than one from her male counterpart? Once again, the counsellor referred to painful motherly incidents seared into her son's memory banks. Occasionally Simeon was prevented from using the school lavatory and arrived home with soiled trousers. Unsympathetic, mother couldn't cope. In sad resignation shaking her head –

'You *make* work for me.'

In 1945, Mrs Hogg at age 34 bore a son. She already had two daughters aged 9 and 13. Simeon, the 'gypsy's warning', was the subject of a frequently recycled family tale involving this pedlar with her unwelcome and inconvenient prediction. A baby was the last thing Alice Hogg wanted. At that time Mum and Dad were busily involved in a partnership with Philip Daniels, an emergent successful retailer taking full advantage of the economic climate at the end of the Second World War. Cash was plentiful, but ladies outerwear, coats, gowns and costumes, were not. Alice, a born saleslady gifted with a vibrant controlling personality, was a valuable asset to her new friend Phil. Hogg family mythology spoke of a golden period in which cascades of cash crashed onto a working class couple who had only ever known a meagre hand-to-mouth existence, the usual lot of coalmining stock.

'They spent it as fast as it came in from those crafty Jew boys. Alice took over £100 a week selling Phil's stuff on Ilkeston Market,' commented one of several cousins who lived in the pit village of Stanley Common.

The most visible monument to this sudden wealth was a brand new detached house, costing just a few hundred 1939 pounds, proudly towering over the many terraced rows of humble colliery cottages. Researching this family narrative put Simeon in mind of Viv Nicholson, the 1961 Yorkshire housewife who won the equivalent of three million 2019 pounds on the football pools. Viv and Alice shared a rags-to-riches-to-rags-again story.

In 1958, Alice and Jack Hogg were back in one of those dowdy terraced cottages - two up / two down. She was still a saleslady in a Derby shop and Jack was happily doing what he did before the war, driving a bus.

Back in 1948, for some reason, the grand house was sold and the family moved to less impressive premises in Belper. Forthcoming relatives and family friends advanced controversial theories contrary to the official family line which Simeon had always been given to understand. Put simply, it is their belief that Philip was the *real* owner of the new house and probably the owner of the Belper property.

Late 1954 saw yet another abrupt change and downgrade of circumstances owing to, rumoured at the time, bankruptcy. The family moved to a somewhat dingy flat above a small shop on the main street of Heanor, a grimy colliery town with a rough reputation.

Simeon reached the conclusion that, before the war, Phil met Alice, was charmed by her sales personality and saw an opportunity to invest in several tax efficient initiatives. He flattered her and boosted her ego by building an eye-catching house cheaply in a local coal mining village. The family was installed. It said to the pit populace of Stanley Common - 'Here is the imposing residence of Jack and Alice Hogg - their impressive reward for sudden success - that of selling ladies clothes on Ilkeston Market Place.' Phil anticipated and took advantage of the dramatic inflation which engulfed post-war Britain. By 1948, he probably quadrupled his money when he sold the house.

Like his son, Jack had a powerful sexual appetite. He indulged in several mistresses. Years later in Detroit, mother spat out the following -

'Your Dad ruined the business!'

'How?'

'He squandered all the money on his fancy women.'

This corresponded with one distressing scene played out in 1957 when an enraged tearful Alice harangued Jack about his treachery. Simeon had never seen her so upset. Although he hardly ever spoke to Simeon, for balance, it should be pointed out that father never spoke ill of mother. Even so, she never forgave him for infidelity with these various unpleasant fishwives. These fishwives behaved to Simeon with total indifference - sometimes worse than indifference.

Ian dug out one clear memory. A seafront boarding house in Blackpool; Simeon was about five-years-old. Both parents were absent - but two women had put him to bed. It was a chore. One of them scowled back at him, approached the bed and suddenly whipped back the bedclothes revealing what many little boys do in bed. He was playing with himself.

'There you are! Just look at that! What did I tell you? *Dirty* little bugger!'

Causing excruciating damaging cruelty, it was one incident of several Simeon came to associate with rough common females who, for some reason, hated him. It was certainly an act of spite inflicted by one of the fancy women.

Alice was guilty of similar humiliations degrading her son. One mortifying example left an ugly scar on his psyche. It happened during the worst period of his life, December 1957, when he was 12. On a daily basis, the sadistic Mundy Street master entertained himself by engineering lynch mob style attacks which brought despair and thoughts of suicide. This perfect storm of a disastrous situation could only exist with the connivance of an indifferent father and hostile mother. They were ashamed and loathed the son who was not a proper son, who could not defend himself with bare knuckles in the playground and hated football. The following sound bites spat out in pit talk were typical.

'What sort 'o lad 'ave we got! Aye [he] couldna kick a ball.'

Jack could hardly bring himself to speak Simeon's name. If it was necessary to reference the despised miserable child, he would, with clear irritation, nod towards him and say 'im'.

It would have been a Saturday or Sunday morning. He'd just got out of bed, not yet dressed, but for a vest which barely covered genitalia - no underpants. Few Heanor boys wore underpants. Hearing the kettle whistle, he descended to the kitchen where mother was mashing [brewing] the morning tea in a large brown pot. As usual, she received him in aloof silence as would have been common in most colliery class homes. He poured tea into a mug, adding milk from the milk bottle and settled to a pleasant stupor sipping the hot liquid in a few moments of tranquillity in the relative safety of the first floor flat.

Suddenly there were sounds of giggly girls bursting into the property. Relatives never knocked; they simply entered. He dived under the table for cover in an attempt to maintain some semblance of dignity. Undercover of the tablecloth, the deception was a success as long as the boy remained perfectly quiet. He had escaped. He waited for mother to invite her guests into the front living room, giving him a chance to make a bolt for the safety of his bedroom. Knowing the sensitivity of an adolescent, most mums (even the ones who disliked their offspring) would have spared him the agony of humiliation. Instead, Alice Hogg decided to inflict maximum suffering on a helpless victim. She said -

‘Look under the table’.

Simeon’s mind went forward to an ugly incident in the early 1990s. One of his colleagues was given tragic news, the sudden death of her mother. She collapsed into a flood of tears, was inconsolable and had to leave her teaching duties immediately. She was helped out of the staffroom and taken home. All other teachers were distressed and rushed over to be supportive, kind and sympathetic.

As a witness to this event, Simeon was also distressed – *but not in the same way*. He was distressed at his own extraordinary response to this upsetting scene. He did *not* feel sorry for the poor woman; on the contrary, he resented her! Why? Because he knew he was ‘damaged goods’. Notwithstanding, Simeon was no psychoanalyst, unable to probe the Freudian darkness, to examine the monsters that lurked inside his own id. Was this hostile reflex connected with a comparison? Let us assume that Simeon received similar bad news – his long standing partner has died. Dare *he* weep? Dare he show pain, as *she* did to the sympathetic heterosexual majority? Would he risk admitting to a ‘degenerate’ relationship, an unnatural closeness?

Back in Granddad’s carnal kitchen of December 1957, Simeon’s parents received support from an unexpected source. After threatening to kill himself, the old paedophile made a case for Simeon remaining alive and running the daily gauntlet of Mundy Street Boys School.

He made a contrast between Simeon and his classmate Chunky who was a frequent visitor to the erotic harem. The former was adequately clothed, reasonably well shod and well fed in a house which was kept clean and warm. Granddad acknowledged that Simeon was despised by disappointed parents, but at the same time, was also cared for by people who took their duties seriously.

When it came to motherhood, Simeon always acknowledged that his mother was on ‘automatic pilot’. In this sense, she was generous. The subject of his homosexuality was never openly declared. In consequence, there was never a confrontation in which he might be ordered to 'pack ya bags and get out!' He explained to Ronnie that, to his personal knowledge, several gay sons were suddenly ejected from their home. Put to the test, Simeon did not believe that Alice Hogg would have kicked out her son.

Other Mundy Street boys in 1957 were in a worse situation than Simeon. Chunky and his 'mam' were often beaten by a brutal dad. He was ill-shod, ill-clad, ill-nourished and occasionally starved which explained his frequent appearance at Granddad's fish and chip suppers. Simeon witnessed several ravenous attacks on food placed before this impoverished child who wolfed it down like a starving dog. He was moved to pity for this classmate, a rat-like scruff who had never done him any harm.

They were both groomed in erotic arts and were united by the expediency of buying protection with sexual favours. He was a misshapen ragamuffin of defective bone growth dashing around the playground. Chunky's twisted appearance was a shield to cruel treatment. It was bad form to target a cripple, but Simeon was seen as fair game. He was whole but 'different'. And that difference inspired in the mob a frisson of sadistic pleasure. A merciless element was all the more ferocious when fired up by an evil schoolmaster.

Ian highlighted damaging trauma originating from females in or close to the family core - principally Simeon's mother and sisters. During carefully probing conversations, he dug out several excruciating incidents such as the sudden disappearance of Jack Carrier.

In 1958 the Hoggs moved from Heanor back to a humble terraced cottage in the colliery village of Stanley Common in the shadow of the grand house which had been their former home. The following year saw Simeon a frustrated, deeply repressed 14-year-old scruffy chicken. Sent on errands, he had become accustomed to a shy and gentle postmaster called Jack Carrier who had tended the village Post Office-cum-shop for as long as anyone could remember. One day he was there - the next day he was gone!

'What's happened to him?' he asked his mother.

'That one! Huh! Good riddance,' she snapped. 'E were one of them funny sorts. No good to any woman,' she growled.

'Well, 'e were allus [always] nicely spoken and polite ta me,' sniffed Aunty Brenda, taking another swig of tea.

The effect on this adolescent? Well, it was the same as the effect on hundreds of thousands of gay boys like Simeon. He hid inside of himself. He became withdrawn and tried to pretend to desire girls. He drifted into a secret world of fear and insecurity.

Clearly Jack had been discovered in some way, denounced and driven out of Stanley Common by ignorant homophobic outrage. In those dark days of rabid gay hate, it was considered quite natural for a heterosexual to 'chat up' a woman. However, if a homosexual engaged another man in conversation, *that* was seen as 'soliciting for an immoral purpose'. Many victims were entrapped by the CID in plainclothes and humiliated in the local press. Did this happen to Jack?

The Carriers had been postmasters in Stanley Common since 1924 and John H Carrier was born in 1920. Years later as an adult, Simeon asked relatives about the disappearing postmaster only to be met with a wall of silence. *Somebody* in Stanley Common *must* know what happened to the inoffensive, mild mannered Jack Carrier who suddenly disappeared in 1959.

Author's Note: The Jack Carrier Mystery was eventually solved in a half page feature printed in the July 2019 edition of *Ilkeston Life* - one of the author's Information Sheets number 167 - link below.

http://tiny.cc/InfoSheet167

Having descended from riches to rags and now back in their terraced rented pit cottage, the Hoggs decided to emigrate to

Detroit to be near their daughter who had been in the USA since 1954. Simeon arrived in November 1963 and docked the day before President Kennedy's assassination.

Years passed. The 1960s blended into the 1970s and Simeon's double life carried on in much the same way as before - a sort of ongoing fragile truce. The homosexual son was akin to a disfigurement which had to be endured.

Jack Hogg died in 1972. It fell to an unmarried son to care for and administer the affairs of his newly widowed mother. If Simeon had not seen the significance of the relationship between his parents and Phil Daniels, further dramatic clues would now present themselves.

It was a shock to discover that Alice Hogg was unable to write a cheque. She had *never* written a cheque! On the other hand, she could still sell and was a saleslady at a Detroit chain of fashion stores for women. As ever, she was always employed, loved to work and loved to spend. She had a store credit card loaded to its maximum of $500 and costing monthly interest at a horrendously high rate. Simeon did the sensible thing - he paid it off. Mother was a shopaholic constantly buying things she didn't need. She had always denounced dad as stingy - 'He'd skin a flea for its fur!'

During his lifetime, Simeon had as little respect for Jack as Jack had for the son he despised, but in death ... well, he was beginning to appreciate the problem with mother. One month later, the credit card was again over $500. It was paid one more time and thereafter ignored as the only way to stop Alice spending.

Sometime in this period, Simeon was arrested on a charge of gross indecency in a public toilet. Within the Detroit gay community, the 14th Floor of Hudson's Department Store was a well known meeting place. Occasionally handsome young officers in plain clothes were dispatched to the men's rest rooms to tempt 'degenerates' into committing an 'immoral' act. Alas, on this particular ill- fated afternoon, he yielded to the promise of instant ecstasy; very foolish because he had heard of this type of entrapment.

But Simeon was unable to believe that a police officer could stoop to such deception. On BBC TV in the 1950s, he had been brought up on a steady diet of *Dixon of Dock Green.* The fictional PC George Dixon was a warm, human, typical old style 'bobby' whose absolute honesty and dependability over the years had seeped into Simeon's conception of a police officer.

Agents provocateurs were undercover agents of the Detroit Police. They could safely get good results from wholesale easy ensnarement of homosexuals with a gentle disposition. This was the City of Detroit - the same high-crime-rate Motor City famously averaging 'three murders a day' in the 1970s. It held an appalling reputation for violence, gangsters, Mafia, muggings and general hooliganism. It even had its own 'Pink Mafia' sub-group.

Like so many before and after, in shock after disclosure of a police badge, mouth dry as dust, Simeon's world suddenly collapsed. He came quietly. They all did. Homosexuals are very easy to hurt. Before being escorted into a cell with hardened criminals, he was allowed one phone call. Tragically, the only number available was the number of the last person he wanted to call. Five hours later, sister and brother-in-law bailed him out with the standard $100. He was released and escorted to the main desk in the foyer. The relatives, utterly disgusted, had come - and gone.

The prisoner stood alone before a towering Police Desk Sergeant. Behind his elevated fortress, the officer's head was ten feet above Simeon's head. The former inmate was seen as half-living slime which had dared to creep out of the gutter. That high countenance twisted into an expression of execration such that the young man flinched from the assault of its sheer malice. Three words were uttered. And those words were invested with all the bitterness and venom available to the man who spat them out –

'Call your sister.'

Reeling from the impact of such a tongue lashing, frozen to the spot for several seconds, the detainee realised there would be no formal dismissal and, in fact, he was free to go.

Homosexuality had always been a useful stick with which to strike Simeon. The next day he paid his sister the $100 and offered to be candid and admit the folly of his conduct at Hudson's. True to form, she took full advantage of distress and misery to denounce his weakness, his useless life, his sordid behaviour and his deviant personality which had disgraced the family name. For a woman who had been the principal source of lifelong character assassination, that arrest and concomitant humiliation was a gift from heaven.

Simeon graduated from university in 1975 and obtained a post teaching Black History in a private Catholic school. At long last, he had a chance to save money and hopefully return to Derbyshire realising a long held ambition. In all 13 years of residence in America, chronically homesick, he managed to visit the UK for as long as funds would stretch - usually about six weeks each summer holiday.

Alice was given plenty of warning that she would be on her own in the autumn of 1976. Daily life was lived in a haze of siege mentality. When her daughters, nieces and nephews visited the house, the 'elephant in the room' withdrew into an extension which had been built in the 1960s. In this sense, he was truly invisible - and glad to be so.

Alone with mother, following the years after her husband's passing, a few words were occasionally exchanged prompted by a natural need for companionship. Alice found Simeon's existence tolerable enough to meet this need. There was no affection. Now in her mid 60s, she was mellowing, coming to terms with a young man who, at least, kept his homosexuality well hidden and attended to general household needs. He had replaced Jack with a level of reasonable satisfaction - no praise, but no complaints.

As the date of departure approached, it was necessary to discuss practical matters - necessary finances, household bills, the car etc. Mum could not drive. Most of the time, Simeon chauffeured her to and from work; other times the daughters helped out. These arrangements were problematic because he was on speaking terms with Mum only. He made it perfectly clear that the family would need to take on the responsibility of an elderly lady needing close supervision in his sudden and permanent absence which was fast approaching.

He was going for good. Alice needed to fully understand the implications and how it would affect her life. In all conscience, her son did not think she fully gathered how she would need to depend upon daughters, nephews and nieces. Simeon braced himself for a grudging family conclave to discuss the ramifications of this new situation and insisted to mother that she *must* warn the family and call for this meeting.

Unfortunately, Alice was inert. She did nothing. She waits for others to organize her, to do for her - as her husband and Phil Daniels did. During one stressful confrontation she snapped -

'Why don't you take me with you and look after me?

This sounded like a line which had been deliberately fed to her. It was unexpected and called for a careful rethink. Simeon's initial reaction was to stick to Plan A and rid himself of the family for good. That said, the possible advantages of Plan B began to take shape. It occurred to him that a family conclave had, in fact, *taken place in his absence* with the demon daughters seeing a golden chance to offload motherly responsibilities. Alice always presented herself as very popular, ever needed, ever wanted by her doting children and grandchildren. Up to this moment, Simeon was taken in by self-promoting ongoing propaganda and began to see Alice in a different light.

Accordingly, in July 1976 the house was sold. Mother and son set sail on the QE2, both hoping for a new beginning and an improving relationship. For a while, it did seem that way. Cautiously he bought a small terraced cottage in Belper so Mum could be near old friends and relatives in Stanley Common. The purchase left sufficient funds for Alice to return to the USA if the plan failed.

In the autumn of 1976, Simeon met Tom who was married with children. The trauma and shock of coming to terms with Tom's life-long repressed same-sex attraction triggered a breakdown and several weeks in a psychiatric hospital. Electric shock aversion therapy was suggested as a 'cure' for his homosexuality.

Established in the new home, away from the malevolent influence of American relatives and certain poisonous family friends, the chemistry between Simeon and Alice had improved. Make no mistake, homosexuality and Mundy Street still cast a dark shadow over the frail relationship, but they were reconciled to a routine of civility and mutual cooperation. They didn't like each other, but open hatred increasingly took a back seat.

Following his divorce, Tom became homeless. The tiny two up / two down cottage was hardly big enough for mother and son, but, notwithstanding, Simeon asked her if Tom might come and live with them. Without hesitation, she readily agreed. It was no surprise. In that way, Alice was always generous. And then something extraordinary happened. The addition of Tom made a dramatic change to the relationship dynamic. Heretofore, there had been little joy in the mother / son equation; now the house received a boost of warmth transforming it into a home.

Alice liked Tom and Tom liked Alice. She was able to accept him as a 'best friend'. That was okay. He was Simeon's mucker, his mate, his pal. The world would see it that way. All would be well. Tom was also practical; he could make things and mend things. As an electrical contractor, he had a 'proper job'. He could mend a puncture. He could lay bricks. He was as butch as a brick. He was a 'proper lad'. Jack Hogg would have been proud of Tom.

Tom lived with them for the best part of a relatively happy but chaotic and troubled year. They were support for each other.

With limited access to his boys aged 6 and 9, they were seen infrequently at Alice's cottage. One memory is poignant. Simeon was looking out of the front bedroom window when Tom arrived with his sons. Traffic roared both ways with intensity making him anxious for their safety. Having difficulty crossing the busy A6 Derby Road, Tom took firm hold of their little hands until a suitable gap appeared making it safe to approach the front door. Something about that man holding on to his precious boys wrenched Simeon's conscience. It was symbolic of a man desperately holding his loved ones together against an overwhelming tempest of homophobic circumstances which had been tearing that unit asunder.

Mum spent quite a lot of time with her pit village relatives until her brother, Uncle Arthur, died, closely followed by Aunty Brenda and their son Ken. These losses were a blow to Alice. Eventually, in 1978, Simeon obtained a teaching post in Worksop causing him to buy an isolated house (Magpie House) near an old fashioned pit village called Clowne about ten miles from his school. He visited Alice at weekends but she had become increasingly isolated from all she had known in the USA.

A combination of family deaths, isolation, advancing years and a yearning for the flashy materialistic lifestyle of American living led Alice to entertain a return to her daughters. Simeon was asked to sell the small Belper house and she returned to Detroit in 1981. He never saw her again.

Chapter 7

Duck

Hearing about Simeon's existence in a clandestine world where all was caution and camouflage, Ronnie was still intrigued by the way one queer met another queer.

'How did you get to know that married bloke, Tom?'

After 13 years of living in Detroit, Belper seemed a quiet conservative backwater at a time when the nearest 'gay' scene for a non-drinker, such as Simeon, was located at the Derby Turkish Baths ten miles south. In Belper, a small mill town, the only gay venue was the home of an old-fashioned elderly man who hosted an open house for secretive repressed visitors, warmly welcomed into his picturesque cottage, anytime day and evening. Anonymous men were treated to tea, cakes, friendly conversation and the occasional massage in Jasper's bedroom. He resided in a maze of narrow lanes which climbed up the steep rise of the Derwent Valley, this gentle and kind gentleman of repellent aspect was also known as the Belper Crone. His penetrating leer reminded Simeon of the old witch in Disney's *Snow White*. He was a bent, humped, effeminate, gangling, toothless old queen presiding over the comings and goings of shy shadowy types in and out of his quaint old cottage.

'To the best of my knowledge, at that time,' said Simeon to Ronnie, 'it was the only safe way to meet other gay men in that conservative community. Over his mantelpiece there was a brass plate bearing a few trite words. As I recall them, I can still see the nodding head and hear his squeaky croak - *Make new friends, but keep the old, one is silver, the other gold.*'

As with many of Jasper's other visitors, Tom was a married man with children. In his late 30s, coming to terms with a lifelong double life was a crushing trauma, too much to bear. He suffered a breakdown and spent several weeks in hospital where electric aversion therapy was suggested to 'cure him' of his homosexuality.

'Did he find any other queers in that old cottage? I mean some other bloke to shack up with?'

'I don't know, Ronnie. We drifted apart when I moved to Clowne. If he did discover that one special person, more than likely, he'd have had to be reconciled to a partnership which could never have been monogamous in the heterosexual sense.'

Simeon went on to outline how gay people met each other in the street, or at the fair or even on Ripley Market Place. Between 1963 and 1976 he returned to the UK each summer for an annual holiday of as many weeks as he could afford. The exception was 1965. Having completely missed 1964, the 19-year-old had been away from his beloved Derbyshire for over 18 months and returned to a quaint world redolent with childhood nostalgia - smells, sounds and sights of scruffy folks crowded into quirky picturesque nooks and crannies such as Ripley Market Place. Simeon was intrigued to enjoy this thrilling reunion with his early boyhood days. After a sterile existence in a well scrubbed United States, he was fascinated by the friendliness of crooked oddities who constantly addressed each other as 'duck' - pronouncing it 'dook'.

The colliery cultural accent is thick and rich. A principal feature is the 'closed U', sounded 'oo' as in 'took', not the sound as in 'boot'. The native tongue makes no distinction between the past tense of take - 'took' - and 'tuck' - something to eat. To the Derbyshire ear, the 'open U' or standard pronunciation of 'tuck' sounds rather like 'tack', a short nail. Accordingly, when Ripley folk say 'duck' (which they often do) it sounds like 'dook'.

Detroit offered nothing like the variety of odd bods interbred over generations from mining stock. Simeon felt he had arrived in a fairytale world of curiosities resembling toads, goblins and gnomes, more medieval than 20th century clean cut American youth, more Grimm than US glitz and glamour. Here the crooked coal-encrusted indigenousness seemed to be older, uglier and have more character, making them all much more interesting.

Wandering around Ripley Market Place, pondering these quirky contrasts, he came on one stall which specialised in sweets, chocolates and all manner of confectionery busy with people and a cacophony of trivial chatter.

'Umbug?' [humbug] said the man behind the counter. 'Tuppence, duck.'

'Arr [our] Fred wants it, you know,' replied his customer, 'no teeth, but he can still suck. Thanks, duck. How's ya mam?'

'Bit better today, duck. It's a fortnight since she took bad.

'Ooo, duck. An you we no 'ands! A think you're a brick, a do, duck.'

This was a magical experience, made all the more magical observing this common place exchange dominated by the one word 'duck'. The old hag's nose seemed to meet her chin giving a witch-like appearance. Her cackling inappropriate comments highlighting a serious disability made a contrast to the stallholder (with no hands) whose cushy caring voice seemed to blend with a downy personality. This ductile chap (known only as Duck) made an immediate impression on Simeon. Somehow it made him feel safe and secure. Conceived in this moment was a lifelong friendship with plump, cosy Duck who was always kind and considerate.

Well away from the endless flatness of Michigan, a short conversation with Duck transported Simeon to the child he once was when he explored the old osier bed alongside the slow, green River Derwent which had, in 1905, been transformed into a beautiful garden in Belper. It was a delight of glades, rock formations, alcoves, islets, avenues and terraces. Simeon enjoyed the contrasts between the open promenade, lovers' walk, the fish pond, the fountain bordered by special nooks and crannies. Here the imagination could run riot. There were rocks picturesque and rocks grotesque. In an ecstasy of exploration, the child hunted out hidden glades. Here he would see deep, spongy moss growing on damp boulders. Here he imagined stories about the 'little people', the fairies. Bright sunlight became dazzling bright green when reflected off the ubiquitous fern. Such unusual illuminations complemented various dank corners and black caves. Little Simeon was told that if he had enough faith, if he tried hard enough, if he believed in the spirits of nature, if he was lucky enough, he might just get a glimpse of elementals in human form. The small boy was very happy. He recalled the warmth of the sun, the cool of the shade, the light and the dark, the scent of wild garlic, the music of birdsong stirred by the gentle coaxing voice of nice, cushy Duck, gentle Duck. He never saw fairies, but Duck was real enough and they became lifelong friends.

Back on the Market Place, the old witch, satiated with her time killing trivia, moved on, leaving Simeon and the stallholder to have their first conversation.

'But how did you know this man was gay?' asked Ronnie.

'Good question - with no simple answer. I suppose he was a bit camp.'

'Pardon?'

'Camp? It's a theatrical term meaning ... err, slightly effeminate - but Duck was much more than that. He projected warmth, oodles of affection within a halo of safe snug comfort. He was totally free from any pretentiousness and you felt you had known him all your life. Not well educated, in many ways a simple man, but Duck was a good listener. You could confide all your secrets.'

'You told him you were gay?'

'It wasn't necessary. In the first few minutes of our chat, things said removed all doubt. We were both teenagers but he was old-fashioned, looking and acting much older. He was comfortable talking about his baby arms ending in stumps. He mentioned that he was born with one leg, but walked quite well with a prosthetic limb. Naturally this disability curtailed his social activities in the gay world.'

Duck was just one of the several curious characters of Derbyshire - goblins, hags, crones, gnomes, fairies, toads and other oddities. He was a regular visitor to Blackpool. Like Coney Island, Blackpool could be garish, cheap, tacky and tatty.

Unlike that American equivalent, this glittering and cheerful resort of the North West held Simeon's affection. It had a past - Simeon's past. As a child, various half remembered carers had brought him here to sample the thrills and spills of the Pleasure Beach. They walked his little legs along the promenade full of shrieks of joy and jammed with the working-class at play, jammed with amusements, ghost trains, shooting galleries, dancing girls, palmists, vulgar postcards and the salty smell of jellied eels.

Ronnie seemed quite intrigued by the mystique surrounding Duck.

'Was there sex? I mean you and ... this Duck ... or shouldn't I ask?'

'It didn't *actually* happen. I'd better explain. He suggested we meet at the local pictures - the Ripley Hippodrome. Something of a flea pit! Bad choice,' sighed Simeon. 'It was always doomed to failure. You do daft things when you're young. You don't think things through properly.'

'What happened?'

'Embarrassment happened. I still cringe to think of it. Poor Duck. He tried to grope me with his stumps. I feigned fear urging caution. "This is a public place!! We might be seen! It's against the law, we could go to jail," - that sort of stuff. Had it been Fabian - **wow** - I'd have thrown caution to the wind.'

'Fabian?'

'Fabian was an early 60s teen idol - stunningly beautiful singing sensation. Drop-dead gorgeous guy with a soft sexy speaking voice oozing seduction. Oh God, Ronnie! He drove me *nuts*. Trust me, Duck was at the extreme bottom end of the Fabian-Duck continuum of desirability.'

Eventually, Simeon was invited back to meet Mrs Duck at the Duckery just round the corner from Ripley Market Place. It was just Duck and Mrs Duck, no Mr Duck. Occasionally, they were visited by a robin which hopped on to the window sill. Duck said -

'Ey oop, Arr Mam, look - it's me dad, it's me dad coom back.'

Simeon was encouraged to visit anytime. He just walked in. He saw two large eggs. These eggs with faces were deeply reposing into a cosy sofa and Simeon had formed the impression they'd been sitting there forever. Each face wore a smile of welcome. Both fat faces were devoid of a single wrinkle which caused the visitor to wonder about the age of mother. Over the long years of friendship, Duck never changed. He had always looked the same. He was just ... Duck. The 'Mam' egg cocked up her legs which could not quite reach the floor and spoke first.

'Eee it is nice ta see thee, dook. Are ya all right then, dook?'

The Duck egg appeared to do a quick funny wriggle with dancing shoulders.

'Shall ya ave a coop a tea, dook? Put kettle on, Arr Mam.'

'No, Dook. Ave joost sat down. *You* put kettle on shall ya, Arr Dook.'

'All right, Arr Mam, I'll put kettle on.'

'You've made it really nice here,' said Simeon. 'So very cosy and comfortable.'

The Duckery was fixed somewhere inside a time warp, in this case possibly mid 1930s. Cosy and comfortable were apt terms here. Everything was soft and cushy. The conversation in this room was all ductility, well matched to the occupants, mild and downy. It became a favourite place for Simeon Hogg. In this old fashioned feathery room, he felt cushioned from the hard knocks of life. Nothing nasty or hurtful ever came from Duck, friendly podgy Duck, ever mellow and mellifluous.

At worst, on the occasions in which he *did* criticise, he would begin with his characteristic wiggle, dancing shoulders and the one word - 'Meself' Like now, regarding the subject of Annie Oaks and her pricing policy

'Meself, a think she's a bit dear. Don't ya think so, Arr Mam.'

'She is, Arr Duck! Them eggs were five pence cheaper int' town. She teks advantage. She knows a can't walk far.'

The conversation continued to touch on similar inanities which included the thoughtless Vivienne whose bouncing ball often annoyed 'Arr Mam', a dripping tap which Fred the neighbourly fixer had promised to fix last month and an unpleasant character in a popular 'soap' who was -

'Nasty! Is really nasty. No need ta be like that. It's oopset Arr Dook, 'e 'as, ant 'e, Arr Dook?'

These trifles amused. Concerns about a person on television who does not exist and an endless stream of minutiae had a soporific effect. The Ducks were warm and generous, non-contentious and undemanding. The quaint chatter was balmy and mildly entertaining. Simeon was always happy in The Duckery.

Chapter 8

Teenagers Together

'Who else?' asked Ronnie. He wanted another example of how a homosexual could meet up with another homosexual.

'I suppose I could tell you about Froggy,' replied Simeon, somewhat doubtfully.

'Froggy! Do they all have daft names?'

'They all have *false* names because they all lead double lives. Froggy comes to mind because I met him at the very end of that same 1965 holiday.'

October 1965 was more than normally very cold, misty with ever longer nights and shorter days. When the fair came to Heanor, it was dark before seven. Anonymously bundled up with a thick black bomber jacket under a black woolly hat, Simeon gravitated to his favourite ride, the Waltzer. His garb was part disguise and part trying to keep warm on a chilly evening. Recognition from Howitt School friends would be welcomed, but the Market Place fair was just a stone's throw from the menace of Mundy Street Boys School. Irrational anxiety perhaps, but even after eight years, the horror of any hostile confrontation was still inhibiting and haunting.

This visit had complex reasons. He had come to the centre of the old mining town out of a ghoulish curiosity, together with a nostalgic compulsion to reconnect with his onetime boyhood excitement - to soak up all the fun of the fair. He had enjoyed the October fair of 1959 with his Howitt mates, crammed, cheek by jowl into one of the Waltzer cars spinning furiously with assistance from one of the rough fairground lads. These sexy greasy gaff boys, in their tempting tight blue jeans, were an important part of the erotic atmosphere. With poise, these standing ruffians rode the whirling Waltzer waves - round and round - perfectly balanced as seated Simeon strained to catch glimpses of beautifully formed buttocks. Butch bums - they were irresistible.

It was the same now in 1965. The strains of Helen Shapiro lamenting *I Don't Care* conjured a dangerous cocktail of menace and magic mixed with high energy of concentrated crowds of collective excitement. Dangerous, because brawny bottoms can quickly become violent if deviant desire is detected. Simeon had long since learned to avoid eye contact with the alluring features of a yob who needed little excuse to punch a poof for the amusement of his fellow thugs.

This tangle of titillation and terror had roots back to the 1957 Granddad days when fairground boys were enticed by offers of cash to sample the pleasures of a toothless old paedophile, just around the corner from their place of work. It was an erotic side show of its own, performed in front of a group of regulars including plenty of protective muscle. Big beefy Blubba, top dog of Mundy Street was there with Stonch, just as brawny, just as dangerous, both making sure that Gaff shot his load, took his money and 'fucked off'.

In safety, illuminated and warmed by Guzzly Granddad's eternal cheerful fire, Simeon was able to have his fill of a lust inspiring scene. The fully inflated manhood of Gaff was swallowed up in a succulent slobbering toothless grotto, whilst two well trained urchins put their naughty little fingers to good use. All sensitive nooks and crannies of bliss were explored to hasten a climax of pure joy. Such delight transformed an unsmiling cruel, coarse face bearing scars of past violence.

That face, focused on the ceiling, was now ecstatic and handsome. Closed eyes and an open moaning mouth with arching back signalled a special moment.

Simeon the voyeur, excited as hell, was galvanised by such a lascivious sight. His ear thrilled to the sound of that final, long, cavernous groan of pleasure rumbling from somewhere deep within the caverns of an experienced old slut. True to Guzzly Granddad's routine, following this powerful scene, a mouth full of Gaff spunk was quickly joined by Blubba spunk, Stonch spunk and lastly Simeon spunk. Their need was great. The old man, dribbling and slobbering down his ancient soup-stained shirt, couldn't get enough.

Gaff was gone. He saw none of this. Moments after discharge, he pulled up his close-fitting jeans, grabbed the ten-shilling-note from between Granddad's fingers and stormed off without a word. Simeon, consumed with lust, was envious of the ragamuffins who had pleasured that rough fairground arse. At that moment, he luxuriated in great relief from a consummate cock sucker.

Watching the Waltzer and that untouchable gaff boy, Simeon recalled the frustration of eight years before in Guzzly Granddad's carnal kitchen. Gaff boys aroused him with a lewd longing which had never been satisfied. Trying to sneak a crafty peek at a tantalising butch bum, he noticed a different type of lad in the crush of others on the Waltzer gantry.

It was a small face. It was a pretty face under a bobble hat with a few escaping strawberry blond curls. In the moment when eyes met eyes, Simeon felt empathy and sympathy for this little chap with the button nose and cheeky grin. Was it a girl? No - definitely a boy. Small for his age? Perhaps. What *was* his age? Could be 12? More like 14. Be careful, Simeon! This is Guzzly Granddad material. Could be very dangerous. Perhaps he *knows* Granddad?

Simeon muscled through the crowd along the gantry making slow progress to the place where sweet bobble hat was last seen. His nostrils were assailed by the odour of crushed bodies blended with hamburger, hotdog, candy floss and diesel. Raucous yelps and screams blended with generators and blaring pop records - all contributing to the unique magic of a fairground.

Bobble hat had gone! Not there! Simeon felt sudden panic. Where was that young, peeping pale face which could have been pre-pubescent? He pushed his way out of that mob of humanity and launched into a chicken hunt to track down a child with a sweet, wan, cheeky face. Where would such a chicken go? He wandered over to the ghoul infested frontage of the Haunted House with its artwork of skeletons, skulls, gravestones and various bloody impressions of the living dead.

Several mesmerising minutes passed as Simeon scanned the crowds trying to locate his chirpy chicken. Almost giving up, he found himself mildly entertained by crude, if captivating, third rate images of tacky horror promoting the Haunted House.

Simeon was suddenly jostled. Silly giggling girls surged forward. A scraggy creep at the entrance urged them to part with their silver sixpences. Touched by somebody else, he recoiled in irritation. But this was *not* a silly girl. It was a small smiling bobble hat, very close, straining upwards, up close to his face making a funny noise - 'Eeeee!'

Simeon made an immediate judgment. This diminutive boy was odd - very odd! He assessed him as child-like rather than childish and was reminded of Dopey the mute dwarf of Disney fame. In gentle reassuring tones as if addressing his words to a frightened child, he said -

'I'm Simeon. What's your name?'

'Froggy.'

'Froggy?'

'Froggeeee!'

'That's an unusual name.'

Froggy stuck out his tongue - immediately electrifying, sparking every erogenous fibre in Simeon's being. In that first glance across the Waltzer, he had established a certain understanding, a feeling that here was a kindred spirit on the same wavelength. Not simple, not a feeble mind, but a character who has cleverly adapted himself to survive in a cruel homophobic working class world.

'So you felt he was gay?' asked Ronnie.

'At that moment, I couldn't be certain. After our experience in the Haunted House, I was *absolutely* certain. Shall we go in? I suggested to the Frog.

'Eeeee,' was the response. I took that as a yes and tendered a shilling to the creepy greasy man behind the pay box counter.'

The creep leered over at his young customers. He had a hooked nose and a lumpy chin. A brief comment, somewhat conspiratorial, somewhat puzzling was lisped out.

'Keep away from them daft girls as just gone in. Feel along the right side and take the first turn to the right. Go straight on until ...' here he lowered his voice to a whisper, '*until ya get touched.*'

'What!'

'Oh just get in,' ordered the creep, suddenly impatient.

Simeon took Froggy's hand and pushed the spring-loaded jet black door with his other hand. As they were plunged into total darkness, he detected a certain tension in the hand of his new friend.

'We can go back if you'd rather?'

'No sweat. Am alright,' said Froggy. 'You'll look after me, won't ya?'

At this, the boy seized his companion with a strong hug burying his head into Simeon's chest. Then, on tiptoe, the lad stretched up to find his mouth immediately plunging into an earnest long - wet - kiss. There was desperation and urgency in this sudden carnal assault, quickly followed by small hands groping around to detect an expected reaction. Small hands were not disappointed. They found and gently fondled a disturbance in Simeon's jeans.

'Ooooh,' breathed Froggy, his naughty fingers exploring the outline of distended manhood - and struggling to locate the fly zip.

'Steady up, little scamp,' responded Simeon, reluctantly resisting these delightful proceedings. 'That creep means us to meet somebody who might be listening to us. I need to find out what this is all about. There is supposed to be ... ah, here!

The right turn was discovered and Simeon led his sexy lover down another black hole of total inky darkness. The structure was only wood, yet the sounds of the fair had receded to the background - but for another sound, very close. It was a cough. Not a youthful cough, not a throat clearing cough. It was an 'I am here' cough.

Simeon lowered his lips to find the boy's ear. He whispered a barely audible instruction.

'Right, Froggy! It's truth time. There's a man ahead, an old man who wants to touch us. I think I know who he is. I'm not sure. If you're uncomfortable with this, we should just go back the way we came. If you're interested, let it be a one off. Don't try to see him again.'

'As 'e 'ad you?' (Has he had you?)

'A long time ago. I think you're too young to get mixed up with his crowd - aren't you?'

At this, Froggy took hold of Simeon's hand and guided it to his crotch in which a concealed randy weapon, equal to his own, was clearly begging for action.

'Wow! You're older than I thought.'

'It's me nob. A call it Froggy's Nob. Nobbeeee!

As they approached the dead end of this short corridor of stygian blackness, a rustle of clothes suggested someone had leaned forward to detect visitors from the dark. It was a thrust forward in eager anticipation of the juicy morsel at hand.

Without words, with no pleasantries, no niceties, the Frog was quick. He jumped in first, unzipped and released his rampant prisoner. Clearly he was no stranger to this extraordinary sensation of yielding to an anonymous long practised master of his art. Nobby plunged into the warm wet darkness of deepest Granddad. Simeon felt the thrill, the tremble of his little body, but in pitch blackness, could only imagine the roll of beautiful eyes as he pulled his new lover up close.

'Stay with me, Simeon,' he murmured softly. It was almost pleading, a small, shaky, broken voice trailing off with - 'Help me, touch me, tease me ... do it ... do it ...'

Simeon could not see, but, from fond memory could only imagine that drooling slash of toothless mouth with the snake of oscillating tongue. It was a tongue which invited, beckoned and urged its prey to enter. It was an old tongue which caressed, stroked, slurped and finally drained with oodles of Jurassic slobber.

As with so many gay men who loved anonymous sex, it had to be acknowledged; there was, deep in Froggy's sexual psyche, a perverse desire to be touched by this mouth-watering old man wanting and willing to work. And work he did. He worked well with tongue and clever crafty hands. Naughty fingers, sticky with drool, searched and slid around the nooks and crannies of bliss, as the boy's half focused unseeing eyes idly explored the dense gloom of that jet blackness. He was now reverberating with crashing ecstasy. All these sensations were enjoyed, greatly enjoyed, safe in the knowledge that the worker would remain low, far away, far below navel level.

After a few precious minutes of pleasure, the Frog finally succumbed. He succumbed to the succulent sounds of guttural slurps and slobber. He succumbed to overwhelming touches, tickles, titillations and the soothing sounds of a slurping old slut. It all ended in that last sound, that finality, the escaping sigh, the last, long, low - murmur.

During his acquaintance in the seedy world of 'teens together' sharing an older superior sucker, Simeon found that the younger teen, having spent, often lost interest in the orgy and quit the sexy scene. Froggy proved better than that; he stayed and made reciprocating efforts to enhance the pleasure of his new lover.

Without delay, Simeon's inflated weapon was wantonly sheathed in the well practised, well lubricated orifice affording supreme ecstasy. It was well known that Guzzly Granddad's toothless grotto was embellished directly after each youthful orgasm. Accordingly, previous spunk enriched the qualities of lubrication to encourage following spunk.

Conscientiously, with both hands, Froggy fingers were all over a bare bum, gently stroking with pats and pets, touches and tickles to delight the anus. Naughty fingers on the other hand tenderly tickled the balls.

If not audible, Simeon's concluding moments of high delight were indicated by evocative body language. Froggy's fondling detected an arching of back, a bracing spasm of joy gripping the youthful body. An open mouth issued a silent scream of rapture from the very foundations of his stiff stake struggling to further impale that old sitting slut. His deep guttural groan of gratitude signalled a milky gush, his reward for services rendered.

No gratitude, no word at all came from the recipients of those services. Quickly, Simeon pulled up his jeans when, by touch, he noticed Froggy was still rude and bare, wide-open for business - *more* business. He had not pulled up. He wanted seconds. Guzzly Granddad, now vacant, indicated his willingness to resume duty with that famous fat tongue all ready to go again. Still exposed, much dribbling with excitement, naughty Nobby slipped down the slippery throat of the greedy slut eliciting from the Frog a small moan. It was a moan of appreciation complemented by a deeper grunt of anticipatory pleasure escaping from the old man.

Back out on the noisy fairground, the sinful couple were looking slightly sheepish after such a lewd interlude only yards from dense crowds of heterosexual revellers. Simeon now had an opportunity to assess his intriguing companion under bright festive lights. He was clean and well dressed. This spoke of parents who took their duties seriously. Froggy appeared to be well fed and was well shod in a cultural climate where such adequate standards were not always reached. Seven years on, Heanor was still relatively primitive.

Feeling the need for a quiet chat, Simeon suggested they stroll to the park just behind the Market Place where silence and darkness would be more conducive to a much needed heart-to-heart. As expected, young Heanorians were all concentrated in the raucous brilliance of thrills and spills, leaving a benighted town park peaceful and safe.

The park gates, illuminated by a single weak yellow street lamp, showed a clear view of that cheeky face, frequently thrust into the other face with an unending chirpy chatter on a variety of subjects. At 19 to the dozen, he rattled on about fair rides, slot machines, the weather (lots of weather) - and now his latest boyfriend.

'Eeee, lookeee; look wot I got!'

From somewhere on his person, Froggy produced a newspaper cutting. Many times folded, it was a frayed photograph of a young man, an impressive fellow with dream boat features. Simeon looked long and hard at this greased, groomed familiar image of a fantasy boyfriend. Now in the park, just visible from the street lamp, Froggy burst into sudden song and dance -

'Like a tiger, oooh, oooh, oooh, like a tiger - WOW! I wanna **growl**...'

With oodles of enthusiasm, he launched himself into several orbits around Simeon - hopping, hoofing, skipping with twirls and whirls in an ecstasy of homage to his teen idol.

'What teen idol?' asked Ronnie.

'He was THE teen idol,' replied Simeon, 'and I'll bet you've never even heard of him.'

'Elvis?'

'Nothing near. The hunk causing Froggy to do cart wheels around me was American, but, unlike Presley, only a one-hit-wonder. Truth to tell, by 1965, this kid was already passé. His short reign was early 60s - but - oh God! His dazzling beauty! Ronnie! I kid you not, he drove me crazy! He had a decent singing voice, plus a mesmerising speaking voice - soooo sexy! It was smooth yet tremulous like on the edge of orgasm. He was 17 and *oozed* eroticism. Oh! to be young again.

'Listen, Ronnie, this dream boat - he shone a bright light on this drab soot stained pit town, and, for that matter, every town in the western world. What's a Fabian?'

'Pardon?'

'That's how he was packaged - promoted. First we heard "What's a Fabian." Later it was, "Fabian is coming" and then "Fabian is HERE."
'Then the record came out. Everybody was singing - "Like a tiger, oooh, oooh, oooh, like a tiger - WOW! I wanna **growl**..."

'This is sounding familiar,' said Ronnie.

'It should. I remember it being played endlessly on the jukebox in the Milk Bar. For a couple of years the world went Fabian mad. To help Froggy, I made out not knowing much about his obsession to give him space to elaborate and enthuse.'

'Fabian's got seven LPs, three gold records and he's made a film!' raved Froggy.

Both friends ambled further into the park and deeper darkness.

'More sex?' suggested Ronnie.

'No. The mood was different. We found a bench and Froggy became serious losing some of his child-like chatter. I saw a different side of this little chap. As with many of us, he had an alternative personality to show the world.'

'Like you, Simeon?' ventured Ronnie. 'I mean,' he added quickly, 'Simeon behind the stern mask, the strict schoolmaster rather than Simeon the human being I've come to know.'

'Spot on, Ronnie,' smiled Simeon. 'The boy I've described was real enough, but he had depth and revealed a heartrending history, disclosing a staggering catalogue of cruelty. He suffered emotional trauma since an occurrence in his earlier schooldays. He was seen kissing another boy. That's it, just a simple kiss. This incident triggered months of appalling bullying extending beyond the school gates into his home with gay hating abuse and bricks through windows. The family was forced to move to Heanor where they were unknown. Now in his 40s, unable to work, deep trauma has adversely affected this victim's mental and physical health - a life ruined by ignorance and bigotry.'

As the friendship between Simeon and Froggy developed and deepened over the years from 1965 up to 1995, further disturbing details of that ruined life came to light. In the 1970s, a clandestine gay bathhouse opened in a Nottinghamshire mining town which was a godsend to the secretive schoolmaster who had to motor many miles north to places like Manchester and Blackpool to enjoy orgiastic sex in the steam room. This more convenient Turkish bath deep in colliery country was located on the edge of town in a rundown one-time warehouse with a plain somewhat ramshackle exterior.

Like the Windsor steam bath over the river from Detroit, the building looked derelict with no windows and no sign indicating any business. Nothing suggested habitation or any activity within. To all appearance, a solitary strong steel door of non-existent use barred the only possible entrance. Careful examination of the right hand jamb disclosed a small unobtrusive button. Once pressed, you pushed the door at the sound of a buzzer - and you were in.

For decades, without being aware, dowdy frumpish women and dull dirty working men shuffled past that anonymous dreary door. Few people had any idea of what occurred within. Heterosexuals who heard rumours took the view it was reserved for the degenerate only. To gain entrance, homosexuals had to *know* about it by word of mouth. But to Simeon and Froggy, this portal of salacious sin and sodomy was the entrance to a palace of pleasure where carnal coupling could be enjoyed in comfort, secrecy and safety.

Aware of Froggy's orgiastic preference, Simeon drove his little friend to this safe house of touches and tickles where they enjoyed years of happy orgasms at the hands of *real* men, masculine unpretentious coarse hairy-arsed coalminers, the raunchy rough and ready. No ceremony - no messing about ...

'Cum 'ere, ya little slut! Let's ave ya. Grab owd a this fucker!!'

Devoid of the civilities of city types, these were the uncouth, crude, lascivious and loutish that quickly passed through the portals of pleasure with flat caps pulled down over upturned collars. The majority were married with children and grandchildren. Evenings in the pub would see them raucously asserting their macho heterosexuality, swilling beer with mates laughing at homophobic jokes at the bar.

Over the years of enjoying the crude coalminers' bathhouse on Saturday, its busiest day; Simeon drove to Heanor and picked up Froggy in the market place. From there, the car descended steeply down to dismal Langley Mill, up the hill through Eastwood, heading east, deep into the grimy Nottinghamshire coalfields.

For more security, Simeon parked his car about a mile away from the town centre in a middleclass neighbourhood adjacent to a park. Leaving the baths, they followed a familiar ritual walk in which Froggy was usually chirpy and chatty with child-like enthusiasm. Even so, there came a day when he was more serious and clearly wanted to unburden himself. It was after one sauna session in 1989, walking back to the car, that they had a long and significant conversation. Simeon was already well acquainted with the horrors of Froggy's life, but on this particular Saturday, for the first time ever, Froggy poured out an appalling litany of cruel events which occurred in his early childhood. This disturbing revelation was triggered by two recent events both within the previous few weeks.

The first was a painful incident in a Matlock cafe. It should be remembered that Froggy, like Dopey the Dwarf appearing decades younger than his years, was always going to be a tempting target for cruel louts looking for fun. This particular instance was especially humiliating for a man, albeit child-like, approaching 40 with a strong sense of his own worth and dignity. These were the days long before the 21st century advent of hate crimes and hate incidents which now attempt to protect gay victims. Froggy fled that dreadful drama, his meal half eaten, to a chorus of homophobic taunts, catcalls, jeers, whistles and shouts. Everybody witnessed the scene - many laughed - some were silent - nobody tried to stop it.

'For evil to triumph, it is necessary only for the good man to do nothing.' Edmund Burke.

The second upsetting event was a compulsory summons to a Social Services interview which included an extensive discussion along the lines of - 'Why can't you work for a living?'

He had been attending such meetings over a period of 20 years, but this one included an element of extra pressure from a particularly zealous interviewing panel. Fortunately, one official with more compassion steered the questioning to morph into a sort of counselling session in which Froggy revealed highly confidential information.

On that Saturday after the baths, Froggy's sad story was also told to Simeon who was deeply moved by the following disclosures. Whilst fresh in mind, he jotted down the gist of the main points.

The sexual scandals of Jehovah's Witnesses first appeared in the public domain in 2014. The most notable was the serial child abuser Jonathan Rose an elder of the Jehovah's Witnesses who was convicted and jailed. Full information is on the internet. Froggy was the son of Jehovah's Witnesses.

Reading back his typed up notes, Simeon found the piece unbelievable - but his friend's words had the ring of truth. For the most part, he believed Froggy, a damaged man with a long history of mental illness resulting from physical and mental abuse. It is worth mentioning that Simeon only knew what he was told and was unable to confirm any of the appalling allegations.

On several occasions, Froggy's Mum punished her son for not concentrating properly on the Jehovah's Witnesses children's bible at the local Kingdom Hall. He was taken to the lavatory and beaten with a large metal spoon. He was often punished by the withholding of food. A minor offence - no pudding. More serious - half portion of the main meal. At age of about 16, during an intimate moment, an older boy was shocked by his protruding ribs and generally poor state of health. Froggy claimed that his diminutive frame was due to partial child starvation.

Between ages six and eleven, he was sent four separate times to a ‘home’ [clinic / assessment centre] to correct / deal with his bad behaviour. In each home he encountered both kind and abusive staff. Transport to and from these ‘homes’ was provided by a Jehovah's Witnesses taxi driver who frequently stopped the car in a secluded spot and demanded that Froggy pleasure him. Froggy himself was never touched. The driver was in his late 50s.

On one occasion Froggy complained to the driver about regular beatings from his dad. The taxi driver persuaded him (at age six) to go to dad and ask a certain question. If he said, ‘Are you a twat?’ then dad would be nice and give him lots of chocolates. Froggy was shocked when dad responded to the question with a good hiding. Violence was often used to punish the child in his own home. The driver was a sadistic paedophile. He enjoyed tormenting Froggy and warned him that nobody would listen if he complained.

‘They’ll take no notice. They all know you speak rubbish. You *are* rubbish!’

The taxi radio was on all the time. A 1959 hit record *(Till) I Kissed You* by the Everly Brothers was played again and again. The lyrics resonated, taking him back to that one momentous event back at school when he was seen kissing another boy - his first meaningful kiss. Froggy said -

‘The memory of this song has never gone away. The more I listen to it, the more I think of what happened to me.’

Froggy’s bad behaviour as a child consisted of minor vandalism. On holiday he once suffered severe sunburn on his back and blames his parents for not exercising due care. He had no recollection of any sun cream being applied. The following day he was in agony on a boat trip with no recollection of any cream provided to ease the pain. In his anger and agony, he peeled and pulled off a considerable area of paint from this already old decrepit boat as it chugged through the waves. Eventually, at the end of the trip, this deliberate damage was discovered by an enraged boatman. Froggy was beaten severely by his father, in front of other passengers, to show the boatman that he was a 'responsible' parent.

At about age 12 in school, Froggy, keen to be one of the lads, eager to increase his self-esteem, was persuaded to grope a teacher. Prior to this assault, he had steeled himself to be hauled before the headmaster and endure consequential punishment. As it turned out, no punishment followed because the teacher did nothing except say - 'You rude little boy!' He probably took the view that more harm than good could follow a formal complaint to the Head - or backed off simply due to embarrassment.

Simeon was told about Froggy being taken to a solicitor - a Jehovah's Witnesses solicitor. His parents made him witness the signing of their will in which it was made clear to him that he would, one day, come into the possession of the family house. Having learning difficulties, Froggy had no independent means of checking the wording of this document which would challenge any adult of average educational ability.

'Why be so suspicious?' asked Ronnie. 'If he's the only son where else would the family home go to?'

'It would go to the Jehovah's Witnesses,' said Simeon with some acerbity. 'Jehovah's Witnesses are interlocked not just by intensive indoctrination and brainwashing, but also by a considerable financial interlocking system. The money stays within the cult, make no mistake about that, Ronnie! I believe that brief legal ceremony was to give the boy some hope and confidence that, say, if the parents ever fell under the proverbial bus, little Froggy would never become homeless. And he wouldn't!'

'I suppose wills can be changed,' mused Ronnie.

'Worse than that!' rejoined Simeon. 'I warned Froggy that the property, bought by Jehovah's Witness money, might still be in Jehovah's Witness ownership after the death of both parents. Ergo: Froggy could still be under Jehovah's Witness control in the future. Remember, these parents saw their son as both sinful and mentally deficient. Yes, they might have kept him clean, well dressed and well housed - but they would ensure that their pernicious tentacles could reach beyond the grave to keep their errant child in check - in perpetuity.

'That's horrible!' exclaimed Ronnie.

'Yes,' responded Simeon. 'And yet I must conclude that Froggy was a *survivor.* Unlike gay friends Hubert and Brian in Detroit who were effectively murdered by Jehovah's Witnesses, Froggy came to resent his religious parents and that resentment freed him from their poisonous grip. Ultimately, Froggy constitutes a happy ending - a rarity in cult style indoctrination.'

'Do you still see Froggy?' asked Ronnie.

'I saw him occasionally, up until April 1995 when my little world collapsed. You'll recall that I referred to it as a collapse of confidence rather than a breakdown. God knows where Froggy is now ... '

Simeon trailed off into a thoughtful silence.

'I realise this is hardly comfortable listening,' he continued tentatively. 'I should be grateful my little friend was never entrapped by the police. To the best of my knowledge, he escaped prison. At about that time the local papers were full of John and Billy.'

'Who? What did they do?'

'Not much. John Clarkson and his boyfriend Bill were sent to prison after Nottingham police found a Christmas card which said -

"To Billy, with all my love, as ever - John".

'John was bullied into admitting that he had slept with Billy. Held separately at the police station, each was told that the other one had confessed to an act of gross indecency. In other words, they both gave statements incriminating each other. A trial took place at Nottingham Crown Court, a humiliating trial which involved ushers holding up bed sheets and a clerk pointing out stains to the jury. A jar of Vaseline was passed around. Jurors were told to notice a few pubic hairs. Words like disgust, perverts, slimy, degenerate, vile and abomination - appeared in the press.'

Again Simeon became thoughtful staring into the distance.

'I might have mentioned a funny little fat man we called Dolly. He used to warn us chickens back in 1965 about the police and CID - agents provocateurs. Not really believing it, we just laughed at him!

"Never put anything in writing. A jar of Vaseline is enough to convict you."

'Even Mr Toad took the piss out of Dolly, frequently 'taking him off' using those very words. We fell about in a heap of giggles. Now I know why Dolly and other old-timers were so paranoid about it. One posh high-ranking snob hit the roof when he discovered a list of addresses and phone numbers in my wallet. I resented the reprimand, but can understand it better now. They were terrified. It was a grim time.'

'You're getting morbid again. Snap out of it! Froggy seems to know how to have fun. As far as you know, he was a survivor,' suggested Ronnie.

'Too true,' smiled Simeon. 'He had it all worked out. Having been driven out of one pit town, one of his several obsessions was to organize a hierarchy of local colliery towns and colliery villages. He'd rank them in order of social desirability. Heanor was quite low, but a touch higher than Langley Mill - dead rough - certainly at the bottom. Ripley was slightly less common than Heanor, but Belper was well above Ripley and posh Duffield outclassed Belper. Then he'd do the villages - Horsley Woodhouse and Stanley Common were level pegging, but West Hallam was far superior ... and so on.'

'What about Worksop?' asked Ronnie.

'Out of range! Froggy could only categorize the places he knew - and he knew Langley Mill best of all,' laughed Simeon. 'He once took me to a shabby building he described as a "piss 'ole" - an appalling public house crowded with raucous yobbos, roughnecks, tarts and scrubbers all carousing in a dirty beer stained ramshackle. They were all well tanked up. To screams of merriment, one silly slut actually flopped out her tit! Somebody shouted, "Get thee knickers off ya dotty trollop!"

‘It was near Christmas. I remember some horrible women with varicose veins stuffing their faces with fish and chips. One face, a right roly-poly, rhythmically munching, was forcing her specs up and down on her fleshy cheeks. She shoved her greasy chip paper into the Christmas tree with a shriek, egging on the other crones to dispose of their litter with cackles all round. *Dreadful* place!’ concluded Simeon - temporarily assuming a certain moral superiority. He noticed that Ronnie had creased up.

‘Yes,’ he chuckled. ‘All Froggy needed for a *complete* night-on-the-piss was the addition of you, Bobbie and Freddy in that Langley Mill rat-hole of ill repute.’

Seizing the advantage of sudden cheer, Ronnie reminded Simeon that any piece of writing, like a school lesson, would be more likely to succeed with an element of comedy.

‘Let’s have a bit more fun. Give us a good show! Like back in class when ... how did you say it? You were sailing close to the wind.’

‘Mmm,’ muttered Simeon. ‘I suppose I could summarise the arrival and departure of an effete and irritating, artificial queen. For devilment, I introduced Mr Toad to an attractive but affected effeminate youth called Julian. Consumed with lust, Toad invited us to stay with him one weekend. All went well - until bedtime - when Toad said -

“Should you require an aspirin or any assistance in the night, Julian, don’t hesitate to cum into my boudoir.” He always waggled his fingers when excited. Julian, however, thrust his snooty nose in the air -

“Most unlikely,” said Julian, who sounded just like a girl. “You, Mr Toad, are GROTESQUE. It would be scraping the bottom of the barrel.”

‘During that night, I was awakened by whoops and screams.

“Oooh! Oooh! Oooh!”

‘A camp queen with - HIGH VOICE - was in rapture - impaled on a stiff stake of impressive proportions. Toad - proud of his inflated weapon - was well practiced in the art of inflicting supreme ecstasy upon a willing victim.

'The climax came. Toad's deep guttural groan signalled a milky gush, concluding high delight.

'Alas - a reaction set in. The rapturous rider denounced his delirious gallop to that final moment of PURE JOY. He lectured the ugly loathsome lecher.

"Mr Toad! We have SINNED! We must pray for forgiveness."

'Hours later - breakfast was difficult. Julian, in foul mood, hardly spoke to his host. But the gloating toad was triumphant, nudging his guest with a wicked elbow.

"Ay ay. Last night ay. HOW WAS THAT FOR THE BOTTOM OF THE BARREL? You enjoyed that ride on my stallion last night, didn't you! He he he."

"As Anne Boleyn said to Henry the 8th," responded Julian, "Last night was a sample of what you *won't* get."

"Well - I'm not going to give you the pleasure of refusing me, Julian," retorted Mr Toad.

"It would not be a pleasure, Mr Toad," responded Julian, "it would be - a necessity. For you see, I shall journey afar, to join a monastery, never to have sex again."

'He packed his bags and stormed out of the house. It was the last we saw of him.'

'That's it, isn't it?' cried Ronnie. 'I mean, that's a queer who *deserves* to be called a queer. They're repulsive. I've only met you, but you're not like that - *queer*!'

'You've probably met lots of homosexuals - and never knew it. A masculine homosexual is not likely to admit it. You're confusing effeminacy with sexuality. Julian was a first rate prat, but he probably couldn't help his high voice or girlish mannerisms.'

'I'll bet he could have toned them down.'

'Or - even exaggerated them up. I had a friend we used to call Gorgeous Gary who hated camp queens. I introduced him to one. "How dare you bring that vile excrescence near my person?" he complained. Detroit had a few weird and wacky queens who used to camp it up in the Woodward Bar. One bitchy queen known as Marie was pure acid. I'll never forget a particular awkward incident which took place. There were four of us - Gary, Hubert, Bill Scruggs and myself - enjoying a quiet drink minding our own business. Marie spotted us and screamed out for the whole bar to hear -

"Miss Scruggs! There ya are! Honey am a comin' over. Here comes my BODY."

'We nearly died of embarrassment! Especially poor Bill who'd just had a toupee fitted.

"Why, Miss Scruggs," quipped the queen. "WHAT IS THAT! A rug on ya head arr perceive. Honey, you aint a foolin' nobody - an arr LOVE to pull hair."

'She noticed Hubert. To his horror, she gave him a big hug like he was a long lost friend -

"Ooo so cuddly, nice-big-fat-belly! See it wobble. Look everybody - it's Hubert. Poor Hubert, those evil queens should not be referrin' to you as 'The Lady of the Vapours'. Why that's just not true. You don't go to the sauna seven days a week - no - you take Mondays off, don't you?

"But be careful baby, you've had three re-treads on ya tongue this year to date. Yeah, an those teeth 'll need scrapin' again soon. That cum just builds up and up.

"Well it's true! It is. When I go to the sauna - they hand me a towel. When you go, Hubert, they hand you knee pads!"

'Gary hated such tittle-tattle from the low life of my quirky collection of friends. He had no time for any of this nonsense. He viewed old fashioned Hubert as one of the dregs of Detroit, a shabbily dressed overweight beer belly who broke wind too often.

"For God's sake don't suggest another meeting," said Gary. "I can't take the body odour. He doesn't like me and I don't like him. Have a good look at him. Hubert *is* 'The Depression'. He gets his clothes from the Good Will. He belongs to the 1930's. He should have *stayed* there.

"And PLEASE don't keep talking about Marie. She may be funny to you but, anybody who *is* anybody, avoids her like the plague. A vicious mixture of show-off, spite, chiffon and cheap make-up. ARE YOU LISTENING TO ME!

"As for Scruggs, well, he's just a complete waste of space."

'Gary was utterly frustrated by the social gay scene. His reasoning was simple. If a man wants to attract another man then -

"Why in hell's name do they behave like a woman? Why turn themselves into freaks. For God's sake - that's just what they are - FREAKS! I'd like to punch their stupid faces! I really would ... ARE YOU LISTENING TO ME?

"I'm at my wits end just trying to find one SINGLE-REAL-MACHO-MAN!"

'You have to understand, Ronnie, many gay men are naturally effeminate. Marie wasn't so bad. He was revenging himself on men who'd shunned him, on the streets, out of fear of being labelled a homosexual themselves. I was always friendly with Marie. Underneath that outrageous facade, he was a sensitive and, essentially, a kind man.

'Hubert was nothing to look at. But he was a friend and I enjoyed his company. Like many repressed men, estranged from a disapproving family and sometimes depressed, he eventually fell into the clutches of religious bigotry. Untold numbers of homosexuals have had their lives warped, effectively destroyed by active evangelism and rabid homophobia.

'After years of unceasing brainwashing from Jehovah's Witnesses, Hubert became celibate. He cut himself off from gay friends and gay support. He died a lonely, sad, broken man.'

Former teacher and former pupil receded into contemplative silence for a few moments as they absorbed this intelligence.

'I can understand folk who are freaked out by the screaming queen type,' said Ronnie. 'You won't like this, but, I could easily give that weirdo Marie a mouthful of knuckles.'

'As a younger man,' responded Simeon, thoughtfully, 'I shared those feelings, although not quite so violent, but I've matured and softened. OK - Marie was mischievous and did provoke. He did go over the top. Nevertheless, some years later in this country, I met a teenager called Martin, an outrageous screamer, just the same as Marie. He painted himself with makeup and often dressed up as a girl.'

'Ooo sick!'

'My feelings exactly. So Martin *never* appeared in drag in my presence. Drag means dressing up as a woman. I was nice about it. I explained that make-up and drag was a massive turn-off for me and for most of the gay men in the circles in which I moved. It was the BOY element of Martin that excited me - and - oh God - he was a beautiful boy! And he was a worker, not a drone like me.' Ronnie looked puzzled. 'I mean he was fantastic sex. He did the work. There was me in my mid 40s and this sexy life-and-soul of the party in his late teens was quite prepared to service my carnal needs - WOW! It doesn't get much better than that.'

Simeon went on to describe his friendship with a young man who, over a couple of years in the late 1980s, had a strong influence on his life. Martin had a passion for life. Yes, he was always the centre of attention, which annoyed some people, but this fearless and honest boy was the perfect antidote to Simeon's inherent anxiety and constant worrying about how the heterosexual world saw him - always fearing being 'found out'.

The pleasure of visiting Martin was enhanced by the loving relationship between boy and his beautiful cat. This mollycoddled moggy received endless attention with cuddles and kisses satisfying a chronic need in Simeon's psyche. Simeon was a frustrated cat lover, allergic to cats, and therefore unable to adopt his own animal. Puttums, as Martin called his pussy, was a magnificent blue-grey with striking green eyes reflecting a sharp intelligence. Dark ears, dark around the eyes and cute little nose, he stalked around the house with a lithe liquidity - the birthright of all felines. And this clean cat occupied an ultra clean and tidy house maintained at a high standard by a very special young man who made the heterosexual majority seem so very dull.

'Martin taught me a lesson,' explained Simeon, looking directly at Ronnie. 'He taught me tolerance, he taught me to accept effeminate men who were just as naturally effeminate as I was born a homosexual. He also taught me how to live. He celebrated life in style. He had the confidence I lacked.'

Ronnie noticed a certain tone of repressed emotion in Simeon's voice which was on the edge of breaking. Respectfully, he remained silent for a few moments.

'The 1960's were amazing years in terms of innovation, imagination, hope and happiness,' said Simeon, somewhat perked up. 'And later we had October 11th 1988, our National Coming Out Day.' Ronnie looked puzzled. His unspoken question was answered. 'And in this Worksopian backwater, here am I still cowering from a brick-wall hostility I'm too scared to confront! WHAT GOOD AM I!' he shouted. He continued with what sounded to Ronnie like a poem.

I am what I am
I am my own special creation
So come take a look
Give me the hook
Or the ovation ...

'Can't remember any more. I think something about ... '

It's one life and there's no return and no deposit
One life so it's time to open up your closet
Life's not worth a damn till you can shout out
I am what I am

The quoting of these lines had a profound effect on both men - the homosexual and the heterosexual. Even Ronnie saw a significant analogy in his own fractured, difficult and dysfunctional existence.

'So .... do you still see this youth?'

This question caused Simeon's face to contort into a picture of agony. Ronnie would have called back his words - but it was too late. Uncomfortable moments passed before a considered response had been silently composed.

'How often have I used the phrase "In my world"? It seems that my whole being, my whole purpose in life, is to keep banging on and on until I get the heterosexual majority to understand the reality, the real horrors lurking in the dark abyss of homosexuality.'

'I'm sorry! I really am. I didn't want to ...'

'Don't apologise, Ronnie. You are not at fault. I'm grateful you are here listening to me in such dedicated friendship. My job is to try and explain something of my world to an outsider. Unfortunately, my bitterness often gets in the way of an essential communication.

'Ok. You asked if I was still friendly with Martin. A very reasonable question. Since I hate pubs we met at the Derby Turkish Baths on Reginald Street. He took me back to a very pleasant flat backing onto The Arboretum where he lived alone with his beloved Puttums who had the run of the park. In the gay world, we tend to ask few questions. Once he mentioned being a pen pusher, but never elaborated and never spoke of any family. Like myself, I assumed he had been disowned and turned out. He had a lot of camp friends and showed me photographs of himself having wild weekend celebrations surrounded by screaming queens in various pubs and a few private houses belonging to more wealthy gay men. My visits to him, usually in the late afternoon or early evening, were all impromptu and sometimes infrequent. His chaotic life allowed for no forward planning. He lived for the day.

'There came a day when I received no response to a knock on Martin's door. His usual greetings were after the enthusiastic style of Sandy and Julian in a *Round the Horne* episode. I returned on another occasion to the same ominous deadly silence. I enquired at the doors of three neighbours. Two of them grudgingly spoke with disapproving hostility, almost shutting the door in my face. The third, an elderly neighbour, spoke kindly of Martin who had not been seen for more than two weeks. More sinister 'no news' came from a chicken hanging around the local cottage.

'He's gone!'

'Where?'

'Don't know. Just gone'

'Just consider this scenario, Ronnie. One of your mates, perhaps Bobbie or Freddie, disappears without trace. They live at home, so parents and relatives will be at the police station demanding action. And a search would ensue. It would be in the papers. Perhaps even on radio or TV. Most likely the boy would be found dead or alive. It is unlikely that a homosexual youth would be reported to the police by other homosexuals, or even by such as the kindly neighbour ... '

'So he was never found?' interrupted Ronnie. 'Didn't turn up anywhere?'

'Martin vanished in the late 1970s. In 18 years, having asked dozens of people, I must conclude nobody has seen or heard of that poor lad who enjoyed such a zest for life. It's possible that he's located somewhere, but more probable that he is dead. Dead he might be, notwithstanding, Martin will be resurrected, commemorated and honoured in the pages of my book.'

Chapter 9

Public Outrage

Any utterance of Jehovah's Witnesses plunged Simeon into a combination of gloom and unbridled fury. Ronnie had noticed it before. After the welcome humour of outrageous screaming queens, the quick sharp contrast disturbed him. There followed a few moments of silence. After Simeon's brood, his thoughts turned to Ronnie's stabbing during the period of Mrs Thatcher's premiership somewhere around 1985. He mused on how badly it affected his pupil's mental health.

'Ronnie! About the time you spent in hospital; I wondered if you were upset by that James Bulger business?'

'Who was James Bulger?'

'A little boy who had a strong impact on my life. I'll never forget it. It was around February time, miserable cold wet dark days. It would be early 1990s. He was only two-years-old. James Bulger was led away from a Liverpool shopping centre by two ten-year-olds. We all saw it captured on grainy CCTV images. It burned into the nation's conscience. It also seared into *my* conscience. Somehow, I took it very personally. This little toddler, so trusting, was holding on to the hand of one of the boys. They walked him two and a half miles through busy streets, eventually to a quiet canal towpath. They tortured him ...'

Ronnie's face, empathetic, much pained, reflected the emotion in Simeon's choked voice as it hesitated - and then regained control.

'They tortured this poor helpless child. They took pleasure in his anguish, his heartfelt tears and his pain.' He took a deep breath. 'We were given to understand that his hopeless cries for help egged them on. This, the child who had trusted them, the child who had faith in these boys - before they murdered him. How can you *not* have known about James Bulger, Ronnie?

'Hang about! We're not all news swots. I don't watch the BBC or read big posh papers with small print - like you!'

'I'm sorry, Ronnie. I was out of order there. We're so close together on this biography stuff ... '

Simeon's apology was genuine. As a gay man, he, of all people, should know about not asking too many intrusive questions. He must try to get a handle on it. He tried a different tack.

'Ok - we news buffs - we were all too aware of the moral decline at that time. With Bulger, Britain's self-doubt had taken on a horrible shape. How can I put it? A blighted economy, grim times - felt as if nobody was in charge. Crime, poverty, boy races in cars terrorising law abiding people in their own streets - even in Clowne. I suffered a plague of screaming motorbikes. Yobs removing baffles. It was physically painful - like - anarchy rules. Even the police seemed to give up!

'For several days, the sweet little face of James stared out at us from newspapers and TV news reports stoking up public outrage. The populace were inflamed. Furious crowds screamed abuse and banged on the police van which brought the boys to court.'

'Grim!' said Ronnie, possibly struggling to find a word strong enough to reference such a dire situation.

'Grim indeed. Occasionally, we feel that a particular heinous killing says something about the moral state of the nation. It must have been at about that time, I heard a new word, an *ugly* word - underclass. Some MP put it quite well:

"This is a hammer blow against the sleeping conscience of the nation. There is a growing sense of moral decline."

'I know you might be a bit touchy about this,' hazarded Ronnie, 'but, well ... you told me something about problems with sixth formers which wound up your teaching career. *That* upset me! No kidding. I wanted to sort them out ...'

'I know, Ronnie. And what you just said means a lot - it really does ...'

'But we didn't give you an easy ride ... I'm really sorry ...'

'Forget it, Ronnie. No sweat. *Your* disruptive behaviour, well, you, Bobbie and Freddie were just "rough and tumble". Malice was never in it. Just look how easily we suddenly started to like each other! The sixth formers ... they were older. Only the lads, it was never the girls. The yobbish element was nasty and cruel spurred on by some of the more laddish members of staff. I suspected one sarcastic colleague and one other who I surmised as traitorous. There must have been a certain amount of familiarity, unprofessional anti-gay banter between them with an inner circle of favoured boys. To some extent they instigated a witch-hunt culture against me.'

'You mean ... dirty talk. They called you names?'

'Along those lines. It was OK to rag the queer. Open season on faggots. One of those lads, I'll call him Ken. He would be 17 - thereabouts ... well, he'd been in one of my tutor groups. I'd had pastoral responsibility of Ken since he was a first year, age eleven. In those six years I did my best for him. I liked him. He liked me. He trusted me and I trusted him.'

Simeon looked at a puzzled Ronnie who was clearly trying to understand what kind of caustic comment could be so devastating as to destroy a 17 year teaching career.

'It hit me like a thunderbolt,' continued Simeon. 'In the Sixth Form Block Central Square, there is a pigeonhole receptacle for attendance registers. At registration time, all tutors based in that block approached them to retrieve their particular register. In the same area, various sixth formers would mill about waiting for the end of registration to enter their classrooms. They'd be a little bored, aimlessly circulating, exchanging desultory remarks.

'I walked up to the pigeonhole, took my register and walked down the corridor to the classroom where my group were waiting to be registered. Out of a hum of conversation, one comment came out loud and clear:

"You took a chance there, Tom!" said Ken. "What ya mean?" said Tom. "Ya turned ya back on 'im." "Shush" from a third party who demonstrated a scrap of shame.'

Ronnie took a few moments to construe the scene.

'Taking the piss.'

'In the worst possible way. A fellow teacher was horrified. He said the heterosexual equivalent was - "Watch out, Girls! Cover ya tits. Hogg's coming."

'Some days later, a few sixth formers were crowding around a locked classroom because their teacher was late. One asked me to unlock it. As I approached to oblige, he said: "Bums tat wall." As a method of self-protection, I pretended not to hear it - but it was clear to all that I *had* heard it. Still recovering from the first insult, at this point, I was sinking rapidly. My authority and respect from sixth formers had hit zero. In following days, further humiliations diminished my capacity to sustain further damage.

'I was already losing my rationality when I thought a boy made an obscene reference to me. He denied it vehemently. On reflection, I think he was probably telling the simple truth - but I couldn't think straight. I couldn't do the job. My position was untenable.'

'But you *must* have done something? You kept *us* in order pretty well. Your classes were quiet and well disciplined. For God's sake! You were known as a strict and well organized teacher.'

'Yes. And you know what, Ronnie? That was very much part of the problem. An old-fashioned schoolmaster like me is a tempting target. After getting "suitable advice" from a teacher, Ken approached me with an apology, an apology given in private. His devastatingly pornographic outrage was thrown at me in front of an audience. He received the mildest of reprimands from a senior member of staff who told him: "That was a silly thing to do".

'The second culprit was easier to deal with. I went straight to his mother who worked in the school. She was horrified and supportive. I obtained a proper apology in writing.'

'But you were knackered,' said Ronnie in a quiet compassionate voice.

'Well put. I was debilitated, drained and enfeebled. Couldn't think straight - couldn't do the job.

'It was, of course, really a replay of the Mundy Street experience 38 years before when a sadistic schoolmaster whipped up a storm of jeering, gibes and catcalls. As a child of twelve, unable to analyse and rationalise, I saw self destruction as the only possible escape. I've told you that it was the old paedophile round the corner who talked me out of it.

'When Ken delivered his fatal blow, I was 49. Resignation, without hope of a pension, was a drastic solution - but less lethal. Effectively - the scumbags got away with it - but here I am - back in harness!! I should *never* have allowed them to talk me into this miserable "come back gradually" predicament. I should have been brave enough to tell them to get stuffed and get the hell out.'

'Well you've got to do something - or I will.'

'I'm tempted to accept your offer of violence but .... Let's face it, Ronnie, we can do better. We've started a process which has headed off any intention of me returning to the classroom. We are both mentally ill ... Oh no; I don't mean we're mad. We're a team. You've given me hope for the future. Ultimately, we'll reach a position where they'll have to get rid of me with a disability pension.

'I worry about *you.* I worry about both of us. Most of all, I worry about the elephant in the room.'

'Oh! That elephant again.'

Both were stilled by the unknown horror of illness. During another uncomfortable silence, neither of them wanted to go to that dark place. Simeon broke the silence by returning to the mental and moral decline he associated with Prime Minister John Major.

'Of course, nobody expected John Major to win that election. 1992? Something like that ...'

'Well ... was Mrs Thatcher ... gone?'

'Oh don't worry about it, Ronnie. I expect you'd got your own problems. You had enough to think about, without who's in charge at Westminster. Forget it.'

But Ronnie was not appeased. His face showed it. And more so Simeon's attempt to downplay the extraordinary fact that a young man of average intelligence with a moderate education, however disinterested in current affairs, *could not have heard of the current Prime Minister*! Ronnie took a deep breath and asked -

'Did Mrs Thatcher die?'

'No. She became very unpopular over a number of things, the poll tax mainly ... Well; it came to the point where her closest colleagues urged her to resign. Men in grey suits they're called. Of course, she clung on tooth and claw - but, in the end, she had to go. Anyway, we had a new election and the Chancellor of the Exchequer; John Major, became the new Prime Minister.'

Ronnie looked miserable.

'Look, Ronnie, don't fret; the point I wanted to make was the chaos of the time. It was chaos in this place. A scourge of mass window breaking. Cost a fortune in repairs. Nobody brought to book. I remember a certain horrible disobedient slag who was totally out of control. She was put on detention dozens of times but just refused, she just walked out. There was one chilling moment when the Senior Mistress said: "I've had it! I can't cope anymore."

'She left the building never to return. Some sort of mental breakdown we were told. The slag, of course, stayed on to inflict her disruptive reign of hell. There were other staff casualties including one who had to be *carried* out of his classroom - I-kid-you-not! It was an appalling incident. He was strapped to a Victorian looking restraining chair by the proverbial men in white coats who rush mad people to the loony bin. It happened not far from here. I saw it myself. The whole Sixth Form Block had to be evacuated. Some thought it was a bomb scare.'

'Crikey! This teacher ... do I know him?'

'Of course you do. But - forgive me, Ronnie. I can't name him. In my final manuscript, I just want to outline the awful breakdown of discipline in the 1990s.'

'Understood. At least you can't hang that on *me*! I mean, me being a bad lad an all that. When it happened, I was long gone ...'

Ronnie's voice trailed off. Again the subtext of his mental condition asserted a menacing reality, which at all costs, had to be avoided. He cast around for a change of subject and found homosexuality to be a useful diversion.

'What about this law you keep going on about - emm - that it let blokes like you have it away with each other? You know the one I mean ... ?

Simeon smiled. It was interesting how Ronnie could somehow manage to be two separate personalities. This one was the 14-year-old he remembered teaching, the inarticulate boy who struggled to express himself. At other times, through Simeon's mist, he sounded and even looked like a man in his mid-twenties, a Ronnie who had made a reasonable effort to improve himself.

'You mean the 1967 Sexual Offences Act,' explained Simeon. 'Yes, it was an important step in the right direction, an important milestone in the battle for gay rights but it only *partially* decriminalised homosexual acts between men over 21. The trials and tribulations of gay people over the last two centuries go on and on. In some ways it got worse. Derbyshire Police already had a secret list of 'known homosexuals', who were 'active'. As a naughty teenager in the early 1960s, I was certainly an 'active' homosexual and more than a little acquainted with several busy public lavatories of the day.

'Older acquaintances showed us newspaper cuttings revealing tragic stories of men who were convicted and punished for committing crimes labelled gross indecency and buggery.'

'Buggery! As in "bugger off," smiled Ronnie.

'You probably know it better as bumming! Buggery is anal intercourse - up the back passage. I doubt my Aunty Brenda knew the true meaning of the word bugger. The Derbyshire version is bogger. She'd often say "Bogger off, ya soft old bogger."

'Anyway, my early years in America imprinted me towards oral rather than anal sex which probably saved me from dying of AIDs.'

'You don't bum?' asked Ronnie still grinning.

'I don't criticise those who do,' laughed Simeon, 'but I certainly picked up the prevailing Detroit prejudice against "hitting the dirt road" as my old friend Hubert used to quip.'

They both laughed out loud.

'All this talk of bumming reminds me of ugly homophobic rants in the Lords and Commons up to the passing of Sexual Offences Act in 1967. "A Charter for Buggery" complained Montgomery. "I suppose it would do less harm to tolerate buggery over the age of 80," Monty added.

'Mischievously, *The Times* reminded its readers that the old soldier was 79! Biographer Nigel Hamilton, citing some evidence, suggested Monty was a repressed homosexual.'

'I've heard of that bloke. Wasn't he a general in the big war?'

'Field Marshall Montgomery - top man. And he wouldn't have been the *only* gay Lord in The Lords. We're told that Lord Arran proposed the bill and also sponsored another bill for the protection of badgers. He was asked why the badger effort failed whereas the gay sex bill had succeeded. Arran replied - "There are not many badgers in the House of Lords."

More laughter and then a sombre seriousness descended as Simeon recalled being shown a newspaper cutting from that period.

'I saw a sad picture of a fire gutted building which once held happy memories in the early 1970s for those of us who needed somewhere safe to go. Formerly a cricket pavilion in Shardlow near Derby, it was known affectionately as "the handbag club" run by a committee of gay men. For people like me that retreat conjures up mixed memories - our joys and sorrows...'

Simeon relapsed into a moody introspection, but was jerked back by Ronnie.

'I want to learn! That 1967 thing must have done *some* good? Why are you so down on it?'

'I'll try to explain. Gay men were criminals. That criminality led to an underground culture which allowed myths and stereotypes to flourish unchallenged. The associations of gay men with effeminacy, dressing up as women and touching up little boys became rooted in the public consciousness. For the record, Ronnie, I've never had a desire to wear women's clothes or act like a woman.'

'And little boys?'

'I prefer BIG boys.'

They both laughed.

'That's better,' said Ronnie.

'But there was not much to laugh about. You never told anybody. You couldn't defend yourself. The police, the law, the church, society, everybody was against you. It was the blackmailer's charter.

'Nearly 30 years on, I'm now more in tune with the fears and horrors of the older men who cautioned me years ago.'

'Like Dolly?'

'Like Dolly - and several others. Like a Canon I met in the Turkish baths. A Canon is a sort of high ranking vicar in a cathedral. He told me a distressing story. He was warning me:

"Once your name is in the paper, your job has gone, everything has gone. The only way out if you got caught ... well, a lot committed suicide. A man came to talk to me in the cathedral. He said he was gay. His family was against him. The next day, I picked up the local newspaper and read that the man had hanged himself."'

'Anyway,' said Ronnie, 'either gay sex is legal or it isn't legal. How can it be half legal?'

Simeon began to rummage through copious notes he had accrued from newspaper cuttings. In this complex answer, he half addressed Ronnie and, whilst shuffling several sheets of A4, half addressed his scribbles.

'Well, to start with, the age of consent was unequal. Heterosexuals could indulge at age 16. Homosexuality was outlawed for all under 21. The 1967 reform applied to England and Wales only. It didn't include the armed forces or merchant navy, where sex between men remained a criminal offence. Gay military personnel and merchant seamen could still be jailed for behaviour that was no longer a crime between gay civilians.

'Centuries-old anti-gay laws were **not** abolished in 1967. They remained on the statute book under the heading "Unnatural offences."

'The two main gay crimes continued to be anal sex, known in law as buggery (bumming) and gross indecency, which was any sexual contact between men - other than bumming. Gross indecency includes wanking off the other chap or letting him wank you - or doing it together. The posh term is mutual masturbation. Just fondling each other, naughty touching ... even kissing comes under the heading of gross indecency.

'There was also the offence of procuring: the inviting or facilitating of gay sex. Bizarrely, the 1967 reform decriminalised anal sex in certain circumstances, but banned men from procuring lawful anal sex for other males, such as arranging a gay sex date for a friend.

'The law against soliciting and importuning remained in force. It was interpreted to designate homosexuality as an immoral purpose. It criminalised men chatting up men or loitering in public places with homosexual intent, even if no sexual act took place. You could go to prison even if nothing happened! Men were convicted under this law before and *after* 1967. You could be charged for merely smiling and winking at other men in the street!

'In the 1950's, I recall a popular cheery song -

Standing on the corner watching all the girls go by ... giving all the girls the eye ... brother they can't lock you up for what you're thinking, nor for the Woo! look in your eye ...

'During the whole of **my** life, I've had to be very careful not to be seen watching **boys** go by. Being arrested by the police, I admit, would be unlikely. On the other hand, if being rumbled or "picked up," as gay parlance goes, increases the risk of verbal abuse from Joe Public, or worse, violence from yobs looking for an excuse for entertainment.

'There were other arrests under ancient legislation against indecency.

Gay and bisexual men continued to be prosecuted right up to the present day under public order and "breach of the peace" laws. You could be hauled in for public displays of affection, such as kissing and cuddling. Many aspects of gay sex remained criminal even **after** 1967.

'I'll tell you this, Ronnie, the repression got **much** worse after 1967! At about that time, I enjoyed a friendship with a retired schoolmaster. He was as old as the century, holding conservative views on homosexuality. Finger wagging and sternly disapproving, he cautioned against cottaging and my naughty woodland walks.

"Be careful, Simeon. They've made it legal in private. Mark my words, the police will now step up their efforts to entrap homosexual men who meet in public places."

'There were police stake-outs in parks and toilets, sometimes using "pretty police" as bait to lure gay men to commit sex offences. For example, a famous actor called Wilfrid Brambell was entrapped by the CID and arrested in the November of 1962 on a charge of intending to commit a lewd act of gross indecency. As a teenager, I read about it. I was fascinated by the idea of one man wishing to have sex with another man, but, in the macho, coalmining coalfields of Derbyshire, wisely, I kept that fascination closely to myself.

'The Brambell incident was splashed over the front pages of the popular press. It reinforced the generally held prejudice that a 'homosexual' looked and acted just like the shambling, dirty, decrepit, toothless, unshaven old man, who was better known to the nation as **Albert Steptoe**.'

'Old man Steptoe!!' cried Ronnie, suddenly coming to life.

'The very same! Shortly after the arrest, watching the rag and bone man on the telly, "Ooncle 'Arry" came in and said:

"Ton that dotty bogga off!" [Turn that dirty bugger off]

'Doing all this research, I've discovered that enemies of people like me are in all classes of society, not just the religious, not just the lords and ladies, but also the common ignorant people who inhabit my background. The Wolfenden Committee recommended decriminalisation of consenting male homosexual acts in private back in 1957, but the Tory government was unwilling to change the law. Many Labour MPs opposed changing the law because - "the miners would not stand for it". You and I, Ronnie, are from coal mining stock.

'After the 1967 Act, gay Turkish baths continued to be raided. Disorderly house charges were pressed against gay clubs that allowed same-sex couples to dance cheek-to-cheek.'

'A disorderly house?' queried Ronnie. 'As a boy, I used to hear about people getting into trouble for keeping a disorderly house. I imagined the police charging into a house and arresting a woman if it was untidy, or she was too idle to put stuff away. But isn't it something to do with sex?'

'Spot on,' laughed Simeon. 'The woman wasn't typical Mrs Housewife who'd let her house get to be a tip, she was a "Madam" managing a brothel and living off immoral earnings.

'Anyway, in 1967, I was still a chicken, in fact, a 22-year-old with only a hazy understanding of "consenting male adults in private". Standing at a urinal, another chicken stood next to me. He looked down at me. I looked down at his manhood, full mast, and up to his handsome face, smiling encouragement. He spoke -

"It's legal now you know."

'In fact it was **not** legal. He was under 21 and a public lavatory is not a private place. The 1967 Sexual Offences Act contained a definition of privacy for gay men which meant that you couldn't have sex in a locked hotel bedroom, a locked car in isolated, secluded woodland or even your own bedroom in your own house when another man was present in another part of the house!

'Now let me see, where is it?' mumbled Simeon fumbling through his notes. 'Got it! In 1966, the year before partial decriminalisation, 420 men were convicted of gross indecency. Seven years after the Act, the number of convictions soared by over 400 percent to 1,711 in 1974. The authorities were determined to ensure that the limited liberalisation of 1967 did not give a green light to what they still regarded as a vice.

'The Law Lords ruled in 1973 that gay lonely heart adverts in magazines were a "conspiracy to corrupt public morals." Despite the reform of 1967, homosexuality was declared by their lordships to be only partly legal, not moral and contrary to the public good.

'Anti-gay discrimination in housing, employment and the provision of goods and services remained lawful by default. There was no legal protection against it. People were denied employment or sacked from their jobs because of their sexual orientation and gender identity. Others were refused rented accommodation or evicted from it. Some were turned away from pubs and restaurants. Gay fathers and lesbian mothers lost custody of their children in divorce cases. They had no redress in law.

'I have personal experience of that particular iniquity. In 1976, I met a married man. They had four children, two girls fostered and two boys. After he came out to family and friends, the girls were immediately removed by social services. Strenuous efforts were made to remove the boys over the traumatic months which followed. He spent six weeks in a psychiatric hospital where he was offered electric aversion therapy to "cure" him of his homosexuality.

'In the 1980s, the Conservative government's "family values" and "Victorian values" campaigns whipped up hysterical levels of gay hate, aided by the moral panic over AIDS, which was dubbed the "gay plague." At the 1987 Conservative Party conference, the Prime Minister Margaret Thatcher used her keynote speech to attack the notion that people had a right to be gay.

'Coinciding with this intolerant anti-gay atmosphere was a massive rise in the arrests of gay men for consenting victimless behaviour.'

'What does that mean?'

'Two blokes agree to have sex. Nobody is harmed. Technically, they've committed a crime. A crime is committed - but where is the victim? Nobody has been robbed or beaten up. It is a victimless crime. The real criminal is somebody like Mrs Thatcher who turned the clock back introducing Section 28.'

Simeon consulted his notes.

'There were 1,718 convictions and cautions for gross indecency in 1989. The 2,022 recorded offences of gross indecency that year was almost as many as the 2,034 recorded in 1954, when male homosexuality was totally illegal and when Britain was gripped by an anti-gay witch-hunt.

'There was also a huge increase in queer-bashing violence. From 1986 to 1991 there were at least 50 murders of men in circumstances that pointed to hate of homosexuals. Police investigations to catch the killers were often derisory. That means they didn't look very hard! Homosexuals were still seen by many law officers as less deserving of the protection of the law.'

'Beating up queers? Sorry, homosexuals ... I can't quite see ... what made folks go and do stuff like that to the likes of you?'

'If the top people, the monarchy, the government, the church, the judiciary and the forces of law and order all hate homosexuals ... what chance do we have? I've lived my whole life in fear. Fear of being rejected by family and friends - which is now the case! Untold numbers of gay men have had to don the cloak of invisibility and take shelter inside the closet of an unhappy marriage. Others, like me, became withdrawn, pretended to like girls and drifted into a secret world of fear and insecurity.'

Chapter 10

Fighting Back

A certain sombre mood had descended imposing a short period of introspection for both parties. Eventually, Simeon spoke.

'Not getting the protection of the law has always irked me. Like the time I was on holiday and was reprimanded for seeking help from the police. I'd been enjoying several breaks each year at an excellent old world luxury gay hotel on the sunny Devon coast. Standing in its own wooded grounds with a beautiful garden ending in a private pathway down to the sea, it was an idyllic setting complete with good food and a busy Turkish bath with friendly understanding staff. It was expensive - but worth it.

'There came a warm night one mid-August, when an appalling noise woke me up at 3am. It roared up through the lush foliage and entered my wide open window. The invisible small car park below, hidden under giant trees, had been invaded by a raucous gaggle of hooligans intent of raising a ruckus to wake the dead. I couldn't see, but it sounded like about a dozen yobbos with no consideration at all for sleeping residents.'

'Hang about! The life you sort lead ... well, I thought you'd be whooping it up in one of those queer clubs, or in the bushes doing a gangbang - or something?'

'I expect some of "my sort", might well be indulging in one of those activities,' chuckled Simeon, amused by Ronnie's stereotypical view of gay life. 'I don't drink and I loathe loud music. That rules out clubs and pubs. I hate crowds anyway - except in a Turkish bath where I'll admit to a taste for group sex - the more the merrier - and I've always been careful about my sleep. Up early and in bed before ten with plenty of wholesome exercise in between. That might sound dull to you but it's the way I've always lived and I hope you'll look as good as me when *you're* 50.'

'I surrender!' cried Ronnie jesting with his hands up. 'Should have remembered. You've told me that stuff before. It's just that ... *yobbos* - a bit close to home.'

'Point taken, Ronnie. But let me make my point about gay folks being afraid to call the police. I struggled over an hour trying to get back to sleep. The yelling and yawping went on and on. You'd hope the hotel owner or, at least, one of his staff would have called the police in thoughtfulness of their slumbering guests. At something well after 4am, the party of pandemonium still raged and I decided to take matters into my own hands. After descending the plush staircase, the telephone in the hall was the only solution. Admitting to the 999 operator that the ongoing bedlam below the hotel was not life threatening, notwithstanding, I requested immediate police assistance on behalf of the whole neighbourhood who were entitled to a night's sleep.

'It was at this point that the bedraggled gray faced sleep deprived hotel manager, in his dressing gown, suddenly appeared like Marley's ghost.

"HANG UP! HANG UP!!" he screamed at me in sheer terror.

'Clutching a mug of tea, he had emerged from the hotel kitchen taking shelter from the ongoing mayhem outside.

"STUPID IDIOT! YOU NEVER, EVER RING THE POLICE FROM A GAY HOTEL! YOU **NAMED** THIS HOTEL!!"

'Oh dear!' said Ronnie with a half smile. 'And did the cops sort out the yobs?'

'That I'll never know, Ronnie. After the drama, the panicking manager was braced for a police raid. He feared they would sort out the gay hotel - and all within. I was guilt ridden - but still angry, very angry and indignant about my rights as a citizen who was entitled to the protection of the law.

'Going down to breakfast a few hours later, the owner of the hotel invited me into his office for a private chat. I liked Alan. As with his staff, he was warm and amiable running a successful business of which I had been grateful for over a decade. Diplomatically, he carefully explained the hazards of a police visit to a homosexual hotel. Word could get out that his hotel had been raided. Many of his guests depended on the discretion of management and staff employed by the Cliff House Hotel. Not all visitors would give their correct names. Many led double lives and needed to be anonymous.

'Whilst maintaining the principle of a gay (good-as-you) man entitled to the protection of the law, I was swayed by Alan's careful, judicious and polite argument in which he effectively defended the conduct of his manager.

'Did the police go to the hotel?'

'Not to my knowledge, neither did they deal with the nocturnal noise. I'll tell you this, the incident made me reflect on the Cliff House Hotel's enormous contribution to the gay community over several decades.'

'What do you mean by that?' asked Ronnie.

'I mean all the good Alan Wilson and his team did for people like me. He'd built up something to be proud of. Homosexuals could safely meet other homosexuals resulting in lifelong friendships. Often it was more than friendship. Many marriages were made at the Cliff House Hotel which transformed lives. Like me, people looked forward to a very special holiday where they were treated with respect; they could be their true selves relaxing in heavenly surroundings miles away from the cruel realities of a hostile heterosexual majority. Can you imagine the culture shock for me? A scruffy kid from the slag tips of Derbyshire, suddenly finding himself in a tropical gay paradise of palm trees able to meet up with his own kind!

'But you said it was expensive?'

'Alan was running a business, not a charity. Yet his business did more than any other Torquay hotel. His luxury home was a refuge for damaged lives. He and his staff had been improving the lives of gay men, lesbians, and bisexuals for decades. As an isolated teenager in the 1960s, unlike heterosexual boys who met girls in dance halls and public houses, I had to meet *my* friends in public toilets and the Turkish Baths on Reginald Street in Derby. We were barely tolerated in the passageway of the Corporation Hotel in the old Cattle Market. I can remember being frozen out by my own kind. These were the superior, secretive, sneering, professional men who, in a climate of fear, rehearsed their artificial vowels in the Friary Hotel in an effort to demean the 'lower orders'.

'The Cliff House Hotel rescued me and probably thousands more from all that. I'm so grateful.'

Ronnie got up and wandered to the window. In fear of his former pupil getting bored with the ongoing retrospection, Simeon wondered what time it was and was about to suggest an adjournment to the next day.

'Folks in that hotel,' ventured Ronnie, 'it seems to me they might be a bit on the pansy side. You've said how much you're turned off by that type.'

'The Cliff House had a good mixture,' mused Simeon, recalling holiday memories. 'But then, the homosexual community is a surprising hodgepodge of all types. Decades back, as a teenager in the shadow of the slag tips of darkest Derbyshire, in the half light of a hidden world, I found gay men wearing hobnail boots. They were common, roughly spoken and masculine. Unlike mincing types, they were *real* men, butch men who looked and behaved like men.

'I don't condemn the limp wrists for their lack of hobnail pit boots. I don't really mind their flamboyance and effeminacy: but, mark my words, they do us **no** favours! Many of them are funny. Some make a living out of it! I've enjoyed characters like Mr Humphries and Larry Grayson.

'Did you know, Ronnie, that homosexuality is still seen as a terrible disease even though the World Health Organization declassified it as a mental disease in 1992 only three years ago? Make no mistake; many still say the world would be a better place without queers. Some say we are incapable of love and caring about other people. If a foetus could be shown to be genetically predetermined to be gay, many would advise parents to abort it.'

Simeon took a deep breath and rested for a few seconds.

'For too long, we homosexuals have been on the margins of society. We've always been the voiceless, powerless victims of those who could inflict their humiliations with impunity. We don't fight back because we're afraid to declare ourselves, afraid to lift the cloak of invisibility.

'You used the word yourself - queers. We are almost universally seen as mad, bad and sad. Same sex relations are deemed a sin, a crime and a sickness. I'm haunted by a comment once heard to the effect that it was not necessary to kill off queers because, if you wait long enough, they'll kill themselves. His name was Albert. Typically, he'd had a terrible life and once suffered a painful incident in a local cafe wounding with emotional damage. Like Froggy, some gay people, a bit different, a bit odd, are always going to be a tempting target for cruel louts looking for fun. This particular instance was especially humiliating for an older man with a strong sense of his own worth and dignity.

When I heard about Albert's ordeal in that cafe, it took me right back to Mundy Street Boys School - the torturous screaming and name-calling. He fled that dreadful drama, his meal half eaten, to a chorus of ignorant taunts, catcalls, jeers, whistles and shouts. Everybody witnessed the scene - many laughed - some were silent - nobody tried to stop it. I am reminded of what Edmund Burke told us over 200 years ago:

"It is necessary only for the good man to do nothing for evil to triumph."

For a few sad minutes Simeon was silent as if grieving for a lost friend. Ronnie maintained a respectful silence until the other seemed to come awake.

'Oh! Did I answer your question?'

'I think so ... yes; you answered it well,' said Ronnie, 'with passion.'

'Good. I can't remember the question!'

Simeon looked down at his notes again.

'The gross indecency law of 1885 had been used to convict the computer genius Alan Turing in 1952 and, before him; it was used to jail the playwright Oscar Wilde in 1895.'

'What did the computer genius do wrong?'

'He won World War II!'

'He was arrested for that? You're not making sense!'

'Turing was a war-hero, a mathematical genius and a Cambridge University teacher whose secret work was of vital importance during World War II deciphering codes encrypted by the German Enigma machine. It's generally acknowledged that Turing's contribution to the war effort was instrumental in our victory.

'In 1952 he was arrested, tried and convicted on a charge of gross indecency. In other words, he was punished for being gay. The judge suggested the prisoner should be made to see the error of his ways. To avoid a lengthy prison sentence, Turing agreed to undergo a 'cure' for his homosexuality – oestrogen injections to neutralise his libido – a form of chemical castration in the interests of his "rehabilitation".

'After two years of a cruel, Nazi style cure, Alan Turing, the once brilliant visionary of the modern computer, was reduced to a depressed, disgraced and broken man. He saw only one way out of an intolerable situation – self-destruction. He ate an apple laced with cyanide.

'Being arrested for consensual sex is an excruciating and traumatising experience. I should know. It happened to me.'

'I know. You told me. What I don't know ... that is, what is more difficult for me ... is how you put up with it all? Didn't *anybody* fight back?'

'Most of us didn't. Too scared. That's why we are where we are - still cowering - shit scared. Hang on! I've just remembered the militant lesbians.'

'Good! They sound promising.'

'In 1986, a rabidly homophobic Staffordshire Tory Councillor, Bill Brownhill, had said that all gays should be gassed. There is an article here ... somewhere?' Simeon fumbled. 'Got it! It's dated January 1987 and shows the level of hatred towards the gay community, using the AIDS crisis as an excuse to call for the mass extermination of gay men and lesbians. Brownhill advocated a method favoured by the Nazis during World War II, the Gas Chamber. No disciplinary action was ever taken by the Conservative Party against William Frank Brownhill.'

Ronnie read the cutting.

GAS GAYS STORM

The Tory leader of South Staffordshire Council, Bill Brownhill, is in the centre of a political storm following his call for the mass extermination of gays. His comments followed a meeting of the council's Health Committee at which a government film on AIDS was shown.

Brownhill said, “I should shoot them all... those bunch of queers that legalise filth in homosexuality have a lot to answer for and I hope they are proud of what they have done. It’s disgusting and diabolical. As a cure I would put 90% of queers in the ruddy gas chambers. Are we going to keep letting these queers trade their filth up and down the country? We must find a way of stopping these gays going round yet we are making *heroes* of some of these people and some are even being *knighted*!”

‘Here is another article,’ continued Simeon. ‘It’s about some members of the Gay Liberation Front who formed a protest outside the home of Bill Brownhill in December 1986. Twelve of them were arrested and locked up over Christmas. All charges were later dropped. One of the people arrested received £30,000 for the way she was treated by the police.’

‘I remember it well,’ continued Simeon, ‘It was about the time that an obnoxious bigoted politician from Northern Ireland called Ian Paisley was ranting “SAVE ULSTER FROM SODOMY!”’

Author’s note - In Northern Ireland, the ban on anal sex was finally repealed in 2008.

‘Good for the girls!’ cheered Ronnie. ‘Is there more upbeat stuff like that? I’d like to hear more.’

‘Do you know - there *is* more. I can’t reveal his real name but let’s call him Sam who made a brave stand back in 1985. Being university educated in a professional position, Sam had a lot to lose when he was approached by a lad in his early teens. At my suggestion, he wrote a full account of his adventure which I thought might be useful as a later statement to the boy's headmaster, his parents or even the police.'

Sam's Story

After a routine walk into town, having shopped for a few items with laden rucksack, in shorts and boots, I slowly trudged up the hill from river level. At the foot of an ancient, deep, steep, cobbled jitty, I noticed a boy sitting on a low wall. He looked at me; I nodded, and continued to slowly ascend.

'Excuse me,' said this boy of rounded features who was dark, about five foot, eight inches, and inclined to puppy fat. I returned, descended a few steps to hear more. The boy was nervous. 'Forget it. It doesn't matter,' he muttered with slight sibilance waving me on my way.

Attempting to lighten the moment I responded with -

'Now I'll be wondering all day what you were going to tell me!'

'I think you're very sexy," he whispered, adding 'Are you gay?'

To deny my sexuality is akin to the Pope denying his Catholicism. So - I parried in light up-beat tones in an attempt to ease the tension of this, clearly, angst ridden individual.

'Yes. And thank you for the compliment!'

Any further conversation was abruptly terminated by the sudden appearance of another youth of similar age with fair hair who had been running and was out of breath. He ignored me and barked out some urgency about a social development – some meeting which was imminent. They both ran off with an impressive speed which only teenage youth can achieve. If anyone can identify this fair boy of, I think, sharp features, his evidence would help corroborate this statement.

Thoughtfully, I continued to trudge up the hill worrying about this homosexual lad who had courageously made an attempt at communication with the gay world. We all know about the misery and stress of social isolation and homophobic bullying. Had we not been interrupted, I would have told him about a new charity for homosexual welfare. It was a confidential support group in Derby for gay men which also had a social subgroup for teenagers run by professionals totally separate from the adults. Derby Friend [established in 1983] was only two years old.

Make no mistake; I, a man of 40, was fully cognisant of the perils of this encounter in my particular situation. Just the same, this gay boy needed to be brought into the protection of a responsible gay friendly fold and meet boys of his own age – not a man old enough to be his father. Staffed with professionals / counsellors and carefully vetted volunteers, Derby Friend was geared up to help youngsters like the boy I describe.

Three weeks later, Sam composed a letter addressed to the Headmaster of the local comprehensive. It was headed with Sam's address, his phone number and delivered at the School Reception where he asked for and received a receipt.

Dear Headmaster,

This is about an event which has caused me distress and cost me sleep. The following incident took place last Friday at 6.00pm. It involved a boy and a girl who, I'm told by neighbours, attend your school.

I walked down to the corner shop at the foot of my street. As usual, there were youngsters hanging around. In fact two were sitting on a low wall – a boy and a girl. I made brief eye contact with them. The girl, quite a pretty girl with obvious make-up, flashed a smile. On recognising me from a brief encounter over Easter [see my enclosed statement] the boy was visibly distressed and instantly looked away. They were still there when I left the shop and walked up the street. My home is probably about a quarter mile up the hill. Halfway, I, and neighbours who are not keen to be witnesses, heard what sounded likc loud abuse which appeared to be aimed in my direction. Turning into my driveway, a glance confirmed that it was that same couple, apparently in pursuit. Safely in the house, I was able to observe their progress to the top of my drive. She retraced her steps, walking back down to the shop. He hovered, looking at my front windows. He spat on the pavement and reluctantly followed the girl. I can't be sure it was a contemptuous spit – possibly just a feature of his habit.

That said, **I have no intention of tolerating this appalling conduct** and am quite prepared to send a copy of this letter to the police together with the enclosed statement describing the Easter incident. I am informed that there are trained officers who have special responsibility and experience in dealing with homosexual matters - officers who have a more progressive attitude to homosexuals like myself who are not prepared to lead a life constantly hiding their sexual orientation. I am a professional man. All my colleagues know that I am a gay man. In my case, threats of blackmail are a waste of time.

If it can be achieved, I would like a spoken and written apology from your pupil where, naturally, you or a senior member of your staff was present. If you think it advisable, I'm quite happy to discuss the matter with his parents.

I can make a positive identification of your pupil. I would be somewhat less confident in spotting the girl. It may be that he has divulged his sexuality to trusted pupils - one of your staff – or one of the auxiliary staff. Whatever, he needs help and **I** need to be able to walk to my corner shop and anywhere else in my town without fear of abuse from an angst-ridden / guilt-ridden young man who needs specialist help. I hope you can investigate this sensitive matter.

A reply from the Headmaster did not arrive until the passing of nearly four weeks.

Sam's second letter to the headmaster

Thank you for the reply to my letter of xxxxth. Mindful that this is a very busy part of the academic year and having not heard from you, I took matters into my own hands and contacted the police last Friday. They responded on the same day! PC John Smith was helpful and very supportive in this distressing matter. His report is filed under – Incident xxx – X/X.XX.

I welcome your willingness to assist the police in their enquiries and would remind you that I am able to make a positive identification of the young man who approached me during Easter and verbally abused me on Friday, XX Xst.

Shortly after the initial incident on that Friday, I conceived a plan to deal with the youth in question – a plan which has been approved by PC Smith. Having encountered this boy twice inside of three weeks, it is likely that another encounter is on the cards soon. When we meet again, I'll hand him a shortened version of the original statement to you [covering both Easter and XXX Xst] minus my contact details, although, of course, after the pursuit he now knows where I live.

From this, he will be informed in writing that his conduct has been noted, reported to you, to the police and that an apology would be a step in the right direction in resolving the problem. He will also know that I am willing to discuss the matter with his parents or guardian.

As stated in my original letter, if it can be achieved, I would like to receive a written apology from him explaining his behaviour and, hopefully, expressing regret. In the presence of you, or one of your staff, or a parent, or police officer - a spoken apology would also be beneficial in clarifying his feelings / motives and might bring some form of closure to this sorry business.

Triggered by this incident, PC Smith suggested that the Local Community Officer might liaise with your school to address the wider issue of gay hate which, as we all know, is endemic in all schools.

Sincerely ...

The headmaster never replied to Sam's second letter and he received no further follow up to the recorded homophobic incident.

'Sam never set eyes on this gay pupil after that incident,' said Simeon to Ronnie. 'Yet, it was entirely likely he *would* have seen the boy as Sam was often in the area of the local comprehensive. I suspect the boy, now a man in his 20s, was immediately moved to another school, perhaps another town, after consultations between the head teacher, the boys' parents and PC Smith. I don't know - just a guess - but it fits the facts and is not without precedent.'

'So this youth got clean away!'

'It's not as simple as that, Ronnie. What was done was probably done for the boy's benefit. Let's hope he learned his lesson and was able to find a safe way into the gay community - perhaps even to find a partner.'

'Well, at least Sam stuck up for himself. Good for Sam!'

'Yes. But it would have been better if the whole business could have been made public as an example to other older gay men who would have buckled under the strain.'

'What do you mean?'

'I mean that most of my friends would have tried to ignore his appalling conduct and hope it wouldn't happen again. In some cases, it would be the gay MAN who would have been forced to move to another town. In the main, gay folks are timid. They buckle.'

A new day dawned for Simeon and Ronnie. It was bright and sunny, lifting the spirits of the two colleagues. And it was now feeling like colleagues rather than pupil and teacher. A brief discussion of the Valley staff gave Simeon a chance to introduce another good example of a gay man fighting back.

'He was a retired teacher who taught at a school in a town not far away from here.'

'A friend of yours?'

'Yes. And his big trouble brought us closer together. Indeed, it produced a small militant gay group not unlike the aggressive lesbians who gave bellicose Brownhill some grief. I'm rather proud of my small part of the action.

'John Jones had been retired over a year from his comprehensive when he decided to write an account of his school woes.'

"That's right, Simeon. I'll be damned if those bastards are going to get away with their crucifixion. I'm going to complain and complain loud in print *and* also in the public press. I'll write a pamphlet - or a book. Yes a book! And I'll get it published or, if necessary, publish it myself. To hell with the cost. Anything is better than this constant brooding."

In the mid 1980s, John Jones wrote and self-published a book which shocked the local people. They had no idea that the Mr Jones who had taught generations of their children was a homosexual. In his introduction and blurb on the back cover, he set out his reasons for this assault on conventional thinking. Having taught English at his comprehensive school for nearly 40 years, he took the view that many of his former colleagues, former pupils and their parents would be interested in an autobiography written by a long-serving member of staff. He warned readers that, without mentioning names, he would describe painful incidents which, in his view, forced a premature retirement. He also warned readers that, if they were looking for any homosexual titillation in terms of anything graphic or prurient, they would be disappointed.

After completion, he contacted the local newspaper and spoke to a young reporter about his book entitled *Homophobia.* John explained the origins of that new word meaning homosexual hate or fear of homosexuals. He first saw it in an article in *The*

Times in 1981. Originally, it was coined by a psychologist, George Weinberg, in the 1960s.

The reporter responded with interest and enthusiasm. This conversation was followed by a couple of further chats on the phone, two letters and another face-to-face visit in the reporter's office where she took delivery of a copy in preparation for her review. John was photographed for a feature. Days later she asked for five further books for a competition.

The feature was due for publication on the following Friday. On the strength of this good news, a delighted manager of WH Smith in the town centre ordered 40 copies of *Homophobia*.

"We'll need them. Books fly off the shelf when they receive the benefit a big feature in the newspaper. I'll make a good display in the window and also inside the shop with the page feature."

'I'd known John for years,' said Simeon to Ronnie. 'Several of us, his close friends, were so excited about *Homophobia*. It was extraordinarily brave of him. There was a celebratory atmosphere pervading our secretive, if cowardly community. So tragic ... '

'Why?'

'Come Friday – no feature. Nothing! Come Monday, John telephoned the deputy editor.'

"We are a family newspaper. My editor has decided that your work is inappropriate for our readers. He has cancelled the feature. We'll return your five books by post."

John was devastated. He wrote to the reporter who had already acclaimed the book.

Dear Reporter,

I had considered writing this to your editor. Would it do any good? Perhaps you could intercede? Let him see this letter. Is there any chance that he might re-consider his decision? I'm a little man, easy to knock down, but, I get up and continue the fight against bigotry, prejudice, discrimination and homophobia wherever they are to be found.

I'm sorry that your editor has wasted your time. He has wasted my time and my money.

Family newspaper? I am part of a family. I have been with my special friend for the last 34 years. Effectively we are husband and husband. He - together with our close friends - are family.

This is censorship plain and simple. If my former pupils and the people of this town are prevented from learning about the problems, the harsh realities, the trials and tribulations of homosexual life – how can they ever be educated? How can they recognise and combat homophobia? How can they possibly know what it is like to be me? How can they feel *my* pain: such as the time when a group of ignorant pupils once shouted out at me, as loud as they could, in the local supermarket – JONES IS A GAY BASTARD?

During four decades of my teaching career that was one of several similar attacks. An unmarried teacher who keeps his private life *very* private, a strict traditional schoolmaster who is not afraid to punish, not afraid to make his pupils work in silence – that schoolmaster is a tempting target to a disruptive minority.

If your ignorant editor would do me the courtesy of reading *Homophobia*, all of it – he will find that it is not sordid, never gratuitous or prurient in its intent. It is intended to be realistic, to educate and to break down barriers in, hopefully, an entertaining way.

The manager of WH Smith is bravely supporting me. She is trying to sell 40 books without local publicity. It won't be easy.

Your time has not been completely wasted. I enjoyed meeting you. It is a pity that many people have been denied the chance to read your work; notwithstanding, thank you very much for your interest in *my* work.

Sincerely,

John Jones

There was no response to this letter. The five books arrived in the post inadequately packed but undamaged.

'A failure!' said Ronnie

'Not exactly,' replied Simeon. 'Adversity can bring a beleaguered people together. And of this, I *can* be proud. Had it not been for John's courage, I doubt I could have been inspired to pen this little piece - albeit with a request to withhold my name and address.'

Simeon produced a newspaper cutting.

Dear Editor,

I was horrified to read a rabidly homophobic feature printed in your paper last Friday. The intemperate tone of that item clearly incites gay hate and may well fall foul of the criminal law.

This ignorant and bigoted rant concerns a picnic site called Fanny's Grove on the Budby to Cuckney A616 near Worksop in north Nottinghamshire.

An anonymous woman claimed she was shocked to see perverts dressed in women's clothing committing buggery over a car bonnet in the glare of her headlights. Absolute and complete nonsense! As a gay man, I can assure her that most gay men are not the least titillated by men dressed in women's clothing. The average homosexual is only interested in a man who looks like a man. *If* she saw anything at all, she saw heterosexual copulation bringing disgrace and shame on the heterosexual community.

The writer said the site has been a Mecca for such unholy activities since the 1970s. This allegation is supported by a photograph of a tree with the one word GAY recently sprayed on to the trunk by a vandal who will certainly *not* be homosexual. This type of graffiti is commonplace.

Living in the nearby village of Clowne, I cycled to Fanny's Grove a few times after hearing that it was a meeting place for gay men – and, occasionally, I did meet a kindred spirit. We enjoyed *conversation* – not sex. Neither did I see any activity of the kind described. The anonymous witness should remember that gay men and women have precious little opportunity to contact their own kind. Some countryside venues are seen as a relatively safe place to socialise.

The tone of this disgraceful article is entirely consistent with the past homophobic conduct of YOU the editor. You wasted the time and money of local author John Jones. In spite of your spite, he has now sold out all copies of his splendid book *Homophobia*.

'Wow! That's telling him,' said Ronnie. 'I'm surprised he printed it!'

'So was I. In fact - he didn't. And he wouldn't. For some reason he wasn't there. Possibly got the sack! Somebody else was the Acting Editor - and something else. There had been a flurry of complaints objecting to that vile article. Look at this one - '

Dear Editor,

I too read that disgraceful article and I too accuse your medieval paper of inciting homophobic hatred. In fact, your piece was very likely to lead to homophobic vigilante attacks on those at Fanny's Grove.

I have informed your head office and the police that you are involved in a criminal act by publishing that appalling article and I denounce you as a homophobe. We will no longer tolerate the sniggers, the smirks and elbow digging which have dogged us all our lives. Enough!

Regarding the writing of letters to challenge hatred of homosexuals, we should continue to write more of them. I take inspiration from the words of Ed Murrow when he spoke of Churchill:

'He mobilised the English language and sent it into battle.'

Chapter 11

Crude Common Queen

On the following day, Ronnie, cheery and chirpy, bounced into the small classroom to find Simeon somewhat subdued.

'What's up?'

'God! I think I'm losing it. What happened to the weekend? It can't be school *every* day.'

'It's school today. Look - there are kids drifting into registration. Why bother?'

'I bother because we've been rabbiting away for ... God knows how many days and I can't recall a weekend - there *has* to be a weekend and what happened to it? I used to enjoy my weekends. I looked forward to them. Don't you?

Immediately Simeon knew that he had stumbled into an area which was simply too challenging for Ronnie. The pained look on the lad's face showed it. Simeon did not know what day it was. It occurred to him to ask Ronnie but strangled the question at birth before it disturbed them both. Some days they *did* know the day of week as it naturally occurred in conversation - but not this day.

An uncomfortable silence ensued. Ronnie recalled Simeon once saying 'aren't we a couple of crocks' and considered making a jocular comment as a way out of the silence - but a vague fear stilled his tongue. He then reached for something funny and jolly which always lit up both faces and had them rolling in the aisles.

'Tell you what - let's have some more of that little slut ... Simon Tonks! That's the name.'

'I'm appalled!' said Simeon, suddenly coming alive in mock horror in an affectation of the stern upright schoolmaster he once was. 'I can't believe the filthy language I descended to going on about that obscene tart. Oh dear! I hoped you might have forgotten all about it. My authority as a teacher in this school is now zilch.'

'You love it! You know you do. Come on! Let's have more dirty talk. Finish that story about beer babies.

'Beer babies,' chuckled Simeon. 'If it weren't so funny it would be pathetic. I suppose that sums up Simon Tonks. He's a character of tragicomedy locked inside a hostile relationship with his harridan-like-fish-wife mother. He told her everything! Every time, after every sexual experience, he went home and laid bare to Olive Tonks the graphic details of his obscene lifestyle.'

At this point Simeon caught a twinkle in Ronnie's eye. They looked at each other and collapsed in a heap of giggles.

'Alright, you win, Ronnie. By heterosexual standards, I confess being promiscuous, but my experiences were never as colourful and certainly never discussed with family.'

Simeon recalled his first sight of Simon Tonks - a child's face. It was a simple face, almost a cartoon which could have been drawn by a child: three buttons, two for eyes and one for a nose. As he became more use to this oddity, the child became a boy and the boy, with a cartoon head cocked on one side, became a man.

Nobody knew the age of Simon Tonks. He was one of the mysterious freaks of the Derbyshire homosexual underworld. Bitchy queens in their forties (who looked their age) had cottaged with him before the war. They swore blind that Simon Tonks must be at least 45. In 1965, he hunted for men with a new generation of teenage chickens, who assumed that he was one of their number - just another chicken, just another common slut ever searching for that next cock. Within living memory, Jasper Wormall had always looked old, bent and hideous. So it was that Simon Tonks, within living memory, had always looked young and pretty.

We now go to the cosy primitive kitchen of Olive Tonks in her mediaeval little stone cottage. It was, in fact, a musty Victorian space. The only illumination in this cave-like dwelling came from a blazing fire in an ancient grate which, perhaps, would have been acceptable for a 'working man' one hundred years before the 1960s. Indeed, the bellows at the side appeared to be from a previous century.

The open fire heated a cast iron boiler on the left to provide hot water. A cooking pot, hung from a chain directly above, transported any visitors into a secret world which could have been penned by Jakob and Wilhelm Grimm. It could have been the dwelling of an old witch; indeed, the horror within had a nose and chin which seemed to meet. Dark corners, nooks and crannies of that ancient chamber were ornamented by crackling, flickering flames producing shadows and grotesque shapes dancing across distempered walls.

On the right of the blaze was an oven for baking and cooking. It supported a crude hot plate upon which a big kettle gently simmered just off the boil. All made their demands on that single, cheerful glow raging in the grate. It was a fire which, with free coal, was kept burning night and day – the prerogative of a coal miner's old widow.

Above, on the mantelpiece, were two unlit candlesticks and a tea caddy. Above them, a few items of washing dangled from a line. Underneath and centre stage, a heavy kitchen table neatly accommodated four simple chairs which sat on a bare floor of quarry tiles. Before the hearth lay the ubiquitous, dirty, darkened, home-made pegged rug - so typical of all humble homes.

Beyond the fire, dimly seen, was a large wall-clock slowly measuring the time with an easy heavy tick-tock, just audible above the crackling, comfortable blaze which both warmed and lit this rudimentary kitchen. Under the window, a shallow stone sink stood next to a large fluted cast iron hand pump indicating a well beneath. This primitive contraption was probably in disuse, because a crude twentieth century tap overhung the ancient sink.

On the left, nearer to the fire, were two comfortable looking antique Windsor chairs in which reposed the old hag Olive Tonks and her very odd son Simon.

'Chesterfield's dead rough,' said Simon Tonks to his grim faced mother. It's not safe for a little queen like me. I mean, last night, two big strapping toughs grabbed me!'

'Did ya try to struggle free?' spat out Olive with an edge of sarcasm. 'Did ya scream for help? Nay lad, and I'll tell you why, because you're a dirty SLUT!'

'Ooo, our mam, have some pity. These two hunks had got big muscles. And little me so weak.'

'Weak willed more like. Muscles you were looking at were between their bloody legs - that where **you** were looking.'

'Well, I did notice they seemed to be well equipped in that department. And they threatened me! They did. One said, "You look like a randy common tart." Other one said, "Wot's it gonna be then? Is it gonna be this (Simon demonstrated by thrusting his fist up in Olive's face) or this?" (He repeated this aggressive action, but this time, the clenched fist was clearly meant to represent a hard cock) 'Ooo it was terrible! Big brawny lads, all muscle, they dragged me to that lavatory next to the crooked spire church and bent me over the bog. Pushed me head right in the bowl they did. Ooo they banged me something awful, one after the other. Straight in, no manners, no ceremony - just brute force and ignorance and there's me, an innocent helpless little queen with my head in the bog!'

Simon cocked his head and twinkled at his God fearing mother, an enthusiastic reader of Leviticus and avid student at Salvation Army bible classes. Dumbstruck; she needed a moment to absorb this unwelcome vision of Sodom and Gomorrah. Perhaps the apocalypse had come!

'They were abusive as well, our mam, adding insult to injury. One said, "You're as bent as that bloody spire, ya common cow." Then the other said, "Come out! You've had long enough. It's my turn to ram into that scrubber." Ooo mother, I felt so ashamed. One after the other. No respect for me. They treated me like a spunk-rag, they did.

'But, I will say this, one were nice at the end. He said, "Eee you've given us a good time, lass. Pull up your knickers, lass. **I bet you feel such a slut!"**

'I should bloody well think you did feel a slut!' exploded Olive who had now recovered her voice. 'A son of mine,' she said in a more gentle pathetic tone, 'getting a good "seeing to" like that in a public bog! The shame! The shame! I don't know where you get it from. I don't. I hated sex. They all said how marvellous it was going to be. I thought I was going to see stars! All I saw was your dad's bloody fat hairy beer belly. You were a beer baby. Nowt but a beer baby.'

Olive was further enraged when Simon described his drunken stagger out of that notorious cottage, having difficulty putting one foot before the other.

'Ooo our mam, I could hardly walk to the bus stop! And when I sat down - it **squelched**.'

'SQUELCHED! What do you mean, squelched?'

'Ooo, our mam, have a bit of pity for a poor little trollop. It was all the spunk coming from me bum hole and wetting the bus seat. That squelch was loud. Passengers might have heard it!'

'Serve you right if they did hear it!' snapped Olive. 'And your little bum hole ... it must be sore,' she muttered more gently, recalling the onetime little baby in her lap of long ago. 'And to think,' she continued, chocking back a sob, 'to think how I used to powder that little innocent bum'ole, that little bum without sin ... '

'Never mind, our mam. Don't take on. I'll go to the pox clinic.'

'You'll go straight to the vicar, that's where you're bloody going to confess your filthy sins. Now get ya bloody kegs [underpants] off and I'll muck out that dirty bum hole.'

She reached for the cloth from under the sink and vigorously attacked his wanton bottom in an attempt to expunge the sin, all the time muttering malicious epithets including 'sins of Sodom, shameless shag bag, abominable arsehole, loose bitch' etc.

Some adventures indicated a predisposition to attract verbal self-flagellation. Simon was invited back to the home of a gay couple who had heard that he responded to a certain amount of 'discipline'.

In a more respectable part of Chesterfield, Jeremy and Lawrence moved mainly in middle class heterosexual professional circles and would not have touched a lowly common cow like Simon with the proverbial barge pole. That said, they were not averse to having, as Olive put it, an occasional good 'seeing to'.

Simon, the well-known whore, was in awe of the nice house fronted by a nice garden in a quiet cul-de-sac in the quiet leafy suburb of Somersall. Inside he asked for a cup of tea or a drink of some sort. His hosts were not disposed to be polite. They dropped their posh accent and reverted to typical Chesterfield working class speech and accompanying rough rudeness - the true root of their humble origins.

'You'll have drink all right. Oh yes. And plenty of it. You'll soon have a mouth full of SPUNK to drink! Get up them stairs ... two at a time!'

In the bedroom, Jeremy and Lawrence began to get undressed. Simon followed their example.

'What are YOU getting undressed for? Nobody's going to touch YOU. You are here to work - and work you will.' Lawrence knelt on the bed and stuck out his backside presenting a begging bottom. Jeremy gave an order. 'Lick his bum hole, ya slut. And lick it **good** ya dirty cow.' To assist, he distended the orifice and guided the little queen's sweet soft hands to do clever service around the naughty nooks and crannies of genitalia forward of anal areas. Fingers wandered underneath, titillating and toying with scrotum and throbbing, dribbling dick. And so it went on - one hand playing with balls. The other hand was carefully fondling and feeling a massive dribbling manhood, as yet unseen by the rimming ravisher.

'Work! Work! Keep working, go deep, **lick, lick** that arsehole,' urged Jeremy with lewd language as Lawrence began to moan with pleasure - round and round, up and down, in and out laboured that enthusiastic tongue buried in buttocks bringing that kneeling man nearer and nearer to his climax.

Suddenly, he turned round and brandished his bobbing weapon in Simon's face threatening him with an imminent sexy spurt of sperm.

'Suck, suck, suck it, strumpet. Take it, take it, trollop!'

Obediently the lascivious slave eagerly consumed the dribbling shaft to the orders of SHOOT! SHOOT! Nearly choking, but he managed to swallow his promised mouthful. Exhausted, Lawrence, breathing heavily, collapsed to the edge of the impressive emperor sized bed to recover.

Poor little Simon, he was given only a few minutes rest before being pressed to further duties, this time, to pleasure Jeremy who insisted that he 'wiped *HIS* arse properly' and had no need of a slut to lick him clean. Jeremy ordered -

'Suck it, you lowly loose bitch,' as he yielded to the delicious ministrations. Occasionally the slut's fingers, well practiced busy fingers, assisted, tenderly tending and exploring hidden secrets of pleasure. Each nodule of bliss caused a small moan of gratification to escape from Jeremy's mouth.

Simon, who worked hard manipulating these men in a thousand ways, had resigned himself to being the sex slave receiving nothing in return. He was wrong. He was delighted to discover that Jeremy was a bum bandit!

Now it was the trollop's treat when commanded to fall to his knees making the threesome a tableau of perfect joy. Lucky boy! Thrusting out his bottom, Simon was impaled. He bounded, wriggled, twisted, sighed and cooed – and begged for more at the approach of another crisis of pleasure. Horned up with oozing love juice, Jeremy was desperate for relief when he urged his champion further into the Tonks arsehole, a well poked grotto of succulent ecstasy.

Finally, they were able to reach a wonderful mutual moment, to spend, at the same time, to enjoy each other's utterances of pleasure.

Side by side by side, bollock naked, the three lay back on the great bed and bathed in the delicious / delightful slaver and slime, the pleasant aftermath of having received 'a good seeing to'. The peaceful silence was broken with a small pleading voice.

'Excuse me,' ventured Simon in pathetic tones, 'there are not many friends in this world. I feel that I'd like us to be friends. Couldn't I come back to this nice house in this nice part of Chesterfield? Couldn't I visit you ... as a friend?'

Alas, they reverted to their posh accent as two superiors wanting to get rid of a common cow - just a piece of meat.

'I'm afraid not,' said Laurence in his Sunday best clipped sneering accent. 'We entertain. We have guests. It would not be convenient. You are so different from our exclusive circle of close friends - people of quality. Anyway, it's time for you to go. We need a shower. You've got to shove off.'

Feeling used and abused, Simon told the whole story to his mother.

'They had a bloody good time, our mam. I worked HARD. My legs ached! Not a civil word they spoke to me.'

'Didn't they give you a drink, even after your dirty stuff?'

'No drink. I was dying for cup of tea after slobbering round Lawrence's bum hole and sucking on Jeremy's tool.'

'I call that pig ignorance!' snapped Olive. 'And such pissy names - Jeremy and Lawrence. Folks like that make me sick. They'll get my bloody fist in their face if I ever find them in Chesterfield. That they will. Didn't they let you have a wash in that posh bathroom?'

'No, our mam. They said they were having a shower - and showed me the door.'

'I'd better put you in that bloody sink and scrub you with the dishcloth again,' threatened Olive.

On the surface, Ronnie continued to be amused by this crude collection of obscene anecdotes. On a deeper level, he encouraged Simeon to speculate on the psychology of a promiscuous son who felt compelled to assail his mother with the sordid details of his sexual shenanigans.

'All this stuff ... it's not *usual* queer life ... is it? I mean, didn't something go badly wrong between him and his mum?'

'I'm not qualified to answer. I'm no psychiatrist, but I'll fumble about and see what I find. It's clear to me that Simon was a seriously damaged lad. He certainly had a very erotically charged sensuous nature and a gift for comedy. He was hilarious! His mother was an audience, one of several audiences. Getting laughs on the gay scene gave him a buzz. I think he needed to show the drab dreary boring working class world that he led an interesting life. He was a 'nobody' desperately trying to prove that he was a 'somebody'.

'In many ways his mother was an unpleasant ignorant woman. She was easily 'wound up' by the mischievous son who might have been exacting some sort of revenge against her and her gay-hating kind. This is not a hundred miles from my own mother / son relationship. Mrs Tonks might have looked like a witch, but Simon was the *real* witch.

'There was a darker side to Simon Tonks. He was manipulative. He enjoyed stirring up people and setting them against each other. Rows happened where he was. He *made* them happen. He was a sort of Iago type.'

'What?'

'A villain. He caused a lot trouble for Othello. He was a black general in a Shakespeare play.'

'Yeah! I've met the type,' mused Ronnie, 'pulling strings, looking on, enjoying it.'

'Don't get me wrong. Simon was quite popular. When we were together it was like a gentle comedy. I liked him. He was simplicity itself and he gave the *effect* of innocence, it felt like two little boys meeting for the first time.'

'Did you have sex?'

'I'd like to say we never did. But I'd be a liar. He was, in fact, very accomplished at giving pleasure. At the first meeting on a warm summer's day, I was cycling in short shorts through a park in Chesterfield. We sat under warm sunshine, side by side. And then it happened. It happened to my leg. Suddenly, a camp little hand alighted upon my bare thigh. I looked down at the delicate, soft, feminine hand and then up, meeting the innocent, half-smiling gaze of that strange doll-like face with its curled up eyelashes. Entranced and yet repelled by those eyelashes, I fully understood why other working-class lads like me made a dash for the closet and hid in that closet for the rest of their lives.

'I was utterly repulsed by (what felt like) the gentle touch of a little girl. There was also another consideration.

Something about this whole freak show put me on the edge of breaking up into hysterical laughter. He started to sing a silly song - *tickle my tummy and I'll suck your dummy* - with oscillating head cocked on one side and then the other, wearing a child-like half smile. It all made for hilarity.'

At this point, Ronnie was wearing a half smile himself assessing this wacky oddity.

'Oh dear! And I thought *my* family was rough!'

'We are the creation of a coal mining community, Ronnie. Considering our backgrounds, it should be no surprise that our families are, as you say, rough. Some interbreeding. In my grandparents' day, blokes would marry the lass next door. Probably none of them ever left the pit village. Poor with no education, a sink or swim mentality led to dysfunctional and unstable behaviour, coarse - and often violent. Rough sums it up. My people were rough and common. The difference between you and me is an added aggravating factor. In nature, the abnormal / defective chick is starved, pecked by the so called normal chicks and thrown OUT of the nest. Effectively, that is what happened to me. That's why I'm bitter. That's why we are now having this conversation.

'Simon used to speak of his grandparents who frightened him to death! Old Granny with her features chiselled out of stone grimaced while Granddad, with his great fat belly, sank into his chair all day long, an idle farting slob always gawking at little Simon.

"Fucking pansy! What's the good of him? Get plenty of dripping down him; it'll put hairs on his chest."

'Granddad Tonks was a boxer in his younger days. He never had a kind word for weak little Simon, the family sissy who was treated as an object of derision and disgust and deserving of humiliation. He burst into his bedroom one morning and caught the lad wanking underneath the bedclothes.

"As got tent oop lad! It's not just for pissing out of you know!"

Further anecdotes were explored giving Ronnie a flavour of the secret world of Chesterfield's old Victorian cottages, redolent with the atmosphere of past indecencies. In one solid edifice of splendid porcelain urinals and quality coloured tiles on the floor, Simeon was horrified when Simon, from his person, produced a much prized old relic of homosexual history - Nora's teeth!

Nora, an old queen who specialised in fellatio, used to haunt this particular latrine back in the early 1960s. Simon told Simeon that Nora was in this very bog committing a lewd act of gross indecency - when disaster struck.

It was a warm August afternoon. As usual, there was a selection of motionless figures, all guilty, all lined up before the ornate Victorian porcelain in a collective tension of repressed excitement. Old Nora toddled in, quickly surveyed the field and selected a vacant stall next to a chunky figure. He was a powerfully built young man with a handsome well bronzed face which nicely contrasted with a fair complexion. An untidy shock of wild golden hair was distinctive in an age where a Beatle cut was the norm. He was dressed in shabby jeans; clearly hand-me-down, one-size-too-small emphasising tempting well proportioned buttocks. It had given previous owners good service and seen better days. The stranger towered at least one foot over Nora.

In spite of many bad experiences behind him, brazenly, the old cocksucker placed himself next to the young hunk who had been given a wide berth by the other men. Although appealing, the eyes of this newcomer were hard and cruel. One seemed dark as if recently blackened. Those eyes were intently focused on the porcelain and a somewhat brutal expression said – 'keep clear; approach at your peril'! On the other hand, an impressive erection, proud as punch, was mischievously straining to reach as high up the ceramic stall as possible. This John Thomas was giving a different message. It said – 'touch me, tease me, tickle and taste me'. Naughty Nora preferred to heed this second message. Enthusiastically, he threw caution to the wind and executed a sudden deep knee bend. He got stuck in to the job busily loosening constrains of belt and zip to gain free access to all erogenous areas, employing considerable dexterity of both hands well practiced over many years.

'And then it happened,' said Simon to Simeon. 'We often cottaged together and I was right there with him, watching the action when poor old Nora slumped backwards into the smelly gutter. The other watchers and the young man shot out of that lavatory like bats out of hell. They weren't going to hang about for the police and ambulance - not them. I've never used a public phone box so I asked a passerby to call for help. I never could manage that button A and button B contraption - too confusing, too technical. The ambulance men confirmed death and asked if I knew the next of kin - which I didn't. We were good friends on the cottaging scene, but not what you'd call - close. I could tell them where he lived, but not much else and was devastated when the ambulance pulled away.

'We'd been together all that day and I was suddenly so horribly alone. It was genuine grief. I didn't know where to go or what to do. One minute Nora was there - and then the next, he was gone - forever.'

Simon was seldom emotional but broke down when recalling this sad experience. Over the years of friendship, he was an occasional caller when Nora would reveal details of how queer life isolated him from family and heterosexual society.

'Me mam died before the war,' said Nora to Simon. 'After that, it was left to me to care for me cantankerous old dad. He never liked me, always insulting me, but had to put up with me. There was nobody else to look after him. He'd outlived all his brothers and sisters. His last few days were pitiful. He started to talk to me nicely. He'd forgot that he didn't like me! Well - he didn't know me anymore. His mind was going. In his last hours he was crying like a baby and calling for his mam. It was terrible ...'

All this was revealed in that deserted public toilet in the twilight of growing gloom as an autumnal fog was descending on a quiet Chesterfield evening. After talk of death and dying, the atmosphere was eerie as Simon embraced one of his spooky moods. Simeon suddenly remembered the macabre relic in Simon's naughty hand.

'What are you doing with Nora's teeth?'

'Oh! I forgot to tell you,' said Simon. 'I used to hold Nora's choppers while he was busy slurping. After the ambulance drove off, I found them in my pocket. Well! They were no use to him now where they? So - I treasured them as a keepsake, a sort of relic. It was a bit of old Nora that was reminiscent of all the pleasure he'd given to battalions of butch blokes for more than half a century.

'And do you know, Simeon, when I feel them in my little camp hand, I feel close to Nora. These dentures - they comfort me ... and I can get through to him. In life, he haunted this lavatory. In death, he *still* walks ... look! Look over there. Can't you see the ghostly outline of a bent old hag slowly stumbling towards us? There! He's there now! LOOK!!'

'My GOD!' said Ronnie. 'He's beginning to scare ME! I can see now why you said that Simon was more of a witch than his nasty old mam. Did you ... *see* anything in that old bog?'

'Power of suggestion,' smiled Simeon. 'It was that queen's stock in trade. It was already getting dark. In the fog, together with a weak amber glow from an underpowered bulb, I was almost persuaded to see a faint outline of an old man. Indeed, it might have been another old queen stopping by to try his luck. Cottages are always more fruitful in dim light and bad weather.

'Simon was often communicating with the dead - seeing things - claiming supernatural powers denied to the generality - that sort of nonsense. His kind has been with us over the eons. Warlocks, magicians, healers, prophets - most of them were probably gay. And that explains why the church and religion in general is stuffed with homosexuals taking refuge from the harsh realities of life outside the church.'

'Queers going to church?' exclaimed Ronnie in surprise.

'You bet. I know it's a paradox, an anomaly, but just consider the quirky characters I've met in my lifetime, all the sexual eccentrics. Consider what happened to fearful, secretive men who became warped by the unforgiving attitudes of an oppressive and bigoted heterosexual majority. What does it do to a man when he spends his *whole* life denying himself? What happens to a man who has spent a lifetime leading a double life - the constant secrecy - the lies?

'I'll tell you what happens, they hide behind thick gothic walls, chant lots of Latin, sing psalms, hum hymns and pray plenty of prayers to an invisible god they hope is listening.'

'Are we talking about vicars?'

'Vicars, priests, canons, bishops, archbishops, archbigots - the lot. They practically **own** Derby Cathedral! I kid you not. Smells and bells - they invented it. The communists abolished all religion just after the Bolshevik Revolution in 1917.'

'Abolished religion!'

'Absolutely. Lenin, their leader, outlawed all forms of religious practice and - get this - ***made homosexuality legal!***'

'You should have been a red.'

'You're right, Ronnie! That's where I went wrong. But you need a bit of background. In simple terms, at first, Communism was a good idea. Everybody was going to be equal. They had created an ideal society - until Lenin died a few years later. What they needed was democracy. What they *got* was a shambolic catastrophe when Lenin died and a cruel dictator took over, turning Russia into a horrible nightmare for the next 28 years - and longer if you count the various tyrants who mismanaged the country after the death of Stalin in 1953. Does the name of Joseph Stalin mean anything to you, Ronnie?'

'It does! Do you remember being so mad in the library that time? You said something about that Russian bloke ... I think you called him Uncle Joe. Well, me, Bobbie and Freddie looked at you gone out. And then you shouted at us!'

'Sorry about that,' smiled Simeon, 'He's a name, like Adolf Hitler. I thought *everybody* had heard of Stalin. Anyway - Freddie defended all three of you effectively.'

'Did he?'

'Yes. A few weeks before the Stalin incident, you and your gang were talking sport - mainly football. You were shocked that I knew nothing about the teams or players. So, you tried a different sport and mentioned Billie Jean King. It was a sort of test. I'd heard the name before, but had to apologise.'

'Oh yes! I remember now. You said you had no idea who this bloke Billy was - and couldn't place him with his sport!! Shocked! I'll say; we were knocked over.'

'Well, Freddie scored a goal telling me off. He said I shouldn't get tetchy if you and the lads couldn't place a long dead nasty megalomaniac who, anyway, had been dead for years - when I had no knowledge of a live **female** tennis world champion who, born in 1943. She was about my own age. And it goes deeper than that. Billie and I have much more in common: we are both gay.'

'Billie Jean King is a lesbian!?'

'Like most of us, she has homophobic parents. When she tried to talk to them, her mother shut her up with - "We're not talking about things like that." The stress of living a double life caused her to suffer an eating disorder. Her marriage ended in 1987.

'I've told you before that my relationship with you and your pals has been perhaps the most significant lesson in my life in so many ways. The Stalin / Billie Jean King episode cured me of my arrogant ignorance of sporting knowledge. It's a bit like Claud Hoadley's pride in the fact that he doesn't know one car from the other. So there it is.

'You, Bobbie and Freddie have done me a lot of good. Even now - years later, Ronnie, you are a great help to me. You're my best friend.'

A pause descended. Late afternoon and it was close to going home time. A somewhat comfortable silence prevailed as they both stared out of the window at the frail pale autumnal sunshine picking out a few remaining leaves on a prematurely shedding ash tree. A bright clean whistle drew their attention to a robin darting from branch to branch. Simeon mentioned seeing a Jenny Wren a few days back. Then the subject briefly alighted on the farthing, a small coin of his boyhood, never seen these days.

'Well,' he said ... '

'Yes,' answered Ronnie, 'it's about that time, but I'll be back tomorrow.'

Chapter 12

Puzzle Gardens

Interested in his former teacher's activity weekends of walking and cycling, Ronnie steered the conversation to parts of Derbyshire Simeon had explored.

'You'll recall that fat American I used to meet in Harrogate. Bill Bulman was the nearest thing to Tennessee Williams' fictitious creation - Big Daddy. He looked and sounded just like that bombastic plantation owner. Bill was a macho homosexual with a voracious appetite for other macho homosexuals encountered on a daily basis in the Harrogate Royal Baths where I first met him in 1966.

'He hated effeminate men and harboured an aversion to Negroes. He was wealthy and unwilling to disclose the source of that considerable wealth living permanently in the Old Swan Hotel, a short walk from the baths.

'My cycling tour through England was very pleasantly interrupted for nearly a month when this lascivious obesity invited me to share his palatial suite at the hotel. I loved every minute.

'Despite his basic white-trash-education and coarse, plantation-field-hand speech, Bulman was not your average redneck. He was a self-taught man aiming for culture. In adult years he discovered England, English art and was horrified to find that I, a self-confessed lover of Derbyshire, had never even heard of Joseph Wright, the famous Wright of Derby! From a man born in the Mississippi Delta, I heard all about an 18th century artist who was born at number 28 Irongate in Derby.

'Bill waxed enthusiastically on the skills of this painter who created beautiful contrasts between darkness and light. He raved about ethereal moonlight, flames of candles, fire and furnace. In graphic detail, he described 'An Experiment on a Bird in the Air Pump', a disturbing scene which illustrates Wright's skill portraying a range of emotions on the faces of those watching.

'His knowledge of Derbyshire and the different towns visited was considerable. Even so, the big man was disappointed that I had never explored his favourite Derbyshire town.

"Why – you missed the best one!" he bellowed. "Wirksworth is fascinating! Old, REALLY old with a wealth of history. Aint ya seen the Puzzle Gardens? You should. Intriguing. Why - quirky miners' cottages, tiny tiny homes perched perilously on the hillside. Yad think they'd all fall over! They're linked by … how would you say … rabbit warren-like walkways. We don't have them in the States. You have a name for them …ginnys?"

"Jitties and ginnels?" I suggested.

"Right! THAT'S what they call those things. ARR CAN HARDLY GET THROUGH THEM!"

'Most people can't locate them because all accesses, of which there are several, look like a private entrance. This suits the residents of these former miners' cottages.'

'They sound like fun,' said Ronnie who was clearly intrigued.

'If you ever get to Wirksworth, a street map will not help you to find the Puzzle Gardens. They are a well kept secret located about a quarter of a mile north west of the Market Place. You go up The Dale which ends at an old quarry. Ascend until the end of the row of cottages on the right. You'll see a narrow, very steep jitty leading up to a collection of older cottages perched steeply on the hill. Just enter and explore. You can easily get lost - part of the fun - but the panoramic views of the old town to the south east below will always guide you back.'

'It's a shame the cycling club didn't take off. You could have shown us all that interesting stuff. And the books you told us about! What about that rude one? Some posh woman putting the make on a rough workman - or something ...'

'Oh dear! I think you are referring to a certain Lady Chatterley and her naughty gamekeeper. To avoid the sack, I had to filter all the fun out of that one. Just for devilment, I'll give you the unexpurgated version now.'

'What?'

'You'll have the full Lady Chatterley with all the rude stuff left in.'

Ronnie's face and body language creased him into a mischievous imp in anticipation of forbidden text.

'Well, let me see,' said Simeon, searching his memory, marshalling his thoughts. 'I need to go back to your age. I have nostalgic memories of autumn 1960 when, at the age of 15, I attended a Pre-Apprentice course at the ultra modern Ilkeston College of Further Education on Field Lane. The very concept of 'Further Education' was new - a 1950s vision of a bright future. It was a gleaming white building with so much promise.'

A reference to *Lady Chatterley's Lover* immediately flagged up Wednesday, November 16th 1960 when, at lunch time, Simeon paid his 3/6 [17p] to buy one of the 200,000 copies printed after a 30-year ban on that controversial book. It was famously vilified by out-of-touch prosecutor, Mr Mervyn Griffith-Jones who said:

'Is this a book you would wish your wife or servant to read?'

In Simeon's humble tiny terraced cottage opposite Stanley Common Miner's Welfare, the nearest he had to a servant was Aunty Brenda. She came to 'muck out' once a week and would certainly have been disgusted by the 'goings on' between Lord Chatterley's roughly-spoken gamekeeper and Her lascivious Ladyship.

As a testosterone charged, deeply closeted 15-year-old guilt-ridden homosexual, Simeon was entranced with the page everybody was talking about. It was a conversation between the gamekeeper and the gamekeeper's fully-inflated manhood – John Thomas - straining at the bit for access to Lady Jane's womanhood.

'Arrr, John Thomas! Rock 'ard, an lookin' up at me! A know what thee wants – ***cunt!*** *That's what thee wants!* ***CUNT! CUNT!*** *An that's what thee's goin' to get.'*

Boasting possession of the infamous book, Simeon memorised this lewd exchange between man and manhood. In the role of randy gamekeeper, using the voice and mannerisms of Long John Silver, Simeon entertained his fellow students at the Ilkeston College in the style of his Heanor Howitt impressions earlier in the year.

With relish, and access to the caretaker's yard brush for a crutch, he mimicked Tony Hancock, impersonating Robert Newton's interpretation of Robert Louis Stevenson's colourful character Long John Silver, from his 1881 book *Treasure Island.*

"Aarr, Jim lad!" and the occasional *"Avast there!"*

This nautical romp consisted of hopping around the playground with a limp neck and imaginary squawking parrot on ye shoulder screeching *'Pieces of Eight!'* It took off, and soon there were several 'Silvers' capering around Howitt Secondary Modern School playground as Simeon's mates wanted to join the fun.

He savoured his new found influence but had to find new material when the novelty waned.

A half crazed, boggle eyed hermit, complete with stout wooden staff, screaming imprecations after the style of -

"REPENT!! Ye lusting sinners! Hear me! Ye are DOOMED!!" had little impact, miserably falling short of the desired effect, especially when cock of the school Rocky shouted -

"Shut it!"

"Nay, Brethren, give heed, I have seen the light."

"Y'll see my fist in a minute."

Alas, his comic impressions didn't take off in Ilkeston in quite the same way as in Heanor, but some sexy boys were suitably intrigued by that erotic presentation.

Ronnie asked -

'After all these years, how could you know what happened on Wednesday, November 16th 1960?

'The memory is clearly fixed because - November 16th 1960 is **also** the day Gilbert Harding died at the age of 53.

'Who?'

'Thirty five years ago, Gilbert Harding was an irascible broadcaster, always on our TV sets, dubbed the rudest man in Britain. He was **FAMOUS**. He was *so* famous; his name did **not** appear under his likeness at Madame Tussauds. The plaque simply said, THE MOST FAMOUS MAN IN BRITAIN.

'Only a few people knew Mr Harding was gay. I never met him, but at the tender age of twelve, having been abducted into a secret circle of paedophiles, I was one of the few – who did know.

'Mingling with 'rough trade', I heard talk about a gay criminal, 'a swinger' with an appalling reputation for seediness, shotguns and torture. Ronnie Kray took 'what he wanted'. He selected boys with 'long lashes with a melting look around the eyes'. They were plied with drink, shown off at the Society Club in Jermyn Street and sometimes taken to Kray's luxury flat in Walthamstow where show business celebrity friends were entertained.'

Rough-and-ready Cockney lads boasted of their connections, their sexual experience within the mobster underworld and certain high profile figures of the Establishment. One extremely desirable thug claimed intimate carnal knowledge of Gilbert Harding and Lord Boothby.

Simeon was rather shocked to hear Cockney youths bragging of their hobnobbing and sexual shenanigans with hoodlums and members of the top brass. He was especially revolted by one extremely desirable thug who claimed to have made Lord Boothby -

" ... spunk three times! Yeah, straight up. No bovver. Got me tongue in 'is arse 'ole. Moooved it slow ... yeah. Nice an steady. Should 'ave 'eard the old geyser, fair squealed with pleasure 'e did. Easy money."

"You rimmed a fat old man!!"

"Leave it out! When did you larrst pocket a tenner for a few minutes work?"

Chapter 13

King Coal

The conversation about Simeon's cycling trips in Derbyshire took various twists and turns until Ronnie felt confident enough to reflect on his colliery background with bitter family memories of the 1984-1985 Miners Strike.

Teacher and pupil had both lived in the grim shadows of pit hills which featured iconic pit wheels marking a winding engine house above each colliery mine shaft. King Coal had been the life and blood of Heanor, Worksop, numerous similar pit towns and pit villages in Derbyshire and Nottinghamshire for over a hundred years.

From his earliest memories, Simeon's world had been imprinted with images of blackened, dowdy cloth-capped workmen making their way to and from coal mines. Snap tins [food] and billycans [drink] hung from strong leather belts. Kneepads strapped to legs and the sound of pit boots clanking along the pavement were familiar to the boys who were expected to join relatives being lowered into the bowels of the earth. Simeon had grown up with the horror of joining countless ghosts haunting the coal face along miles of subterranean passageways. These were muscular, dust encrusted men who suffered and sweated long dark hours under long gone green fields.

Interrupting these thoughts, Ronnie asked a question which jolted the other.

'That strike must be over by now?' At the incredulous look on Simeon's face, he added - 'Well ... we *were* losing it, weren't we? You're not going to tell me it's still going on?'

Simeon's disturbed thoughts spun around his head in an effort to make sense of this extraordinary ignorance from a young man who was not stupid. Choosing his words carefully, he responded with a question.

'Ronnie! That year long strike has now ended. It ended in March 1985. Surely you remember it? It was so bitter! It was all over the news, the national news and *international* news. Thatcher got her way. She was cock-a-hoop, positively crowing. Scenes of fury, it was painful to watch on TV. The National Union of Mineworkers delegates ... well, they were broken men! At the bitter end, they voted to return to work. They had no choice. They came out of NUM HQ to furious crowds screaming abuse - "Scum! Scabs! Traitor!"

Simeon was taken aback by Ronnie's anguished expression. Something about that twisted countenance made him suddenly remember the significance of that year.

'Hang on! 1985? Is that when you were stabbed and had to spend months in hospital?'

'Yes,' responded the boy. 'I think so ... but ... if it's over? What happened?' he added miserably.

'Well,' said Simeon, thinking quickly, 'if you'll recall, some weeks back when you first came to me, we helped each other sort out the year we are now in? Have you forgotten? Can you tell me what year we are in?' Ronnie looked blank. 'Not to worry. We've both of us suffered trauma, yours being more physical and mine being a mental breakdown. We used to call it a nervous breakdown and my counsellor referred to it as a collapse of confidence. 'Anyway - the result is a mental fog and we're stuck in a sort of time warp with memory loss,' concluded Simeon taking a deep breath.

'OK. Back to the strike and the current year. I can't be certain, some days I can think more clearly, and on other days - I'm lost in a fog. This is a good day - and I'm fairly confident that the coal strike has been over for ten years. We are now in 1995.'

Ronnie looked perplexed and struggled with his thoughts. When he spoke, it was the younger roughly tongued pupil Simeon remembered teaching.

'Well ... me dad, me granddad, me uncles an cousins ... we were rock solid. *We* weren't scabs! We never gave in at Manton. We were proud and strong. Me dad were at Orgreave in a pitched battle wit coppers in riot gear ... an coppers on fuckin 'orses. Bastards! That bitch!'

'I know. She called the miners "the enemy within". Anyway, as far as gays are concerned, you'll know how much we hate her.

'I'm afraid Manton Pit has now closed after 96 years of production. It closed this year.'

'There was some talk about it during the strike,' replied Ronnie gathering confidence, now in more command of his memory. 'Me uncle 'arry said they'll take revenge and close Manton. And so they've really done it!'

'That's right, Ronnie. In 1984, the strike started because the Tories proposed closing 20 uneconomic pits, losing 20,000 jobs. There were a total of 160 deep mines, so closing 20 didn't sound too bad. The militant NUM President, Arthur Scargill, would not tolerate *any* pit closed or the loss of *any* miner. He dug in his feet and so did the 'Iron Lady'. She gave the police the Edmund-Davis award ...'

'What?'

'It was a massive pay increase given before the strike started. We teachers were quite envious. Oh yes! As well as that, she also made sure of huge coal stocks in advance. She intended to win.'

Simeon had always been critical of Arthur Scargill. He decided to use tact and say very little about the man who was sued by the National Union of Mineworkers in 1990 for 1.4 million pounds. It was alleged that Scargill had been cooking the books and had taken money from men who had been led to abject and humiliating defeat.

Simeon gave Ronnie an update of his missing ten years and spoke of the tragedy of blight across British coalfields.

'Scargill's doom laden prophecy was proved right. I think there are now about only 15 pits still working. So much for the proposed closure of 20 pits. Maggie has seen off 145!'

'She's destroyed the coal industry!'

'It's worse than that! Whole communities have been laid waste. I spent my last few precious weekends catching my breath from being ground down in this place. Out of curiosity, for a change, I cycled east weaving along the pretty narrow country lanes of Nottinghamshire and explored Shirebrook. It was like a ghost town! You could almost imagine the aftermath of a nuclear war. In the centre, shops were run down, scruffy and depressing to see. Others were boarded up and blighted by the scars of a thousand vandals.

'I cycled south, down to Clipstone, past the east side of Mansfield and through Thieves Wood. Thieves Wood is a haunt of homosexuals, where I tucked into my sandwiches and chatted to a few of the lads. One big advantage of gay life in a colliery culture is the endemic hard masculinity - butch blokes who don't mess about. No ceremony, just rude rough brute force. None of that prissy *may I kiss you* crap you find in the Derby Elite. NO! Rough working class pit types don't mess about. They talk dirty - they get straight to it. They get on with it - like - *come on, let's ave ya, get ya smackers round this fucker, ya randy sod. Get ya kegs off an stick ya bum in t' air like ya beggin for it, ya slut* - and so on.'

When Ronnie stopped laughing he detected a contradiction.

'You told me that tough pit men, Mundy Street Boys School and that lot had no time for sissy types. You said rough sorts hated queers?'

'It's what we call a paradox,' said Simeon. He tried to explain. 'The horror of homosexual activity was certainly taboo in the mining culture. To be sociable, I once went to a pub called the Jolly Colliers and stood nursing my orange juice ignoring snide remarks from cloth cap chaps knocking back pints. The laddish banter was often nasty, quite often anti - gay, yet some of those men, skilfully blending into a bawdy raucous heterosexual world, would be bisexual or completely gay, enjoying same-sex activity whenever opportunity offered itself.'

'Where might that be?'

'Oh - anywhere where nobody can see them; in the pit head showers or the local piss corner, or in an ultra secret sect near to Mundy Street Boys School in Heanor.'

'Guzzly Granddad?'

'Guzzly Granddad,' replied Simeon dryly. 'Granddad was a rough old retired miner whose lifestyle and habits were governed by his pit background and experiences. His very home, an old terraced cottage in a Heanor back street... It was camouflaged with choking ivy, about 50 years in the growing. If anybody discerned a building at all, it would be assumed to be derelict - a ruin. 'You must remember that Heanor had slum areas infested by scruffs with lots of ragged urchins running about in the muck. It was easy for a bedraggled old man, like Guzzly Granddad, to hide in such a rat hole.'

'Sounds worse than Manton!'

'In 1957 it probably *was* worse than most current coal towns. To be in homosexual society, you had to be ***in*** the secret. You had to *know* it was there. Regular visitors to Granddad's house used familiar shouts and whistling in the dark to inform that all's well, a device probably borrowed from his colliery experience. Before I actually met the old nonce, I was pressed into pleasuring Stonch in the Heanor Market Place lavatory. He'd be about 18 and did all the cooking and cleaning for Granddad and his urchins. A little lad stood outside the bog and did a whistle if an unknown man approached.

'It's like this, Ronnie. Paedophilia and coal mining shared a common danger. Safety–first, team work, trust and eternal vigilance were essential to ward off potential disaster. His very name was an inspired choice for his safety. Granddad! We all had at least one Granddad. When he was mentioned in the Mundy Street playground, nobody took much notice. Before my first initiation in his primitive kitchen, I'd heard some of the boys talking about Granddad.'

'When you'd been initiated, did they threaten you? Like, keep ya mouth shut - or else?'

'From Guzzly Granddad himself, the threat was implicit. That is, he hinted about bad things happening to me if I told anyone about "being rude" or, indeed, about the secret house hidden under ivy. You must remember that I was going through hell every day anyway. I was desperately trying to find a quick way out by suicide. Having that old man take an interest in me was wonderful! Becoming one of his guttersnipes was a godsend. He gave me warmth in an appallingly cold winter. He gave me security, the will to live, self-respect and physical pleasure. He fondled me and was fond of me. I came to love Guzzly Granddad.

'I know how this must sound to you, Ronnie. It was not an ideal childhood. I can't recommend it, wouldn't wish it on my worst enemy - but - that - old - man - saved - my - life. He was the king of kids, the ruler of ragamuffins.'

'What's that supposed to mean!'

'Well ... I mean he had power over his subjects. And he used that power for good. At Mundy Street Church of England School, a regime of cruelty (against a backdrop of hymns and prayers) imposed a system where a boy was esteemed by how much humiliation and pain he could inflict on other boys. You've heard this stuff before, but know this.

'Only a handful of boys from my actual class of 48 were initiated members of Guzzly Granddad's secret carnal club. The most powerful youth was not only the school's top dog, but also the best fighter in Heanor. Blubba was more muscle than blubber, but that was his nickname - Blubba.

'Blubba was ideal as a powerful weapon for protection and intimidation when needed. Rough as a badger's arse, he was Guzzly Granddad's hard-man and policeman. He was not sensitive – not kind – but loyal and obedient to the old man. All Granddad's roughs were accustomed to the reality of hard knocks, a heartless regime and a pecking order in which you knew where you stood. I understood the rules. I'd seen the results of hard knock discipline in the Mundy Street Boys School playground and knew Blubba would not hesitate to impose discipline if required.

'Here is the bottom line. Blubba was instructed to protect Piggy from the cruelty of Mundy Street Boys School classroom and playground.'

'Piggy?'

'That was me. They called me Piggy. For security, all of Granddad's gang were required to have a nickname. A fat slob was on the team. He was called Slob. A huge man of well over six foot was christened Oaf.

'Anyway, after Granddad told Blubba to shield me from humiliation and casual violence ...'

'What's casual violence?'

'There was *dead-legging*, *winding* and *ear-screaming*. Dead-legging was a well aimed kick into the side of the leg which rendered it useless for a few minutes and bringing the victim down. Winding was a sharp punch into the stomach making a boy unable to draw breath and ear-screaming happened so frequently I suffered a lifelong hearing loss – in both ears. This all contributed to the psychological damage sustained in that Christian gulag which was always excused as "a part of growing up".

'In those cold midwinter days in January 1958, I felt extra warmth from the protective reach of a new Guardian Angel, reassuringly like an invisible shield.'

The word 'damage' alarmed Ronnie who noticed yet another brooding introspection with pain etched on Simeon's face. Some things were too personal to share with his companion. In this reflective mood he was revisiting the playground where he was too frightened to use the school toilet. Mortifying incidents had made Mundy Street Boys School lavatory a no-go area for a boy who grew up to be a badly constipated man. Word went around the playground – 'hog's on t' bog'. A crowd gathered to enjoy the sport. Alarmingly, several times, unknown assailants kicked the door causing panic! Violent kicks - loud bangs - *terrifying* bangs! Within that small cubicle, distressing percussion reverberated with no escape. A quick bolt would result in certain capture by a blood thirsty lynch mob. Objects were thrown over the top. Taunting abuse through the gap below complemented a monstrous act of torture.

'Anyway ... where was I?'

'You were telling me about chatting to the queer lads in Thieves Wood,' said Ronnie, keen to change the subject.

'Oh, yes. I was chatting to Jed.'

'Jed! Who was Jed?'

'An older gay man, a scruffy sort, a bit rough, definitely a pit bloke, a butch bloke. At first sight I was hoping for a bit of rough sex. You know, Ronnie, in my world, conversation is taboo. It kills sex, good sex, sex with a stranger. But Jed needed to talk. He was very depressed, indeed, distressed.'

'Why?'

Simeon narrated a tragic story which seared into his consciousness - a story about two blokes. Jed wanted a sympathetic ear to speak about his partner Ben who he had met about 20 years earlier in a rough old pub. They were ordinary working class men from mining stock living in the shadow of slag hills in a pit town which had seen better days. Not well educated, not articulate, not the sort to make wills, just two gay men who keep their heads down hoping not to be noticed in a hostile homophobic landscape. They lived close, but not in the same house sharing mutual love spending most of their time in Ben's home.

In the last few months, Ben became ill and needed several spells in hospital. Just before Christmas 1994, Jed went to Ben's house expecting him to be home. Arriving at the door, as usual, he let himself in with the key he had owned for years.

Something was wrong! Furniture had been rearranged and an angry, ignorant, hostile woman confronted Jed, brutally insulting him with a torrent of abuse including false allegations in a homophobic rant. Ben's sister had rummaged through his personal belongings during the days the house was empty. She was horrified to discover items which clearly identified her brother's homosexual status and his deep love for a man.

She demanded Jed's key and ordered him off the property. At no time during this hateful attack did she draw breath to mention the fact that Ben was dead! Jed's parents and family knew of Ben's passing. To preserve the shameful secret, the demise was never mentioned to the man most closely concerned.

Jed heard about the death of his loved one from chatter in his local pub. He uncovered funeral details from strangers and, for moral support, asked a friend to meet him outside the church and sit with him inside. Like Jed, Ben was an atheist hostile to any kind of religious ceremony.

In the last few weeks up to the festive season, Jed had been profoundly depressed trying to pick up the pieces of his broken life.

Ronnie was stunned by this tragic story and expressed considerable comment.

'Yes,' said Simeon thoughtfully. 'It would have been a few weeks after my illness when I was cycling around the area taking in Thatcher's legacy in late April. Jed was still in a poor way coming to terms with his loss in this ex-mining area. He now suffers isolation together with dereliction that blights once-thriving communities.

'Well - I suppose I did some good listening to Jed. It's sad that we didn't exchange addresses; I would have liked to have kept in touch with him. He seemed a decent sort.'

To explore more of this impoverished landscape, Simeon cycled south west and eventually came out at the colliery village of Newstead which was reduced to rows and rows of empty, boarded up terraced cottages. These were the homes of proud miners, cohesive communities held together by past generations of honest hard working folk sharing a culture of mutual dependence. It put the cyclist in mind of untold numbers of broken men suffering from pneumoconiosis claiming social security. The strike set brother against brother, houses were repossessed, marriages were broken up and kids lived in abject poverty.

Chapter 14

Shocking Question

Another day dawned. Two friends sat in the same place, tete-a-tete. Whether consciously or unconsciously, Ronnie decided to push at the boundaries and asked Simeon about his last day at school, as a teacher, before his current malaise.

'I know you're muddled in fog, but together, we might be able to sort out a few things. Hope you don't mind. It's just that ... well; I think it'll help *me* some. Do you know what I mean?'

'I know *exactly* what you mean! We can help each other. Well ... let me see? The last few months had been terrible. I was losing my grip. You know about the sixth formers. I think they extinguished what was left of my collapsing confidence, sort of, put the tin-hat-on-it.

'I must have appeared pretty grim to the colleague who suggested time off. Everything spoke of it, my body language, stooped bearing and slow painful gait not to mention looking much older. The Nurse, a kind lady, was worried and actually mentioned the possibility of sick leave.

'I recall sitting still in my classroom staring at the TV. It was *my* TV. I was thinking that it was too heavy to carry it into the car. Because, you see, for mental salvation, I'd made a life changing decision. When I left that classroom on that day, I vowed never to return! But the videotape recorder was also mine and that *could* be carried to the car.'

'Never return! But you *did* come back?'

'Not as a teacher. I was reinstated as a mental cripple wasting time with lesson plans which were becoming increasingly irrelevant as you yourself pointed out, Ronnie. My life has to mean something ...' His voice broke, briefly, choking back a sob. He rallied. 'I intended to make a clean break. I shouldn't be here. I should be ...'

'At home? Why don't you go home now, Simeon? Why don't you just walk out of this building - right now?'

This question was a shock! Ronnie *intended* it to be a shock and had backed him into a corner. It was a moment of crossing the Rubicon; the 'elephant' had been confronted and slain. For some scary moments, they looked at each other. Reading emotions; face studied face. They saw a mutual blend of anxiety, affection, pity and resignation. Tentatively, with a gentle smile of surrender, Simeon responded -

'I'll go to the top of the stairs and walk down them - if you'll come with me. Will you come with me, Ronnie? Will you take the risk?'

'Yes,' said Ronnie, struggling to find his voice in a barely audible whisper.

They stood up, opened the door, turned left and went through the door to the top of the stairwell.

'Are you OK?' asked Simeon.

'Hold my hand,' said the other with emotion. 'I'm scared you'll disappear.'

'I *can* feel your hand! It's warm. Look down on the playground. Can you see that teacher walking towards this block? In a moment he'll walk up these stairs and pass us. And here we are, holding hands. Won't you be embarrassed?'

'No,' spat out Ronnie with a scornful giggle. He looked Simeon straight in the eyes. 'He won't notice us ... will he?'

And he didn't. Moments passed as physical contact continued. Simeon acknowledged they were still together, conscious of each other, had not disappeared. They descended, hand in hand, into the open playground still holding hands. A couple of caretakers deep in technical conversation heedlessly passed nearby. Ronnie giggled at the absurdity of the situation. Simeon suggested they make another bold move and risk *breaking* physical contact. His former pupil reluctantly disconnected hands but continued to look into the eyes of his protector.

'Still here,' grinned Ronnie.

'I was right. I think it must be October. There's a fresh nip in the air and ... Look at that! Check out that blaze of colour.' Momentarily they took pleasure in nearby trees; brilliant sunshine illuminated autumnal tints of bright orange and yellow leaves. 'I suppose we can enjoy this beauty because we're looking at it and we're talking about it. Look who's coming now.'

'The Nurse.'

'Yes the Nurse. I wonder?'

'What?'

'I wonder if she'll see us. Have you ever seen the film *Carousel*?' asked Simeon. 'It's about a man; he gets killed in a fight, goes to heaven but is allowed to visit earth to help his teenage daughter understand the circumstances of his death. He's told that the girl will only see and hear him, if he *wants* her to. Otherwise, she can't see or hear him ... '

'No! I don't want her to see us ... please don't ...'

'Don't worry. It's OK. She's not going to see us. Even if we wanted it, I doubt it would happen. Incidentally, that man in the movie ... he was stabbed.'

Ronnie, attempting to come to terms with the reality forced upon him, was struggling to find a response.

'So!' said Simeon, 'we're still here, still breathing in the fresh cool air on this fine day. We exist. We're still able to think, to reason and delight in the senses of living sentient creatures. We touch, feel and smell the autumnal ambience and we see the world pass by. We exist (if not actually live) with the critical faculties to which we are accustomed. Are you cold?'

'No.'

'Neither am I. Perhaps I should be with shorts and tracksuit top on - nothing more. Tell me, Ronnie: in these last few weeks, have I worn anything else?'

'No - and I can't remember being without this shirt and jeans since ... '

'The moment you were stabbed? Yes - and *I* need to discover what happened to *me*. Hazily, I thought I'd arrived at school each day on my bicycle, and, if asked, would have told you it was parked in the history book cupboard just outside my classroom.'

'An accident?'

'Possibly. And yet ... It's all so fuzzy. If I think hard enough ... I think it was deliberate. I might have been ...

murdered. It's just a faint memory - probably me being dramatic. You've heard it said, they walk when they're taken too quick.'

'Murder! I'm interested. Keep talking.'

'It's not a clear memory, but recently there was a nasty incident as I was cycling home along that maze of country lanes about a mile or so outside of Worksop. A car drove past me ... slowly. I saw four youths including the driver, but was not able to identify anyone. A little way ahead, ominously, it stopped. Immediately I considered that one or more could have been either current Valley pupils or former pupils. I was scared.

'You and your mates liked me, in fact we were quite chummy, perhaps too chummy - but, before that Damascene moment when we had the heart to heart chat, you thought like most of my pupils.'

'What do you mean?'

'You thought I was strict, perhaps too strict. Kids with a bit of spirit like you, Ronnie, resent being made to work in silence. That's why we had that bust-up at the back of my classroom with Bobbie and Freddie. OK - *we* sorted it out, but when reprimanded some lads become indignant, especially girls, and some nurse a grudge and become bitter.'

'So....'

'So when that car stopped ... I thought - I was for it.'

'And?'

'And I was right! I continued to cycle on my way trying to tough it out. I tried to be brave and looked nonchalant, not going overly fast, casual - sort of. As I was actually passing the car, the driver abruptly opened his door with the obvious spiteful intention of causing a nasty accident. Fortunately, perhaps expecting something unpleasant to happen, I'd taken the precaution of giving this vehicle a wide berth and safely cycled past the offending door ...'

'Go on.'

'Well - this is the scary bit. I have *no* memory of anything else after that mishap. I can't remember getting home or any other part of that journey or that day. I feel that it happened within the few days before my last day at the Valley. I reason that I must have got home because, on my very last day at school, I'd certainly got there by car because of the television.

You'll remember me sitting in my classroom looking at the TV which, unlike my videotape player, was too heavy to carry to the car. I swore that it was going to be my last day at this place and clearly remember driving away in the car. In fact, I made a point of NOT looking back.'

'The book cupboard is up the stairs we've just come down,' said Ronnie pointing. 'You said you can never remember whether you come to school by bike or car. Let's see if your bike is in that cupboard now. Why not have a look?'

'No reason at all,' replied Simeon.

They re-entered the Sixth Form Block and climbed the stairs. The history book cupboard, actually a tiny room, contained only books - no bike.

'So,' said Ronnie, coming out into the corridor collecting his thoughts. 'You're thinking that a few nutters ran you over or beat you to death?'

'It could be,' replied Simeon. 'But I feel certain that my last school day memory was in the land of the living. It's all so hazy.'

Emboldened by the fact of both of them having the courage to walk around the school, Simeon was prepared to risk a further walk.

'Let's go to the main staff room, I want to see today's date on a newspaper.'

With ongoing anxiety, Ronnie continued to chat nervously and touch his friend for fear of dissolving into the ether. Simeon reminded him that, for the last few weeks, they had been meeting up on a daily basis in the small classroom in the Sixth Form Block. Therefore, there was no reason to suppose the meetings should stop so long as they both wished the meetings to continue.

'After all, Ronnie, we've been drawn to each other by a shared significant moment. Don't you remember? I referred to it a few minutes ago as a Damascene moment - St Paul's miraculous conversion on the road to Damascus. During one of my rants, Bobbie stuck up for you, shamed me - and made me see myself as I was at your age at my Secondary Modern

School, Howitt in Heanor. It was a momentous turnaround for me - and you. Suddenly, I saw you as *I* was at 14, struggling with a chaotic home life - complications and overwhelming problems - like swimming in treacle. In all 20 years of my teaching career, I'd never enjoyed such a shining breakthrough. Verging on unprofessional conduct, we were more mates than pupil-teacher after that experience.

'Tell you what, if we're parted for any reason, I'll go back to the small classroom and stay there until you turn up tomorrow as usual. OK?'

Ronnie was calmed, but stayed close during the walk across the playground.

'Funny, isn't it? I mean us dead and walking like other folk. Shouldn't we be able to float?'

'Good point, Ronnie,' giggled Simeon. 'We are still rooted to the concepts of time and space which governed and ruled our mortal existence.'

'Too right! I should be able to *wish* myself to the Main Block - or China for that matter.'

Enjoying these fanciful considerations, they progressed along the playground and up to the main staffroom in the Main Block. It was the lunch hour. Simeon observed his onetime colleagues with mixed feelings.

'Just look at them! It's so easy to categorize the assorted types. See that group in the far corner, they're known as The Old Guard. Like me, they've been here for as long as anybody can remember. Most of them are from the Technical Department - politically reactionary red necks, right wingers doing what they do best, grumbling and grouching about everything. Their arch enemies are in the opposite corner, the English Department, equally odious in a different way.'

'What way?'

'I suppose we should call them the far left. They're the progressives. *You* should like them, Ronnie. They tolerate noisy classrooms, kids chattering and wandering around - not much work done and reluctant to punish. Sarcastic with an acid wit sums them up. Quite nasty at times.'

'I know them all in the Old Guard, but none in the English group. Where do *you* fit in?'

'I don't. English teachers don't stay long. They move on to better things. Me? Well, historians have their own smaller staffroom in the Sixth Form Block. They're a mixture of the two extremes. I used to *think* I was a good teacher and was comfortable conversing with the old-fashioned tech types. That said, they were hostile to queers - as, of course, were some progressives. Notice a few members of staff who sit on their own - loners. That would be me, if I ever used this room, which I seldom did.'

Suddenly, one of the traditionalists let rip in a plaintive cry -

'Of course, I'm a voice in the wilderness, but if you want *my* opinion, I wouldn't touch that scumbag with a bargepole. I wouldn't stand for it. The headmaster should ... '

'I hated that old fart,' interrupted Ronnie. 'He might have been on about *me*. Do you think I could chuck that big glass ashtray at him?'

'And be an apprentice poltergeist? Not a good idea. Firstly, I don't think you could move anything; secondly, I'd urge you to hold on to what you have left because, whatever we are, we're fragile and vulnerable. My instinct is to keep a tight grip on ourselves and abide by normal rules of conduct. I can't prevent your mischief, but an unseen higher power just might do what you're most scared of. He might blow you away.'

Over the previous few weeks, Simeon had heard a lot about Ronnie's dysfunctional, chaotic life and understood his bitter reaction to the word 'scumbag' as applied to pupils like himself. If Simeon was seen as a degenerate queer by his family and the wider world, so Ronnie, a rough tearaway, had always been rubbished by the bad press of respectable opinion. Was this the tenacious link binding two ghosts trying to make sense of their current situation? The word 'sentient' came to mind. Two ghosts without a body, fragile and loosely hooked up by a common purpose, exploring their self worth. Two ghosts who could so easily melt away! Breaking into these thoughts -

'Sorry, Simeon.'

'No problem. I was just trying to be practical.' Checking *The Guardian* reposing on a coffee table, he confirmed the month and year of October 1995. 'It proves we have some sense of the passage of time. But your darkness, Ronnie; it came some ten years earlier. Put another way, your fog is thicker than mine. Can we take it you have no idea of where you go when we say goodbye at the end of each school day?'

'I can only remember turning up to our meetings. The bike wasn't there, but do you cycle back to Clowne when I've gone?'

'Funny isn't it! I thought I did - but I don't. I dream. I dream of cycling along country lanes hearing a distant cuckoo in spring and dream of my isolated house covered in ivy with the garden all overgrown, impenetrable with shrubs and trees out of control.

'So there it is,' Simeon sighed. 'Our existence is dependent on us being together. Let's go back to the classroom and examine those sheets of autobiographical notes.'

They found the typed sheets in Simeon's briefcase - but he doubted their reality beyond the fact that they were looking at them and could be touched.

'Anyway, *how* would we get the manuscript to anyone in the living world? Has it all been a waste of time, Ronnie?'

'No!! Absolutely not! What is time anyway? We seem to have plenty of it - and I don't think we're wasting it. A bloke writes a book to be read by anybody who can, and wants to read it. I'm interested. I can touch these pages and move them from here to there - see.' Ronnie demonstrated. 'And I can read them. And so can you. That's two people. Perhaps that's enough. We should press on as long as we *can* press on. We haunt this room. Let's *keep* haunting it. It's better than nothingness. I dread that.'

'In life,' said Simeon, 'I never feared death, only the process of death. Why should I dread nothingness, oblivion? What about all the eons of years which preceded my birth? I've no memory of those millenniums before my existence, so what does it matter? You might have a point, Ronnie, about it being enough. At least, we've shared our life stories. If we've been granted time to do that, perhaps we should respect that time. If we dissolve into the ether - so what? We'll never know about it.'

'You're bitter, Simeon.'

'That's true enough. It's a recurring theme throughout my life. You'll recall the old miner who touched me up when I was 12. I was in abject despair, planning suicide. He was my only friend and cautioned against such a drastic solution. He told me that a live lad could *do* something, but a dead lad could do nothing. He was right. I'm dead. I can do nothing. I *am* nothing.'

'Stop feeling sorry for yourself! You're something to me. I might not be queer, but I can feel the justice of your cause. Believe me, I know all about prejudice. You once explained it to us in class: prejudice = pre-judging someone, not giving them a chance. We'll stay safe in this room and you can keep telling me about your life. Keep ranting if you have to. I'll listen to your anger, your pain, your loves, your misery and your happiness. It's not *all* bad is it?'

'No, Ronnie. Like all lives it has highs and lows. Being optimistic, we continue to exist and might find a way to get this manuscript into the land of the living. Who knows?'

Epilogue

Fifty years pass. It is noon on July 12th 2045, on a hot summer's day. We return to Clowne High Street which has retained some of the character that made it so distinctive when first seen by Simeon in 1978. However, the people are now different. He would not have recognised it as the same place. The quirky individuality of scruffy people who once inhabited this one time pit village was now a memory of the elderly.

Gone are the lopsided, dirty bedraggled types perambulating up and down the high street. The slovenly and dishevelled are a thing of the distant past. Downtown Clowne, now a pedestrian precinct, still has its ancient cross. After 900 years, it still stands at an intersection of several roads, but is no longer a craggy backwater of interbred crooked colliers. Simeon would have looked in vain for his assortment of fishwives, scarecrows, yokels, crones, hags, louts and simpletons including the obese, the old and the misshapen. Clowne is no longer a craggy coal community - gone are flat caps and slatterns slowly shuffling around the shops uttering inanities in pit talk.

Speech is now more standardised. History books now teach that Britain's rapid decline as a major industrial power in the 1900s had much to do with accent and sharp social divisions based on the way you spoke.

Some 80 years before, Simeon the lowly Derbyshire teenager was in awe of an extraordinary accent of 'cut-glass' diction. He was impressed by an orgy of enunciation, such high art of lavish articulation hitting the boy's Derbyshire ear like a thunderbolt. Today in 2045 he would not hear the rough and common. He would not hear the refined tones of upper class homosexuals (or, indeed, posh heterosexuals) trying to pretend they were something they were not.

Had the ghost of Simeon cycled westwards in this extreme north eastern secluded corner of Derbyshire, he would have encountered a near unbroken urban landscape sprawling all the way to Chesterfield. A route eastwards would have looked more familiar. A 2045 explorer might still be challenged and easily get lost in the maze of country lanes stretching towards Worksop, Whitwell, Creswell and remnants of Sherwood Forest which had escaped the onslaught of new housing to absorb an alarming increase of population.

Members of that population included students Campbell and Colt who, after lengthy discussions with their Counsellor, Amelia, were finalising the requirements of their Clowne Academy dissertation for Academy Graduation.

Traditional formal examinations from the 20th century were not yet extinct, but had largely been replaced by the practice of continual assessment in a move to something resembling a PhD. Clowne Academy sounded rather grand but was in fact the new name for secondary education prior to university education. The very name Comprehensive School, discredited way back in the 1990s, had been superseded by High School and eventually the Academy. Within the last 20 years, a focus on 'original research' had been pressed on the Humanities Departments of Academies.

Counsellors like Amelia invested a lot of time and trouble delving into the interests and inclinations of students like 15-year-olds Campbell and Colt who were embarking on their final two years of Academy education. In the 2030s, there was a vogue towards naming boys after family names, hence the odd sounding pairing of Amelia's students.

It was already becoming more common to *choose* your first name. Colt had legally changed his name to alliterate with Campbell who had been his boyhood partner from the age of 12. They enjoyed a stable and loving homosexual relationship fully approved by friends, family and society at large.

In everyday parlance, the word 'homosexual' had superseded other euphemisms such as gay and same-sex-attraction which, in turn, had replaced offensive terms such as queer, faggot, bum boy, bender etc. In the early 2020s, LGBT + had started to break down as an umbrella which covered a variety of sexual minorities. In 2045, lesbians, bisexuals and transgender people had now achieved the same normality as Campbell and Colt. By a process of enlightened education, almost by osmosis, the horrors which had blighted Simeon's life were simply no longer an issue. Organised religion had withered on the vine and lost its evil power to crush homosexuality.

Simeon, with horror, had looked at the abominations and crucifixions inflicted on homosexual victims in his 20th century. In the same way, Campbell and Colt, in conversation with parents, grandparents and older people in general, had heard of appalling prejudices and unspeakable deeds done to boys like themselves. One day, chatting to Amelia, they wanted to know more about it. At once, she identified a possible thesis which offered the precious quality of originality together with an enthusiasm which might well keep her students focused for the next two or three years.

Fortunately, their Counsellor, born and bred in Clowne, had always been intrigued with the Mystery of Magpie House and had heard something of the schoolmaster who had occupied that Gothic edifice some seventy years before.

Even in 1978 when that secretive teacher moved into that neglected Victorian pile, it was already more than a hundred years old and slowly rotting in the centre of a dense wood. Such an enchanting situation, even then, cried out for comparisons to the Sleeping Beauty legend. Amelia was reminded of that local fairy tale, that cryptic conundrum now more than 200 years back in time! Old timers held to the same reality that it would never be possible to reach that antiquated house - *if* indeed the house still stood. Nobody knew.

Such an adventure would require the use of a sharp chainsaw to cut through the dark density of trees healthy, and trees fallen, to reach the centre of Magpie Wood. But the boys dismissed her fears of hiring expensive professional woodsmen. If equipped with a suitable machete, they were confident a path of least resistance could be found and a meandering track would lead them through to investigate the ruin.

And this they did. Every day they walked from the Academy, past the old church (now a quaint Community Hall) still surrounded by slowly rotting sunken graves (now nearly sunken out of sight) - out of the village for about half a mile until they reached the edge of woodland. All attempts to locate the onetime rough bridleway which wound into the wood - failed.

The bridle path had disappeared together with springtime bluebells, anemones and celandine which had once enchanted Simeon. July still sported ancient deciduous woodland of oak, sycamore, beech and birch together with a riot of scents and midsummer birdsong. All nature was still intact.

Campbell and Colt struggled on day after day for the best part of a week and finally agreed to assistance from professionals with chainsaws who generously donated their time and skill in a good cause. The woodland put up a good fight to keep its secret. Men and boys came to appreciate the enchanting effects of human neglect which enhanced the natural allure of a mature wood.

Areas of dark density and several fallen trees with a mighty violent crash were evidence of an unspoilt world where nature had laid low a great beech or ancient oak with exposed torn roots, thrust up! - was now supporting mosses and fungi.

Men and boys laboured for nearly two weeks before Magpie Wood gave up its long held secret. Day by day, ongoing discussions examined several possibilities. One man, a builder by trade, was certain that nothing better than a pile of masonry would be found - if anything was found at all. Another man, a tree surgeon, was more optimistic, asserting the quality and construction skills of Victorians who intended their work to last for centuries.

All agreed that, whatever the condition, the collective memory of the elderly described mature trees well established just yards from the Gothic dwelling of Magpie House. It was strong and sturdy with stone mullioned windows some 70 years back. Even then, those walls were heavily covered with ivy and Virginia creeper camouflaging the structure making it nigh on invisible. It was assumed that, when discovery came, that moment would come suddenly! And so it was.

This moment was momentous and magical. Years later the boys, now men, were watching an old documentary about the eerie, silent first sight of the Titanic seen from a deep sea submersible. Immediately, they recognised the feeling. That iconic bow, two miles deep, shrouded by ghostly rusticles in a cold alien environment first seen by human eyes after decades of slow decay - yet still intact.

And so it was to suddenly find a perfectly preserved solid Victorian wall buttressed by close encroaching trees, a one-time home of dilapidation strangled by masses of foliage where, ironically, the strangler had, for nearly 200 years, actually protected and preserved the home of Simeon Hogg.

With some difficulty, the boys and their helpers hacked their way around the house. They checked windows, some sound, but many leafy limbs had attacked and invaded the interior. The roof was still there! Badly sunken perhaps, but a complete roof notwithstanding. Giant trees towering above Magpie House had formed a living cathedral of protective branches preserving a manmade canopy - by extension preserving the writings of a long dead schoolmaster.

A solid sturdy front door, securely and firmly locked, was located and its integrity respected.

'No point damaging it,' said one man, 'Look over there.'

The lower massive branch of a large beech tree was thrust through the remains of a onetime French window / glass door designed to give access to the garden.

The act of entering triggered a multiplicity of emotions swirling around the boys. In previous months, after public appeals on radio and in the press, they had already uncovered personal letters sent by the former resident of Magpie House to kindred spirits who secretly shared same-sex attraction. Leading double lives, Simeon's gay friends would have kept such letters in a very safe place only to be discovered by embarrassed sons, daughters, nephews or nieces probably many decades later. Some letters might have been destroyed but other correspondences have a habit of surviving several generations. A prize discovery came to light thanks to a solicitor who chanced upon a secret drawer in an inherited antique writing desk, once the property of his grandfather. The concealed compartment gave up a wodge of letters all signed - 'With affection, Simeon.'

The revelation of a homosexual ancestor in the late 2030s was far less scandalous than the same disclosure occurring in the 1970s. The correspondence covering a period from 1976 to 1995 was seen as an interesting curiosity shining a light on the darkness, pain and suffering of a hounded minority. In fact, it was a potentially valuable historic document.

Campbell and Colt pored over their treasured discovery, an articulate record of the schoolmaster's life before he disappeared into his reclusive home deep in the woods. As a secretive repressed gay man, Simeon's increasing monkish lifestyle began some years before his sudden disappearance one day after walking out of the Valley Comprehensive School on Thursday, April 6th 1995. School records, even 50 years before, had been easy to check. Due to stress and overwork, Mr Hogg had been advised to take his Easter holiday one day early, hopefully to return refreshed on the Monday of April 24th. He failed to show. Unfortunately, the school log made no mention of efforts to contact him. Here the mist and fog of a half century span seemed as impenetrable as the opaque tangle of woodland which hid Magpie House. All Valley colleagues who might have recollections were long dead.

Sparse unverified local knowledge together with hearsay gathered by Counsellor Amelia from her 'old timers' was as close to the truth as they were ever likely to get. Her ability to assist her students was restricted by the rules and regulations governing 'original research'. She *was* able to supply the boys with a list of elderly residents who were willing to be questioned about any recollections of their own grandparents. After careful analysis, referencing and cross-referencing, the gist of rumour and tittle-tattle was this -

'The bachelor teacher was a mysterious woodland hermit. He dwelt in the big house keeping himself to himself. Memory was often vague, years were difficult to pin down, but the schoolmaster from Worksop was regarded by some as a polite educated gentleman, nicely spoken, very civil but disinclined to talk about himself. Moody - he could be sociable but would not talk for long. You could never get to know him. He often went into Clowne to shop. It was not really acceptable to be a 50 something and still be "not married with neither child nor chick." Something not quite right about a bloke who had no interest in football and was never seen in a pub. The more respectable were sniffy about the fact that he never set foot in the church.'

Campbell and Colt shared Simeon's first impression (50 years previously) that Magpie House was derelict and had been so for many years - totally devoid of human occupation. Having just stepped into the old house, they commented on the 'Sleeping Beauty' letter when Simeon was certain there would be no sleeping beauty within.

'A good thing since a sleeping prince, a handsome one, would be more to *my* taste. Anyway - it was the *house* sleeping and I would, if I could afford it, kiss this house into a home.'

With trepidation, the boys explored the ground floor rooms all panelled with dark oak. Hushed conversation was spasmodic.

'Creaks.'

'It's a sinking house! I'll bet the roof is sinking.

'The floor is sinking. Dare we visit the cellar?

'One thing at a time.

'It's old, very old,' said Colt.

'It's still falling down, falling down slowly because it was well built in the first place.'

'It's hundreds of years old.'

'That puts it well. It's described as a gabled Victorian manor house.'

'What's a manor house?' asked Colt.

'A large country house with land, I think,' replied Campbell. 'You'll be more concerned when we go outside and see the sunken roof from the trees. Putting it plainly, it's all decayed.'

Through windows, it could be seen that the woodland had already encroached over a onetime garden right up to the house walls.

'I expect the schoolmaster couldn't afford gardeners.' Cole stopped as if visualising long lost landscaping stretching back to the 19th century.

They both felt a deep sorrow. The house was impregnated with melancholy.

'It all seems so sad,' said Colt. 'And yet, Simeon was excited about buying it! I wonder why?'

'Because he was getting exactly what he wanted! A tumbling down ancient dwelling, in an enchanted wood, with land at a cheap price. It's perfect! It's haunted.'

'Is it?'

'Don't worry. I don't think we'll actually ever *see* anything – but I feel it – and smell it,' said Campbell. 'Ghosts can't hurt you. I'm told fairies can, if they put their mind to it. Get this straight: the ghosts and fairies around this place and wood are *friendly*. Just don't annoy them.'

'Good. I won't.'

'Anyway, a house this old, so crooked, so decrepit … well, it's bound to be a bit noisy. Especially in the dead of night when there's a dead silence. I think it's called *settling*.'

Effectively, Simeon had acquired a museum of 19th century furniture with drawers and wardrobes.

They passed through a cold flagged passageway and emerged into an even colder spacious entrance hall giving on to an imposing south-facing front door. The coldness was everywhere.

But the cold was somewhat mitigated by fine oak panelling which followed an impressive oaken staircase lighted by a large leaded window one and a half floors deep.

Lighting from this excess of glass was somewhat dimmed by advancing foliage. The boys paused on mid-landing to scrutinise the tangle of branches heavy with lichen and rampant ivy. The sun was brilliantly bright, yet here was darkness? In an effort to solve the puzzle, their eyes tried, and failed, to penetrate beyond the knotted convolutions which seemed to end in blackness. More curious still, higher up, blackness was broken by haphazard spots of sunlight picking out brilliant green holly and equally brilliant blood-red rubies of berries somewhat in advance of their usual autumnal stage.

Other spots landed on dazzling brighter pockets leaping out of a stygian backdrop. They were trying to make sense of it. It seemed like a sort of optical illusion. They were facing north. On the north side, effectively, they were in a hole – a big hole. A quarry wall gave a strange quality of night. It was magic!
'I told you we were in the centre of an enchanted wood,' said Campbell.

Giant beeches on *top* of the quarry wall accentuated depth, increasing the illusion of trees reaching to heaven - scraping the sky. Campbell was inspired to quote a memorised line from one of Simeon's letters.

'On a windy day, walk into my beguiling garden, look up, and you'll be bewitched by a ballet of boughs and limbs at what seems like an impossible height!'

'Fascinating!' said Colt completely carried along with his enthusiasm. 'It's beautiful – fairyland. And … are those diamonds?' He pointed to glitter on the right of the canvas.

Diamonds? Oh, I see. That's fluorspar in the rock. It sparkles.'

The first floor landing, formal and generous, was at odds with two crooked passageways leading off in opposite drunken directions - wide at first – becoming narrow, twisting and bending. This was a dramatic demonstration of warping decay seemingly in sympathy with the spirit of long dead decaying gentle folk who had been unable to keep the house straight and true. Campbell imagined a giant picking up the house, giving it a gentle squeeze and twist before putting it back.

One room opposite the staircase was obviously a master bedroom suite. According to one of Simeon's recently discovered letters, it comprised of a bed chamber, a study with attached private library - all described in some detail.

'I'll bet this is where he slept,' said a slightly excited Campbell.

'Let's not ... I mean ...'

In that fearful gap, Campbell understood Colt's unfinished sentence. At some point in that exploration of the old house, they were likely to make the grim discovery of the schoolmaster's remains where he took his last breath. A main bedroom combined with a study and library might well have been Simeon's work place and office where he spent most of his time. Abruptly, Campbell changed the subject.

'You can easily get lost in this rambling house. We don't want to be too long because the men are waiting for us. I don't think we should try to explore *all* the mysterious nooks and crannies ... however tempting they are. Well ... at least not now - not today. There'll be other days. Try not to scream if you glimpse a floating apparition.'

'Don't be daft. Anyway, we have to think about safety. This building is dangerous!'

'Let's press on. Let's be brave.'

With a pleasurable frisson of adventure, they went down the right hand passageway which (after passing a few doors) turned, narrowed, and finally twisted upward to a dead end – or so it seemed. A look to the right revealed a narrow staircase up to the second floor. They clomped up noisy steps and emerged into what could have been a different house, dusty with ancient cobwebs, built for little people.

'Poor servants!' said Colt ducking slightly to keep his hair off the ceiling. 'Of course, it's getting worse, but even years ago, this must have been a cramped and crushed existence for them.'

They investigated this cheerless area and observed how Victorians treated those lesser mortals who toiled to make life comfortable for *their betters*.

As best as the boys could make out, the attic provided accommodation for a cook, scullery maid and three or four other maids. Two rooms on the second floor might have been for a housekeeper. Another room might have been an office.

They returned to the first floor, took a grip on themselves and entered what was considered to be Simeon's bedroom suite. Gothic bleakness with an ornate massive four-poster bed immediately reminded them of the Alastair Sim film, *Scrooge.* Raw Victorian oppressiveness was tempered by another whopping window. South facing sunlit cheer flooded through more mullions, bright brilliance reposing on branches quite close to the glass. They were pleasantly surprised to discover a neatly made bed with no dead body visible.

'There you are,' said Campbell. 'At least he made his bed before he died!'

'Dusty musty and fusty,' replied Colt taking a sniff and pulling a face.

'But not mouldy or mildewed,' returned his partner. 'There's no nasty smell because this group of rooms is free of broken windows unlike other parts of the house. And ventilation from that open fireplace would help.'

The mid July sun was warm and warming to this otherwise stone cold room during the brief times of day when it could navigate around the multitude of tree branches. Just now, it was illuminating a dusty washstand with large jug and bowl. Most of the room was in deep shade.

'Look at that hideous looking wardrobe,' said Colt. It's probably a big as your house. It belongs in a horror film! Hope it doesn't give you nightmares.'

Campbell was not afraid of the wardrobe. This grim piece of gigantic furniture, an extravagance of leering gargoyles, looked as if it had been carved by the same mad-man who had misshapen the freakish four posts supporting Simeon's monstrous bed.

Seeing a closed door, they became immobile as an ominous silence descended upon them. This would be the door leading to the library and / or the office where the schoolmaster wrote his biographical account of a life blighted by homophobia. Campbell broke the silence.

'We don't know where he died! He could have died anywhere. He might not be in this house at all. He might have keeled over into a bed of those tall nettles outside or ... someplace far out in the fields. It is 50 years! Wherever he is, there won't be much left of him now will there?'

'All right. Come on then.'

The first room was the windowless library with bookshelves all round lit only slightly by a large Tudor archway leading into the office. Here a floor to ceiling heavily mullioned ornate stone window, identical to the bedroom window, admitted even more brilliant sunlight to flood the room. It was certainly less cold in this plain more cheerful room. Here again was a fireplace.

And again their eyes dazzled. And those eyes were drawn to the window beaming more brightly from an enhanced sun now sinking in the onset of early evening. It took a few seconds of adjustment to the light before they saw it. The desk. An enormous cumbersome gothic desk facing them in front of an empty desk chair sensibly positioned so that the writer had benefit of natural light behind him. A large typewriter had been pushed forward to facilitate the writing of hand written notes. Various sheets of paper were to hand as was the typewriter which was ergonomically ready for service at the reach of a hand.

It took a little time to discern the remains of that hand. In silence and reverence, Campbell and Colt moved forward to see an ivory global object, which must once have been the head of Simeon Hogg, reposing on the desk.

For some months, the boys had discussed this moment with their counsellor. To prepare for that moment, she had made it clear that they must not expect a complete skeleton anatomically joined up in the style of images seen in countless horror films. This much, they were prepared for. Accordingly, only a few bones were on the desk, no bones at all on the chair and just a few scattered on the floor in the vicinity of the desk. They had also been warned to touch nothing as if they had come across a crime scene.

In deference and respect they stayed several minutes, as one might keep vigil at a grave site, to honour his memory. Some papers were tantalisingly visible; typed notes slightly obscured by dust which, of course, were not touched either.

They had to wait a few weeks to receive a formal Forensic Report necessary with any discovery of human remains. That official statement confirmed that no human or animal had entered the room to remove or disturb the skeletal fragments which had once been the central focus of their school dissertation.

Together with the Forensic Report, Campbell and Colt were presented with 182 fifty year old type-written sheets totalling over 75,000 words. This extraordinary manuscript revealed a long conversation between Simeon Hogg and a former pupil called Ronnie. His family name was never mentioned. There were also frequent references to former pupils, friends of Ronnie, called Bobbie and Freddie.

None of the sheets were dated. Nonetheless, by detecting clues in the text together with a process of elimination and cross reference, the boys were able to date the period of writing lasting about one month, give or take a few days. That month was from sometime in September 1995 to sometime in October 1995. Whereas there was documentary proof of the schoolmaster, nothing could be discovered to verify the existence of the other three 20th century boys - a great disappointment to the 21st century boys who faced the task of interpreting this month long conversation. With assistance from a few homosexual centenarians, contemporaries of the late Simeon Hogg, analysis and interpretation was very successful. Copious notes were taken during interviews, some of which, with permission, were recorded.

Campbell and Colt enjoyed a satisfying exploration of Simeon's life during the following two years which crowned their Academy Education and went on to occupy much of their University Education culminating in a jointly authored book entitled *Double Life.*

ACKNOWLEDGEMENTS

Most of the factual historical information in this novel was supplied by **Peter Tatchell** and **David Edgley**.

Peter Tatchell should not need an introduction. He's a real heavyweight when it comes to human rights and injustices. www.petertatchellfoundation.org'.

David Edgley is the editor of Nottinghamshire's ***Queer Bulletin***. He is also the principal driving force of Nottinghamshire's Rainbow Heritage team. Not least, David is the author of ***The History of a Lesbian and Gay Telephone Helpline*** which has always been an indispensable reference for my campaigning and writing.

David is big stuff! I often refer to him as Mr Nottingham. His presentations have been acclaimed for the entertaining, amusing and informative style we have come to enjoy in the pages of *QB* over many editions. He is also a leading light at Nottinghamshire Rainbow. Members of that team have worked hard many years improving the lives of people who share same sex attraction.

Nottinghamshire's Rainbow Heritage
7 Mansfield Road
Nottingham
NG1 3FB

Notts LGBT+ Network - 0115 934 8485

info@nottslgbt.com

www.nottsrainbowheritage.org.uk

PROOF-READERS and COPY EDITORS

PC Fred Bray is our friendly Hate Crime Monitoring Police Officer, a regular attendee at Belper Golden Rainbows. A tower of strength, his lively personality adds zest to each event, at the same time, offering practical professional advice to those of us who are in need. I thank him for the time and effort he has invested into improving this novel.

Good friend and fellow writer **Allan Morton** has played an important part in the production of *Double Life*. Apart from his valuable technical skills, he has worked hard as a publicist promoting all my efforts which carry an important LGBT message. Towards publication, Allan introduced and managed a special monthly newsletter to generate interest in *Double Life*. Readers were invited to subscribe to exclusive extracts from the new novel and have a sneak preview in advance of publication.

I am grateful for the efforts of **Tony Barker** of Nottinghamshire's Rainbow Heritage who is an experienced proof-reader and copy editor.

In Chapter 8 there is a reference to the gay anthem - **I AM WHAT I AM** from *La Cage aux folles* - August 1983. **Lyrics by Jerry Herman.**

Also in Chapter 8, Froggy raves about the popular singer Fabian Forte who was known as FABIAN. There is a reference to the 1959 hit **TIGER**. **Lyrics by Ollie Jones.**

In Chapter 9 there is a reference to - **STANDING ON THE CORNER WATCHING ALL THE GIRLS GO BY** from the 1958 musical *Most Happy Fella* - **Lyrics by Frank Loesser.**

Sea Change

A Mystery set in Derbyshire 1957 and 1958

Sea Change is a controversial story of transformation: a journey from despair to delight. Adolescence is the change from boy to man. In a sequel to *Lost Lad,* Simeon Hogg escapes from a living hell into an enchanted world of fairytale people inhabiting the nooks and crannies of deepest Derbyshire. Follow him as he transforms from a rough and miserable urchin who - *'suffers a sea-change into something rich and strange'* – as sung by Ariel, the airy spirit from *The Tempest.*

Narvel Annable has disclosed confidential, erotic and embarrassing details which many gay boys of the 1950s have taken to their graves. In this brutally honest autobiographic novel, he goes further. He revisits his Dickensian Mundy Street Boys School ordeal of sex slavery and bullying in Heanor. Cruelty has a cost. Approaching his 70s, the author is now paying the bill. Adventures set in a shadowy gay world uncover a furtive existence. Under the secretive mainstream of homosexuals is an underclass – *a taboo within a taboo.*

With the help of legislation and enlightened education, the LGBT community of the 21st century hopes these horrors, which have damaged so many, have gone forever.

This novel explodes myths and challenges conventional thinking. Whilst not condoning, it does not condemn. At the brink of self destruction, Simeon's sexual abuser becomes his saviour, persuading him, giving him courage to escape and live – rather than to stay and die in a culture where a boy was esteemed by his ability to inflict humiliation, pain and suffering on others.

Another great yarn from the storyteller of gay Derbyshire, Narvel Annable. Interwoven with references to real-life events and history, he writes a terrific mystery novel. I wish we had a Narvel in every region of England to tell such tales.

Peter Tatchell, human rights campaigner
www.PeterTatchellFoundation.org

ADULTS ONLY £10.00

Introduction to *Sea Change*

A woman asked me questions about my new book *Sea Change*. I informed her it was a sequel to *Lost Lad* in which, back in 2003, I had withheld significant details. The principal character, Guzzly Granddad, appeared in previous titles where Simeon Hogg (my character) was in his late teens. Acquainted with the old obesity with a taste for teenage boys, she expressed abhorrence at such 'disgusting behaviour'.

Granddad was not popular with some readers. This was a typical reaction. However, she exploded with outrage when told I was procured by a school bully and initiated into the old man's secret circle of urchins at the tender age of 12. His Dickensian kitchen was conveniently near Mundy Street Boys School in 1957. Eyes blazing, mouth spitting fire -

'I'd take a knife to that lump of lard and castrate him! I'd do it myself. I would. I would. I mean it. I mean it.'

Shocked by this barbaric hatred, I tried to explain the aim of this novel – don't cut off goolies – cut off the supply of boys. *Sea Change* will not condone men who incite boys into sexual activity. Readers are asked to take a step back and consider the big picture. The aim of this book is to slay mythology surrounding paedophilia. The second aim is to explore the folklore of Derbyshire through the eyes of an isolated runaway fleeing an intolerable situation. The third aim (up close and personal) was summed up by Helen Meynell in a *Derby Telegraph* feature about *Secret Summer*, September 24th 2010 -

'His books and campaigns are Narvel's way of assuaging the guilt he feels for keeping quiet for so long. Writing has been cathartic and therapeutic helping him through a lot of emotions.'

Make no mistake – men having sex with children is always wrong – full stop. That said, there is much hysteria and nonsense regarding paedophilia. It is said boys fondled by adults are permanently damaged. We are told they grow up unable to enjoy relationships.

I am living proof this is not the case.

Notwithstanding – I *am* damaged.

In the culture of cruelty at Mundy Street Boys School in Heanor, Derbyshire; you were esteemed by your ability to inflict humiliation, pain and suffering on others. As the following extract from *Sea Change* will show, in such a brutal regime, my status was rock bottom.

'Piggy was too frightened to use the school toilet. Mortifying incidents had made Mundy Street lavatory a no-go area for a boy who grew up to be a badly constipated man. Word went around the playground – 'Hog's on t' bog'. A crowd gathered to enjoy the sport. Alarmingly, several times, unknown assailants kicked the door causing panic! Violent kicks - loud bangs - *terrifying* bangs! Within that small cubicle, distressing percussion reverberated with no escape. A quick bolt would result in certain capture by a crazed mob thirsty for blood. Objects were thrown over the top. Taunting abuse through the gap below complemented a monstrous act of torture.'

On several occasions I arrived home with soiled underpants. My mother, unsympathetic, could not cope. In sad resignation, she slowly shook her head. I can hear her now –

'You *make* work for me.'

I planned an act of self-destruction, yet words like 'immoral' and 'abhorrent' are used to describe the man who warned against such an act. He saved my life. It is subjective. In that old coalminer's primitive kitchen, after initial coercion, I became a willing party to erotic play organised by an adult. At Mundy Street Boys School, effectively, I was a sex slave with no choice. A miserable child was pressed into service pleasuring powerful pupils.

The more culpable villain is the sadistic schoolmaster. He choreographed classroom situations in which I suffered excruciating humiliations. They wreaked emotional damage which will follow me to the grave. To this day, I endure vivid flashbacks, intrusive thoughts causing distress which still disturbs my sleep. If not branded into my flesh with a hot iron, the traumas inflicted by that ruthless Church of England regime are burnt into my psyche. Cruelty has a cost. Approaching my 70s, I am now paying the bill.

Hardly to be recommended - yet it was not the gentle touches of an old man who drove me to wish for death. It was the relentless emotional brutality which will forever be associated with a pious, scripture-obsessed ayatollah of a headmaster. He presided over a bleak midwinter of daily torment where the greatest sin was to 'tell tales'. Result – I bottled up my stress for more than half a century until the emotional problems became deeply ingrained. Until the start of this book in 2010, these highly toxic Mundy Street traumas have never been discussed with anybody or treated by any professional.

Remove that academy of atrocities, and you would have removed the steady supply of frightened children to the nearby scullery of a child molester. *Sea Change* invites you to examine the *big* picture. Don't string up my old Granddad who was kind; sack the headmaster and his monstrous teacher who was so skilfully grooming the barbarous school thugs. That is the 'grooming' to be concerned about. Here in the 21st century - children kill themselves to escape bullying.

In December 1957, I had *nowhere* to go. My unfeeling parents took the view that I *deserved* unhappiness, pain and all the opprobrium I had brought down on my own head due to my own perverse nature.

It must be said, in the material sense, Narvel was always well cared for. However, in December 1957, I discerned the beginnings of character assassination originating from disappointed parents and two older sisters. As *Sea Change* will show - bad press, disinformation, lies and a merciless machinery of denigration was spreading like osmosis, like a virus remorselessly through family channels infecting ignorant family friends with a strong predisposition to rabid homophobia. It was an uncompromising mindset towards the most negative view of an unsatisfactory son. They trashed my life.

They always said – 'Hit them back!' I'm fighting now. I'm fighting with pen and keyboard - but I couldn't fight then. Male Annables were fighters giving a good account of themselves with bare knuckles in the school playground. I dishonoured the family. I was the boy who didn't like football. In working-class, coal-mining Heanor, this was unheard of! Unacceptable – sissy - mardy - queer!

I couldn't spell, do sums and sank to the bottom of the class in most other subjects. That *might* have been forgiven had I displayed any practicable ability – of which there was none. Rough Heanor lads were supposed to make things. I made nothing. Tortured children tend to do badly in school. And I *do* mean tortured! The Narvel of December 1957 was broken, scarred, and will take his injuries to the grave.

This despised lover of boys, this mysterious Heanorian of no name who hid his face in the shadows; he was the *only* person to show compassion and offer practical help during that dire period of late 1957. Hearing of my plan to commit suicide, he was horrified.

'Nay, lad! Ya moant [must not] do that. Life's precious. A dead boy can do nought. A live boy can do something. Why don't you run away?'

Kind words spoken by a man reviled and detested by the majority. Thinking about the grubby harem which dominated my little world 57 years ago, I recall the equally detested Good Samaritan who was the only passer-by to aid a man who had been beaten and robbed. It should also be remembered that unloved children desperate for affection and respect will respond to kindness offered from anyone outside the immediate family. At my Church of England School, I developed a hatred for all things religious and, at that tender age, was unlikely to receive grooming from any paedophilic cleric. That said, I believe the sexual scandals which have come to light in recent years were initiated by untold numbers of miserable children, like me, seeking sympathy and understanding from a compassionate man of the cloth.

Reader be warned! Some passages in this book are harrowing. Publication in 2014 means this novel has been under construction since 2010 when *Secret Summer* was published. If harrowing to read, you can be sure it has been painful to write over these past five years. A 12-year-old reduced to a mindset of self-annihilation is terrible thing. You have to be there to know what it's really like when death is the only escape from an intolerable situation. Actual suicide was halted by fear of failure. The second floor window over 4 Red Lion Square in Heanor was judged not high enough to assure oblivion. Years later, I heard about gay boys snuffing their lives by means of a gun in the mouth. If Sam Annable had owned such a weapon, with its guarantee of certain success, this book would not exist.

I have revisited *Lost Lad* to make a more detailed description of the horrific events in December 1957 at Mundy Street Boys School. In the eleven years since the publication of *Lost Lad*, hopefully, I have become a better writer and able to do justice to an account of the darkest days of my life.

In the book, I explore a possible link between carnal activities in Granddad's kitchen and the sexual atmosphere which pervaded the classroom and playground of that nearby homoerotic school. I was never quite sure which other boys had knowledge of the secret sect. The older boys were more than usually infused with titillating interest often masked by high spirits, mock combat and frisky fun. In rough packs, I often saw the style and method of that rude old man who was there in spirit – if not in the flesh.

One of the most feared toughs was a frequent visitor to Granddad's gatherings. I suspect he was instructed to 'go easy' on me and use his network of terror to subdue the mob. This would explain the small improvement in January 1958 – a situation which could be described as less agonizing, less traumatic.

I fully understand the arguments against sexual exploitation. There are real dangers arising from an imbalance of power and control between a child and a man. Those same dangers exist between any child and any guardian irrespective of carnal desire. For example, the perverted schoolmaster with his non-sexual vicious streak was the very person who was supposed to protect me! Without mercy, he was the sadist who inspired in the rabble a frisson of sadistic pleasure.

We must get away from appalling hysteria characterised by ignorant mediaeval-minded people calling for sudden surgery on a man who – however undesirable - became my friend and saviour.

This friend gave me a 'road map' to a future which did not include cruel bullies, a monstrous schoolmaster and frosty parents who did not want me anyway. Before Christmas 1957, I had something new. I had hope. For the first time, I had tasted happiness in a clandestine community where, for the most part, I was valued and treated well.

In the humble terraced home of Guzzly Granddad, I never considered myself a *victim* of sexual abuse. At the Boys School I was certainly a victim of cruel conduct, abuse from a heartless master who should never have been allowed near children. Whilst taking care not to portray this Dickensian kitchen as an ideal environment for young boys, my book challenges language which supports and reinforces common prejudices.

Over the last 38 years, I have enjoyed a loving relationship with a man, Terry Durand, now my Civil Partner. Distasteful it might be to some readers, I held a genuine affection for my 'Granddad'. At the same time, I was able to concede the reality of that old man's erotic predation. I was not fooled, but, in my opinion, I was more *used* than abused.

My child-like love and loyalty was freely given as a vulnerable rejected child rescued from desperation, very nearly an act of self-destruction. Initial barriers of revulsion from the touch of an ugly, ancient pile of flesh had been overcome by a network of camaraderie and fellowship from other boys, some of them feral, in the child-sex secret cell.

As with previous titles, nearly all names in *Sea Change* (even nick-names) have been changed. Like previous titles, it is autobiographic, a blend of fact and fiction – essentially telling a true story. The following events took place in real places peopled by a fictitious cast. The following caricatured composites were inspired by a selection of the characters I met nearly 60 years ago. However real flesh and blood the original model, who ends up on these pages (after being processed through my brain) is far from being a real person – alive or dead.

Lost Lad mentioned nothing of this covert club. Why? In deciding to expose this grim chapter of my life, this bleak mid-winter of 1957; I needed to examine reasons for a half century of silence. In many ways it was much to do with a familiar journey made by many who share same-sex attraction.

I hid in a dark well locked closet in fear of being exposed, embarrassed and humiliated. Born into a macho, football crazy, working class, coal mining culture; homophobia was not just endemic, it was almost a badge of honour with some people. A thief, thug or murderer would be afforded more respect than a gentle, honest homosexual. After suffering painful incidents, I learned to exist in isolation and stay deeply hidden inside myself.

In the dying years of the 20th century and early years of the 21st century, gay progress in the form of a better press and slow decline in homophobia made it possible to be a little more open about the reasons for being a bachelor. Little-by-little, constantly testing the water, I was always ready to make a quick retreat.

It was one thing to *be* homosexual, another thing to *tell* people about it – and worse, much worse, to *write* about it! In the same way, it could be said - it was one thing admitting sexual contact with boys my own age - another thing to reveal sexual activity with a man old enough to be my grandfather. Such an admission would attract a higher level of embarrassment and disapproval.

As with the heterosexual majority, the gay community tended to disdain carnal relationships with old men, especially those who were seen as a 'danger to boys'.

These were the reasons for the long silence. In addition there were reasons for breaking that silence. For the record, I wanted to place the responsibility for prepubescent misery and near death firmly at the door of Mundy Street Boys School with its entrenched callousness. I wanted to challenge unreasoned panic associated with the taboo subject of paedophilia. The activities of Guzzly Granddad represented a *taboo within a taboo.* He and his friends were an underclass of boy hunters leading a furtive existence subsumed underneath the already clandestine underclass of mainstream homosexuals.

Granddad's regular visitors used familiar shouts and whistling in the dark to inform that all's well, a device probably borrowed from his colliery experience. Paedophilia and coal mining shared a common danger. Safety–first, team work, trust and eternal vigilance were essential to ward off potential disaster.

His very name was an inspired choice for security. In the classroom and playground, I often heard references to Granddad. But then, didn't we all have a granddad?

Across three titles biographically exploring my personal encounters in the 1960s, three groups of homosexuals are identified. On top - the professional men, the sneering snobs of stately demeanour affecting upper-class accents enforcing a safe social distance from the 'lower orders'.

The lower orders included bizarre types inhabiting a sleazy underworld of public lavatories such as Toby Jug, Nobby the Gnome, Mr Toad, the Gutter-Gobbler and the Belper Goblin. Yet this assortment of crude characters were united in carnal desire to taste the flesh of young men who were certainly *men* – well into their teens and well past the stage of adolescence.

The third group, such as Guzzly Granddad and his 'bum chums', was a minority occupying a highly secretive, covert invisible space below more conventional members of the gay community. For perspective, it should not be forgotten that before 1967, at any age, all homosexuality was illegal in the UK. Transgressors risked more than a jail sentence. Violent inmates with a homophobic disposition inflicted their own unspeakable punishments on men whose only crime was to share same-sex attraction.

The paedophile circle into which I entered, as a traumatised child, was enjoyable and supportive. Accordingly, as in previous novels the autobiographic text will include erotic episodes. It will be honest, frank and graphic - but will not stray into the sordid or prurient. It is not intended to be a bawdy book. It will gain strength from *between* the lines, from the unspoken and the subtle. Those lines are not intended to titillate readers disposed to exploit children. This book is the true story of *my* experience – how I was procured for Guzzly Granddad, advised to abandon a plan of suicide and run away – get away from unsympathetic, ignorant homophobic parents who, in 1957, could not stand the sight of me. This flight was followed by adventures composited from encounters with a child trafficking network. Mab was inspired by a real woman. Fairytale Castle was a real place somewhere in Britain by the sea and Edward was inspired by a real man. This is my story, a story only partly told in *Lost Lad.*

As in *Lost Lad*, Mary McLening and Doris Cook are specially honoured by appearing under their own names. Their compassion and kindness is recorded in these pages for posterity.

It has been suggested to me that Granddad and his pals might not have been so gentle and understanding. Pederasts are like everybody else. They come in categories of good, bad and all gradations in between. For me, fortunately it was good. It could easily have been otherwise. Rape is an act of violence - humiliating violence at that. Nothing of that kind has ever happened to me. Accordingly, I am disinclined to condemn people who delivered me safely back to the world of the living.

Arthur C Clarke made an important point about the link between child sex and emotional damage. I kept my mouth shut and was spared the fuss made by irate parents who discover their boy has been, as is often put, 'touched up' by a man. In my case, no questions were asked because Mr and Mrs Annable did not want answers from a son who was unsatisfactory in the first place. At least in that, I did not suffer further abuse and more psychological devastation from *respectable* heterosexuals who would have put my friends in prison and smugly nod satisfaction when they were beaten to a pulp by queer-bashing inmates.

If you seek enlightenment, read my book - but don't expect me to name names. In a hidden world of extreme secrecy, in the thick smog laden days of December 1957; everybody had nicknames. Guzzly Granddad and Edward were survivors. To the best of my knowledge, they died in their beds.

Narvel Annable

First Review of Sea Change

They say that every story has been told and new ones are just variations of old ones, but this is the first book I have come across that makes 'heroes' of 'outcasts' and challenges long held, deep prejudices.

Not many people would dare to write about such a taboo, but Narvel Annable has done so in the best way possible by making it part of an intriguing and challenging 'true life' story – his story. This is a sometimes harrowing account, portraying real people with real feelings and real dilemmas amid real intolerance and real dangers. He has lifted the lid on a secret world which open-minded people will find irresistible.

Life for 12-year-old gay boy Simeon is so bad that he contemplates suicide. But he finds a friend in 'Guzzly Granddad', a paedophile who helps him escape a life of torment in a Derbyshire mining town without pity. On his journey to freedom, Simeon meets others who live secret lives, discovering love, courage and kindness in their twilight world.

The account of Simeon's transition from unwanted, bullied boy to confident adult is moving and inspiring, and furthers the cause of compassion and understanding for people who are perceived to be 'different'.

To say the author struggled at school, this is brilliant writing; a powerful story with a challenging message.

Robert Anthony
Freelance Journalist

Second Review of Sea Change

Heartbreak Hotel by Elvis Presley was still bellowing out from Milk Bar jukeboxes in 1957 and through 1958 - the period for which Narvel Annable's latest novel *Sea Change* is set. It's more like *Heartbreak Heanor* though, as that *Six-Five Special steamin' down the line* is taking us on a rocky rollercoaster of real emotions. From fear and despair to love and understanding; from a culture of cruelty to one of kindness.

Hold on tight as we travel through deepest darkest seediest Derbyshire, out through treacherous snow, into mysterious magical woods and then out again as far as Scotland (or is it?). With your trusty Cresta Deluxe rucksack crammed with essentials and your fleece-lined bomber-jacket, you won't go far wrong.

This challenging ride is not for the faint hearted however, so be warned, but the reward lies in the magic of Narvel's writing and the journey he takes you on as you feel you are transported to the there and then…even though sometimes you'd really rather not be. *Sea Change* is the transformation of a poor, bullied and abused boy into something rich and strange, and *Oh Boy!* a story with characters that you will never forget.

Allan Morton Local Writer

About the Author

Narvel Annable's *Heanor Schooldays* (1998) was autobiographic, covering his unhappiness in a grim, gas-lit, Dickensian, Church of England junior school from 1955 to 1958. Adolescence and the move to William Howitt Secondary Modern School, "A culture of kindness", in September, 1958, was a dramatic improvement, graphically retold in the second half of the social history.

In 1963 he emigrated to the United States and arrived in Detroit on the day before the assassination of President Kennedy. The next seven years saw him in a variety of jobs which included labourer, lathe-hand, bank messenger and camera salesman. In 1975 he graduated from Eastern Michigan University (magna cum laude) and taught African American History for a year at St Bridget High School in Detroit.

In 1976 he returned to Derbyshire to help organise and launch 'Heritage Education Year 1977' at Sudbury Hall. From 1978 to 1995 he taught history at the Valley Comprehensive School in Worksop which gradually became more progressive. Narvel criticises these changes in some detail in his first two books. Seizing retirement at the earliest opportunity, he started to write historical and educational articles for the local Press and has been interviewed several times on BBC Radio Derby and BBC Radio Nottingham. BBC Radio Manchester and Sheffield also invited Narvel to discuss his writing and campaigning. BBC Radio Leicester asked serious questions about *Scruffy Chicken* in 2006.

Death on the Derwent - A Murder Mystery set in Belper 1949, his third book and first novel, was published in 1999. His fourth book, *A Judge Too Far* - A Biography of His Honour Judge Keith Matthewman QC of the Nottingham Crown Court, was published in 2001.

Inspired by *Heanor Schooldays*, Mr Annable's second 'whodunit' novel and fifth book *Lost Lad* A Mystery set in Derbyshire in 1960 (ISBN 0 9530419 6 4) was published in

2003. His sixth book *Scruffy Chicken* A Derbyshire Mystery set in 1965 (ISBN 0 9530419 4 8) was published in 2006. *Secret Summer* A Derbyshire Mystery set in 1966 – was published by The Nazca Plains Corporation in Las Vegas in 2010.

Sea Change (the *real* truth behind *Lost Lad*) was published in 2014.

Double Life was published in 2019

Narvel lives with his husband Terry Durand in Belper, Derbyshire. In September 2019 they celebrated their 43 years together.

LOST LAD

In the glorious summer of 1960, six pals from William Howitt Secondary Modern School in the hilltop mining town of Heanor, decide to cycle up into the high Derbyshire hills. They have a great time. Everything goes well - until they cycle out of the village of Litton, along a narrow country lane and speedily descend the 550ft steep drop into a deep, wooded ravine which is called Water-cum-Jolly-Dale. Six boys were happily racing down the hill, but only five reach the bottom!

In the following hours, the boys make a thorough search for their friend - in vain. Eventually the police are called in and make a careful professional search - in vain. Where is the lost lad?

Forty-three years pass and one of the original pals who has spent most of his adult life in the United States returns to England to re-open the search. An odyssey develops which takes many twists and turns around the lives of different men, some of whom can hardly recognise each other four decades on. An investigation which turns lives upside-down. A quest which eventually comes to a dramatic and stunning conclusion when we finally learn the devastating truth about - the *'Lost Lad'*.

This is an autobiographic, sometimes comic, sometimes erotic psychological thriller; a 'rollercoaster of emotions' from the depths of despair to the heights of happiness. Along the way, Narvel Annable skilfully blending fact and fiction, reveals a secret history and vividly recreates the gritty realities of his youth on both sides of the Atlantic. A local story of long-lost friendship and a Derbyshire travelogue which combines elements of folklore, legend and quirky, crooked old men who inhabit the murky depths of a sleazy underworld. It is all set against the magnificent moody backdrop of a 'howling wilderness', spectacular ravines and lush green valleys. This entertaining and ingenious whodunit will take you through the recesses, nooks and crannies of a life, which, for many years, lay hidden behind the mask of a stern and respectable schoolmaster.

Lost Lad Reviews

"Intriguing. We are made to wait nearly half a century before Narvel finally reveals to us the secret of his devilishly clever conjuring trick. *Lost Lad* is an entertaining, interesting and well constructed novel. It'll be a real eye opener to the folk of Derbyshire.

"I've never featured in a mystery thriller before. I've enjoyed every minute of it."

John Holmes, BBC Radio Nottingham

"Written by a guy who so obviously loves this county of ours, the novel's Derbyshire backdrop is spectacular. It is a blend of fact with fiction and is packed with characters and events which many of you may find familiar.

"*Lost Lad* is a fantastic read. We at the Cash Project have no hesitation in recommending it to you."

Gary Woodhouse, *The Bent Spire*, Chesterfield. Easter 2005

"*Lost Lad* is written with conviction. In its way, it works quite well, and canters along at a reasonable pace. It's just that, the world unlidded for us here strikes an innocent like me as loathsomely tacky. But that at least underscores Narvel Annable's competence in bringing the more revolting characters so horribly to life! All in all, it is an odd book, and, for all I know, epoch-making for its genre."

Maxwell Craven, *Derby Evening Telegraph*, 13.02.04

"Here's a thriller for the fireside. Narvel Annable's easy style, coupled with local knowledge, makes this an entertaining read and will have the reader determined to find out what happened to the lost lad."

Judith Halliday, *Derbyshire Today*, December 2003

"Annable's prose is generally excellent - evocative without being torturous. It is sharp and witty. His characters are well observed and the story - on the whole - unfolds well. Narvel Annable is undoubtedly a talented author."

Mark Michalowski, *SHOUT!* March 2004

"The narrative seamlessly blends fact and fantasy, vividly recreating scenes from a tough and sometimes sleazy youth. The story follows the fates of six friends and the investigation which lays bare their fears and weaknesses, building to a dramatic final twist."

Ian Soutar *Sheffield Telegraph* 10.09.04

"An interesting tale in which truth and fiction are cleverly blurred."

***Derbyshire Life and Countryside* December 2003**

"Some very strange 'goings on'. Narvel Annable weaves his narrative, carefully travelling from the Derbyshire Dales to the urban landscapes of America, and back, through a minefield of intrigue and mystery before the story reaches the final conclusion."

Keith How, *Peak Advertiser* 03.11.03

"It offers a unique insight into the former history teacher's life. The story takes us back to a Dickensian style school which almost drove Mr Annable to suicide. A word of warning: some of the action is not for the fainthearted and is more suitable for adults than children."

James Mitchinson, *Worksop Guardian* 17.10.03

"Compulsive reading for those who have grown up in Derbyshire, but also for anyone who enjoys a good mystery."

Emily Davies, *Ilkeston Advertiser* 30.10.03

"Lost Lad reveals Narvel's lifelong passion for cycling along leafy lanes and his appreciation of natural beauty. The spirit and atmosphere of the novel is cleverly captured by the Shipley Park artist Lesley Robinson."

Pauline Oldrini, ***Belper News*** **and the** ***Ripley and Heanor News*** **30.10.03**

"An entertaining and gritty mystery of a missing cyclist."

Jonathan Dodds, ***Buxton Advertiser*** **19.12.03**

Lost Lad is available as an electronic book at Amazon. It can be ordered from bookshops or directly from the author by sending a cheque for £10.00 to - 44 Dovedale Crescent, Belper, Derbyshire DE56 1HJ.

Scruffy Chicken

A Mystery set in Derbyshire 1965

The year is 1965. Outside, it is dull, wet and cold. Inside the steam room of the Derby Turkish Baths, it is a hissing haze of hot, gurgling, boiling anger, a chamber of pea soup where visibility is down to an arm's length. Dimly seen, a man is resting in the corner, head lolling back, eyes closed, pleasantly soaking up the heat - or so it seems. Various bathers come and go. All regulars, they all know this ugly, effeminate man who frequently secludes himself in his usual corner. They all know the outrageous, the common Becksitch Betty, the local drag act, the acid queen who has inflamed so many passions in the nervous, closeted, gay communities of Derby and Nottingham. Nobody wants to bother this infamous bitch, left to doze in swirls of vapour, left to doze in a miasma of his twisted hate and jealousy.

It was the very last time this hated old hag was ever seen. Nobody saw him dress and nobody saw him leave the building. Becksitch Betty never returned to his mean little cottage in Belper and was never, ever heard of again ... until ... On July 12th in the year 2005, Simeon Hogg is celebrating his 60th birthday. By a fluke, he stumbles upon the truth and solves the old mystery of the disappearance of the infamous, the long-past Becksitch Betty. That same ugly old queen Simeon once knew when he was a scruffy chicken forty years before.

Narvel Annable delivers yet another cracking autobiographic whodunit, which begins in Detroit on the day before the assassination of President Kennedy. Eventually, it takes us into deepest Derbyshire, into a bitchy underworld of crones, queens, toads, goblins, gnomes, feral boys and social-climbing snobs of the mid-1960's - finally concluding just days after the appalling London bombings of '7/7'.

Follow the candid teenage Simeon as he cycles. Meander with him around the leafy lanes of Derbyshire and discovers a labyrinth; a secret, subterranean, fairytale world which could have been penned by Grimm. Meet his unique collection of curious characters, all taking shelter in their twilight existence; monsters, clowns, the high and the low, the pretentious and the pompous, the scented and the sneering, the common and the crude. They are all here, all inspired by real people, all warped by the vicious homophobic cruelty and bigotry of 1965.

***Scruffy Chicken* Reviews**

"A rare pleasure I never thought I'd see: a gay thriller set in Derbyshire."

Matthew Parris of *The Times*

"An excellent book by Narvel Annable! This novel is superb in that it describes the somewhat 'hidden' Gay history of the 1960s. I believe we should not forget what, for many of us, our forefathers experienced. *Scruffy Chicken* documents both the attitudes of the times and the experience of living in a society which derided and negated the lives of Gay men. Annable has created a masterpiece documenting much of our non recorded Gay history.

"It is his second Gay semi-autobiographical novel, and captures life in the mid 1960s, not only here in the UK but also in the USA, a definite first for this type of novel.

"Set in both Detroit and Derbyshire it chronicles the very 'misspent' youth of a Gay young man as he stumbles towards adulthood. The journey, which is essentially what it is, features some rather strange people in extremely bizarre situations. Annable manages to interweave an ingenious mystery as part of the plot, the disappearance of 'Becksitch Betty' a rather nasty drag Queen cum washed up stage act. Not surprisingly, most of the bizarre characters come under some form of suspicion!

"To describe the book as 'a novel' is somewhat disingenuous, it brilliantly documents the homophobia, fear and clear hatred faced by Gay men in the early to mid sixties and cleverly manages to transport the reader to those less tolerant times.

"The journey of Simeon Hogg – the book's central character, and Annable's alter ego – begins in Detroit in 1963, and beautifully describes Simeon's observations – of both Gay life here and 'stateside'.

"The encounters with the 60s Gay underworld will be enlightening for anyone under forty yet very real to those for whom Queer life was so different to today. The Derbyshire, Detroit and Nottinghamshire 'scenes' are vividly portrayed together with the local dialect and it hard to imagine that some of the bizarre characters in the story ever really existed – thankfully, they did!

"*Scruffy Chicken* depicts a time when homosexuality was illegal and as such this alone makes for a darker story. If you are looking for titillation this is not the book for you, although the life experiences, sexual and other are well documented.

"I can truly say this is one of the best books I have ever read and a must for all Gay men, whatever age.

"*Scruffy Chicken* is a real tour de force of a read!"

Paul Hunt, Chief Features Writer - *Shout!* - Yorkshire's Gay Paper, March 2007

"In a quaint old library deep in middle England, a coming of age story is unfolding, casting light in some dark corners of the gay world. The tale being told is sad, sometimes cruel and oftentimes laughing-out loud funny. Local author Narvel Annable, a retired schoolteacher, is creatively portraying characters from his most recent novel, *Scruffy Chicken*, which is inspired by his own story.

"The big picture is about a wide-eyed teenager guided on an erotic adventure tour of Turkish baths and active toilets by a series of unlikely hosts, discovering along the way how discriminatory attitudes have driven some gays to despair and isolation.

"Annable also chronicles discriminatory traits within the gay community itself, including gay on gay abuse in which elderly and unattractive gays are targeted. It is a study of contrasts, old verses young, pristine countryside beauty versus smelly toilet-side fixations and beautiful bodies versus stooped, toothless, lopsided forms.

"Tonight the audience in Derby Central Library is mesmerised by Annable's acting ability. By turns he is an adventurous chicken, ugly troll, vicious queen and arrogant, upper-class pretender. But the most interesting characters are the tormented, unattractive gays Annable encounters during his travels.

"The talk concludes with enthusiastic applause and a very civilised serving of wine amidst introductions and handshakes."

Brad Teeter was writing about his evening at the Derby Central Library on February 21st 2007. It was printed on May 9th 2007 in Vancouver's Lesbian and Gay Biweekly *EXTRA! West* www.xtra.ca British Columbia, Canada.

Scruffy Chicken **is available as an electronic book at Amazon. It can be ordered from bookshops or directly from the author. Send a cheque for £10 to Narvel Annable - 44 Dovedale Crescent Belper Derby DE56 1HJ. Or phone 01 773 82 44 83.**

Secret Summer

A Mystery set in Derbyshire 1966

Here is a heartrending tale of young love. Narvel Annable reaches down into the joys and sorrows of his past to produce an autobiographic account of adventure, passion and pain. A cracking whodunit; it features a missing person and contract killers from the unforgiving criminal underworld of Detroit. Barely out of his teens, Simeon is homesick for his beloved Derbyshire, but falls in love with a mysterious tough-guy called Ahmed. The storyline explores a mixture of magic and menace following two incompatible personalities, desperately trying to make their relationship work in the homophobic landscape of Detroit, January 1966.

Why secret? Because when you are young, when you are in love and if you are gay in 1966 - it must be secret. You lust in secret, hunt in secret and love in secret. See Simeon in love; a rollercoaster, a frantic mixture of agony and ecstasy spanning the Atlantic Ocean. He has no support save for that which was available from the frequently unreliable world of gay men who were riddled with all their own personal problems, repressions and hang-ups.

Signed copies of *Secret Summer* are available directly from the author.

To include P&P, please send a £10 cheque payable to Narvel Annable at 44 Dovedale Crescent, Belper, Derby DE56 1HJ. Phone: 01 773 82 44 83.

"Another quirky corker in the Derbyshire mystery series from the irrepressible Narvel Annable. A Boy's Own story from 1966; it is a most entertaining read."

Peter Tatchell

Reviews of *Secret Summer*

Review from Bradford's *Telegraph & Argus* printed on April 16th 2011

Inspired by a cycling holiday, this is a moving portrayal of a young gay man on the run and ostracised in the 1960s.

Bullied as a child and an adult, Narvel Annable has endured the agony of being treated as an outsider simply because he is gay. He was a guest speaker at an International Day Against Homophobia event in Bradford in 2009 and was nominated for an Equity Partnership award last year. Narvel describes writing his novel as a cathartic experience helping him to deal with painful memories.

Partly set in Bradford, the townscape and terrain of the metropolis is described as –

'A splendid panorama of pinnacles and finials. Most notable was the distinctive Italianate clock tower of the City Hall and the ornate Venetian Gothic parapets and pinnacles of the Wool Exchange. They reminded Simeon [Narvel's alter ego] of an ancient fairytale castle.'

Simeon also discovers Bradford Cathedral and is delighted by its tranquil, peaceful 'secret garden'.

At its heart, *Secret Summer* is a touching story of young love, laced with a well-paced thriller involving a missing person and a gay criminal underworld. It is also a love letter to Narvel's native Derbyshire with beautifully written passages devoted to its natural landscape.

Emma Clayton

Five Star www.amazon.com Review of *Secret Summer* from the Chief Features Writer of *Shout!* Magazine – Paul Hunt – December 31st 2010

Superb - A Must Read!!!

This book really does have it all; joy, pain, sadness and comedy, not to mention true pathos.

I found the characters very 'real' although I do appreciate it is a semi-autobiographical novel.

The book takes you on a historical journey to life before the decriminalisation of homosexuality. The author manages, very skilfully, to explore and convey the sexual, emotional and psychological awakening of Simeon, the central character, and relates in superb narrative those who shape his future.

This book is an excellent read – you may laugh, you may cry, but you will undoubtedly want to explore Narvel Annable's other books!

Nottinghamshire's *Queer Bulletin* - Number 57 – December 2010 / January 2011 – page 5.

See the original on Nottinghamshire's Rainbow Heritage website - www.nottsrainbowheritage.org.uk

Detroit to Derbyshire via the Mafia, Freaks and Young Love

This is the third semi-autobiographical novel to feature young Simeon Hogg. Firstly set in Detroit where he gets involved in a complex, somewhat abusive relationship with a young man linked to a pink mafia. He literally escapes back to his native Derbyshire. Fearful for his life, Simeon goes on the run (well, actually on the pedal) as he cycles through Derbyshire and Yorkshire.

The hidden, secretive, often furtive world is reflected in encounters with some oddball characters who appear in Narvel's previous books, but also with others who anticipated the era of Gay Liberation. We meet – amongst others – Mr Toad, Droopy the Vesuvius vacuum cleaner, Fluff and Nobby the Gnome.

It's history, it's travelogue, it's crime, it's sex (quite a lot of), it's a love story and it's another good read.

If you want a signed copy of *Secret Summer*, you can get one directly from the author by going to his website at – **www.narvelannable.co.uk**

Review / feature from the *Belper News* - October 6th 2010 – www.belpernews.co.uk

Gay author's book published in the USA

Literature can be appreciated by so many different people. It can bring them together, make them laugh and make them cry. In many instances it can even serve to break down negative views and stereotypes.

A book written by a retired man from Belper, quite easily accomplishes all of the above – and more.

Not only is *Secret Summer* the first of Narvel Annable's novels to be professionally published, it is the first to reach audiences in America.

Narvel has achieved what so many British celebrities have tried to do and failed - he has made it in America. The book was snapped up by The Nazca Plains Corporation situated in the bright lights of Las Vegas.

Although this book has more than enough exciting twists and turns to stand alone as a truly gripping fictional read, it also has a very important message – that people's lives can be ruined by the attitudes of others.

Secret Summer is not just a must for the gay community – it also celebrates the beautiful Belper countryside and the surrounding towns and villages are given several mentions. It celebrates Narvel's love of the area.

Katy Hallam

Review of *Secret Summer* from Tony Fenwick Co-Chair of LGBT History Month – www.lgbthistorymonth.org - and **Schools OUT** – www.schools-out.org – January 12th 2011.

In many ways, Narvel Annable's *Secret Summer* is a very different novel. It follows the fortunes and misfortunes of a young Simeon Hogg in the 1960s.

Born and bred in the mining towns of industrial Derbyshire, Simeon moves to Detroit, where he is swept off his feet and taken into a whole new world by the sinister Ahmed, who has abducted the boy and shows his love by taking possessiveness to a whole new level.

Simeon is waited upon and lavished upon and given a complete new life and identity, but he is homesick for Belper and he knows that if he ever crosses Ahmed his life might be in danger. So he plans his escape and the physically repulsive but well-endowed Mr Toad becomes his temporary saviour in the Derbyshire countryside.

There's no cocaine fuelled evenings in the bars and clubs in *Secret Summer*. The novel is a mystery, but the beauty of it is that it gives us a rich insight into what it was like to be a young gay man in the US and in the East Midlands in 1966. Simeon is based on Narvel himself. The colourful and often grotesque locals he describes are real people from his past; only the names have been changed. Moreover, it shows us how people in these times coped with being outcasts and outlaws just because of whom they loved.

Review / feature from the *Derby Telegraph* - September 24th 2010 – www.thisisderbyshire.co.uk

A celebration of Derbyshire as 'pink mafia' go on the rampage

When it comes to gay thrillers set in Derbyshire, author Narvel Annable seems to have cornered the market.

Secret Summer begins in Detroit in 1966. Simeon Hogg is imprisoned by his lover Ahmed, in a luxurious apartment funded by a gay criminal underworld described as a 'pink mafia'. Eventually he manages to escape with a friend, Gary, and the pair return to Simeon's native Derbyshire, where he discovers a thriving gay scene in Matlock's caves. But the mafia are hot on their heels and Gary disappears. Simeon goes on the run cycling around youth hostels under an assumed name.

Narvel is a committed campaigner and his latest book is part of that campaign. *Secret Summer* teaches the heterosexual majority what it is like to be an ostracized minority. His books and campaigns are Narvel's way of assuaging the guilt he feels for keeping quiet for so long. But *Secret Summer* will not just appeal to gay readers; it's a celebration of Derbyshire too.

Helen Meynell

Review from the *Sheffield Star* printed on March 14th 2011

Next time you're browsing a book shop looking for a gay thriller based in Derbyshire, you could do worse that think of Narvel Annable.

The former Worksop Valley Comprehensive teacher's third novel in his 'pink whodunit' trilogy released in the UK by The Nazca Plains Corporation in Las Vegas.

Depicting a flourishing gay scene in Matlock caves and a homosexual Mafia, *Secret Summer* follows on from Narvel's previous efforts *Lost Lad* and *Scruffy Chicken*.

Colin Drury

Review from the *Harrogate Advertiser* printed on May 6th 2011

This dramatic story crosses the Atlantic. It follows Annable's own experiences, eventually bringing his lead character, Simeon, to Harrogate. He meets Big Bill Bulman, an obese American based on Bill Silvey, whom Annable met in 1966.

Bill was living at the Old Swan Hotel and was a regular visitor to the Royal Baths. Annable describes him as a colourful character who enthused about the town in a roaring Deep South accent and thinks many other people who were in the area at the time will probably remember him.

Vicky Carr

Review / feature from *Shout!* November 2010 www.shoutweb.co.uk

The secret of summer

Shout!'s favourite author, has finally arrived. The Nazca Plains Corporation of Las Vegas, a major American publishing house, is hoping to have Narvel Annable's latest novel, *Secret Summer*, on bookshelves around the world.

Paul Hunt

Comments about *Secret Summer* from Councillor Robin Wood – November 3rd 2010

Robin is a former Mayor of the City of Derby. His partner was the venerable Jeffery Tillett [1927-2008] also a former Mayor in 1977 when the Queen granted Derby city status. During their 37 years together, Robin and Jeffery made a huge contribution, cautiously yet bravely improving the quality of life for the Derby LGBT community.

"I thoroughly enjoyed reading *Secret Summer*. It brought back some memories and, curiously, memories of things Jeff used to tell me decades ago. He used to talk about the 'Mansfield Case'. As far as I recall, this was a court case in the 1950s//60s when a lot of gay men were prosecuted. The implications spread far and wide making the gay crowd in Derby and Nottingham very nervous indeed - as exemplified in this novel.

"Perhaps we are all becoming gargoyles and gnomes!"

LGBT History Month Bulletin 76 – October 2010
www.lgbthistorymonth.org.uk

New Novel from Narvel

There aren't many people called Narvel Annable and there aren't many gay men who have spent half their youth in a Derbyshire mining community and the other half in Detroit.

LGBT History Month Co-Chair Tony Fenwick said –
"Our SCHOOLS **OUT** member is an accomplished author with a wealth of experience and knowledge about gay life on both sides of the pond. His characters – heroes, villains, Adonises and monsters – are inspired by real people in real places which are still there. After enjoying *Lost Lad*, I'm looking forward to reading *Secret Summer* immensely."

Comment from Terry Ladlow of *Terivison Productions*, Hunmanby, Filey, North Yorkshire – November 12th 2010

"*Secret Summer* is so perfect! It is sensitive, erotic, poignant, tender and so human. I've been reading it and re-reading chapters to get the full feeling and power of the interplay of characters, feelings and emotions Narvel Annable has created. I felt for Simeon and his tenderness, stimuli, aberrations, and the unenviable intolerance he suffered as a boy. Congratulations on writing such a fine book."

Comment from Sonya Robotham of Derbys Rainbow Fringe Festival – October 2010

"The story told in *Secret Summer* is very important as part of the journey of many LGBT people both locally and globally."

To obtain a personally signed copy of *Secret Summer* for £10 inclusive of P&P – send a cheque payable to Narvel Annable at 44 Dovedale Crescent, Belper, Derbyshire DE56 1HJ. Or phone - 01 773 824483

Heanor Schooldays
A Social History

ISBN 0 9530419 1 3

This book deals with the last hundred years but majors on the author's personal experience of the 1950's and 1960's in which he recreates the optimistic social atmosphere of teenagers enjoying the popular culture of the day. You will also gain insights into the gritty, unpretentious, honest character of Heanor folk.

It is a graphic, colourful and emotional journey from the depths of despair to the heights of happiness. Along the way, Narvel Annable honours the memory of teachers, headmasters and headmistresses who have shaped the lives of countless Heanorians. Disquiet is expressed, as discredited modern teaching methods are contrasted to the successful tried and trusted methods of past years.

Forty-five photographs and fifteen documents will rekindle memories. The work is supported by a foreword from His Honour Judge Keith Matthewman QC and contains first-hand accounts from many contributors, including the one-time local lad, The Rt. Hon. Kenneth Clarke QC, MP, the former Chancellor of the Exchequer from 1993 to 1997. 205 pages.

"I was enthralled. A cracking collection of tales."

John Holmes, BBC Radio Derby.

Reviews of *Heanor Schooldays*

Vivid and detailed memories of a 1950's childhood. Sensitively written, Narvel explores the vagaries of the educational system which helped to develop his character and prepare him for adulthood. This is an important snapshot of social history, and the author brings it to life with recollections of strict discipline, bullying and extreme forms of punishment. A rollercoaster of emotions."

Pauline Oldrini, *Ripley and Heanor News* and *Belper News* 05.11.98

"Mr Annable mixes anecdote with comment to provide an important record of changes made in education as seen from the sides of both pupil and teacher."

Geoff Hammerton, *Derby Evening Telegraph* 04.12.98

"This autobiographic book charts a gritty history and weaves a graphic tapestry of Derbyshire school life 40 years ago. It is littered with colourful characters, interesting facts and first-hand accounts."

David Mark, *Nottingham Evening Post* 27.10.98

"Narvel Annable has managed to do what most authors never could; that is, to make a book about his schooldays a thoroughly enjoyable read.

"In his unique style he gives us a history of people and institutions. He gives us his views on education, past and present, and we are treated to a fascinating glimpse of a school-life in the fifties and sixties, complete with all its sorrows and joys. You do not have to remember those days to enjoy this book: you do not have to be an educationalist to enjoy this book: but if you are in either group, or both, you will enjoy it all the more - and so will your children."

His Honour Judge Keith Matthewman QC November 1998

Heanor Schooldays can be obtained from bookshops or directly from the author by sending a cheque for £10.00 to -

44 Dovedale Crescent, Belper, Derbyshire DE56 1HJ.

Death on the Derwent

A Murder Mystery set in Belper 1949

ISBN 0 9530419 2 1

Join the formidable schoolmistress Miss Florence Calder and her small, cantankerous, hunchbacked sister Miss Madge, as they detect and attempt to unmask a clever murderer in the leafy, ivy-clad, quaint and quieter Belper of 1949.

This entertaining blend of fact and fiction, set against the skilfully described background of spectacular Derbyshire scenery, is both an intriguing 'whodunit' and also a local history. Atmospheric narrative will take you around the nooks and crannies of the old mill town, in both bright sunshine and also in menacing thick fog.

It is complete with a body in a boat, psychic phenomena in the candle-lit haunted halls of the rambling old Bridge House School, a séance, a conjuring trick and all ending in a surprise.

Some hilarious, colourful and quirky characters spanning the social divide from the past poverty of Cowhill, to the opulence of Bridge Hill, combine with suspense and dramatic tension to produce a thoroughly enjoyable thriller. 204 pages.

"So who has done it? Well Narvel has, but he'll keep you guessing right up to the final breath."

John Holmes, BBC Radio Derby.

Reviews of *Death on the Derwent*

"A remarkable murder mystery novel ... gives a new twist to the whodunit genre ... a skilful mixture of fact and fiction ... strong historical interest ... complications and twists, red herrings and false trails. Mr Annable has got himself a real-life, ready-made character in Miss Florence Calder. This could be - should be - the start of a series of Miss Calder novels."

Geoff Hammerton, *Derby Evening Telegraph* 17.12.99

"Peopled with distinctive characters ... meritorious for the descriptive detail. A well-produced book. Worth reading a second time or more to fully appreciate the construction of this ingenious novel."

Margaret Beardsley, *Belper News* 23.02.00

"Great characters!" Bob Attewell, *Belper Express* 13.01.00

"I loved the rich and qualitative language, the machinations, twists and turns of the plot. I was empathetic with the characters as they desperately tried to unravel the mystery Mr Annable has so brilliantly created."

Terry Ladlow, 'Terivision Productions', Wetwang, Driffield, East Yorkshire 22.03.00

"Simon Tonks is the village fool who ends up as a servant to the Calders, Claud Hoadley is the pompous Belper man-turned-snob who teaches elocution so that the townspeople can 'better themselves' and Aubrey Pod is a pushy 'Mr Toad' character always full of himself."

Paul Imrie, 'Talk of the Town', *Derby Evening Telegraph* 23.11.99

Death on the Derwent can be obtained from Derbyshire County Library. Used copies are available on the internet. An electronic version is available at Amazon.

Printed in Dunstable, United Kingdom

80721743R00141